ST. MA...

MINOTAUR
MYSTERIES

GET A CLUE!

Be the first to hear the latest mystery book news...

With the St. Martin's Minotaur monthly newsletter,
you'll learn about the hottest new Minotaur books,
receive advance excerpts from newly published works,
read exclusive original material from featured mystery
writers, and be able to enter to win free books!

Sign up on the Minotaur Web site at:
www.minotaurbooks.com

HARD FREEZE

"*Hard Freeze* makes for great escapist reading . . . [G]et ready to dip into a terrific, take-no-prisoners read."

—*Denver Post*

"Readers looking for two-fisted, take-no-prisoners action should pick up a copy."

—*Milwaukee Journal Sentinel*

"A bristling climax . . . Kurtz makes a riveting protagonist for the non-is-beautiful crowd."

—*Kirkus Review* (starred review)

"In addition to crafting one of the least likeable protagonists you'll ever find yourself rooting for . . . [Simmons] writes action scenes that'll leave your hands clammy on the page."

—*Booklist*

"Hannibal Lecter meets the Godfather . . . [V]iolent, fast-paced, with a high body count, and plenty of sanguinary and pyrotechnic detail, this high-octane thriller should please both hard-boiled addicts and Simmons devotees . . . [I]t's Simmons at his hard-driving best."

—*Publishers Weekly* (starred review)

"This straight-ahead, no-frills read is sure to garner enthusiasm among fans of Richard Stark and Joe Gores."

—*Library Journal*

HARDCASE

"Within the first five pages of *Hardcase*, you know it's going to live up to its title . . . [I]f you're after a hard-core, full-tilt rocket ride, you'll find it in *Hardcase*."

—*Rocky Mountain News*

MORE . . .

ALSO BY DAN SIMMONS

Hardcase

Hard as Nails

AVAILABLE FROM
ST. MARTIN'S/MINOTAUR PAPERBACKS

HARD
FREEZE

A JOE KURTZ NOVEL

DAN SIMMONS

St. Martin's Paperbacks

HARD FREEZE

Copyright © 2002 by Dan Simmons.

Excerpt from *Hard as Nails* © 2003 by Dan Simmons.

All rights reserved. No part of this book may be used or reproduced in any manner whatsoever without written permission except in the case of brief quotations embodied in critical articles or reviews. For information address St. Martin's Press, 175 Fifth Avenue, New York, NY 10010.

Library of Congress Catalog Card Number: 2002023706

ISBN: 0-312-98948-2
EAN: 80312-98948-4

Printed in the United States of America

St. Martin's Press hardcover edition / August 2002
St. Martin's Paperbacks edition / September 2003

St. Martin's Paperbacks are published by St. Martin's Press, 175 Fifth Avenue, New York, NY 10010.

10 9 8 7 6 5 4 3 2

CHAPTER
ONE

Joe Kurtz knew that someday he would lose focus, that his attention would wander at a crucial minute, that instincts honed in almost twelve years of cell-block survival would fail him, and on that day he would die a violent death.

Not today.

He noticed the old Pontiac Firebird turning behind him and parking at the far side of the lot when he pulled into Ted's Hot Dogs on Sheridan, and when he stepped out, he noticed three men staying in their car as the Pontiac's engine idled. The Firebird's windshield wipers moved the falling snow aside in two black arcs, but Kurtz could see the three men's heads outlined by the lights behind them. It was not yet 6:00 P.M., but full night had fallen in that dark, cold, claustrophobic way that only Buffalo, New York, in February could offer.

Kurtz scooped three rolls of quarters out of the console of his old Volvo, slipped them into the pocket of his peacoat and went into Ted's Hot Dogs. He ordered two dogs with everything except hot sauce, an order of onion rings, and a black coffee, all the while standing where he could watch the Firebird from the corner of his eye. Three men got out, talked for a minute in the falling snow and then dispersed, none of them coming into the brightly lighted restaurant.

Kurtz carried his tray of food to the seating area around behind the long counter of charcoal burners and drink machines and found a booth away from the windows where he could still see out and was in line of sight of all the doors.

It was the Three Stooges.

Kurtz had glimpsed them long enough to make a positive identification. He knew the Stooges' real names but it didn't matter—during the years he had been in Attica with them, everyone had known them only as the Three Stooges. White men, in their thirties, not related except via some sexual ménage à trois that Kurtz didn't want to think about, the Stooges were dirt stupid but crafty in their mean and lethal way. The Stooges had made a career of exercise-yard shank jobs, taking orders from those who couldn't get at their targets for whatever reason and contracting their hits out for pay as low as a few dozen cartons of cigarettes. They were equal-opportunity killers: shanking a black for the Aryan Brotherhood one week, killing a white boy for a black gang the next.

So now Kurtz was out of stir and the Stooges were out of stir and it was his turn to die.

Kurtz ate his hot dogs and considered the problem. First, he had to find out who had ordered the contract on him.

No, scratch that. First he had to deal with the Three Stooges, but in a way that allowed him to find out who had put the contract out. He ate slowly and looked at the logistics of the matter. They weren't promising. Either through blind luck or good intelligence—and Kurtz did not believe in luck—the Stooges had made their move at the only time when Kurtz was not armed. He was on his way home from a visit to his parole officer, and he'd decided that even the Volvo wasn't a good place to hide a weapon. His PO was a tough-assed lady.

So the Stooges had him without a firearm and their specialty was execution in a public place. Kurtz looked around. There were only half a dozen other people sitting in the booths—two old-timers sitting silent and apart, and an exhausted-looking mother with three loud, preschool-age boys. One of the boys looked over at Kurtz and gave him the finger. The mother ate her french fries and pretended not to notice.

Kurtz looked around again. The two front doors opened onto the Sheridan Drive side of the restaurant to the south. Doors on the east and west sides of the brightly lighted dining area opened onto the parking lots. The north wall was empty except for the entrance to the two rest rooms.

If the Stooges came in and started blazing away, Kurtz did not have much recourse except to grab one or more of the civilians to use as a shield and try to get out one of the doors. The drifts were deep out there and it was dark away from the restaurant lights.

Not much of a plan, Joe. Kurtz ate his second hot dog and sipped his Coke. The odds were that the Stooges would wait outside for him to emerge—not sure if he had seen them—and gun him down in the parking lot. The Stooges weren't afraid of spectators, but this wasn't the exercise yard at Attica; if they came inside to kill him, they'd have to shoot all the witnesses—diners and workers behind the counter included. It seemed excessive even for the Attica Three Stooges.

The oldest of the three boys two booths over tossed a ketchup-covered french fry at Kurtz. Kurtz smiled and looked at the happy family, wondering whether two of those kids, held high, would offer enough bone and body mass to stop whatever caliber slugs the Stooges would be firing. Probably not.

Too bad. Kurtz lifted one foot at a time onto the seat of the booth, removed his shoes and slid off his socks, balling one inside the other. One of the boys in the nearby booth pointed at Kurtz and started babbling excitedly to his mother, but by the time the sallow-faced woman looked his way, he'd tied the second shoe and was finishing his onion rings. The air felt chilly without socks on.

Keeping his eye on the pale Stooge faces just visible through the falling snow outside, Kurtz brought out each roll of quarters and emptied them into the double-thick sock. When he was finished, he set the ad hoc sap into the pocket of his peacoat. Assuming that the Stooges were carrying handguns and/or automatic weapons, it wasn't quite a fair fight yet.

A Buffalo police officer came into the dining area carrying his tray of hot dogs. The cop was uniformed, overweight, armed and alone, probably on his way home from a day shift. He looked tired and depressed.

Saved, thought Kurtz with only a little irony.

The cop set his food on a table and went into the rest room. Kurtz waited thirty seconds and then pulled on his gloves and followed.

The officer was at the only urinal and did not turn around as Kurtz entered. Kurtz passed him as if heading for the stall, pulled the homemade blackjack out of his pocket and sapped the cop hard over the head. The officer groaned but went down on both knees. Kurtz sapped him again.

Bending over the cop, he took the long-barreled .38 service revolver, the handcuffs, and the heavy baton from his belt. He removed the cop's hand radio and smashed it underfoot. Then he tugged off the cop's jacket.

The rear window was high up on the wall in the stall, was reinforced with metal mesh and was not designed to be opened. Holding the cop's jacket up to deflect the glass and muffle the sound, Kurtz smashed the glass and pulled the metal grid out of its rusted hinges. Stepping up on the toilet, he squeezed through the small window and dropped into the snow outside, getting to his feet behind the Dumpster.

East side first. Sliding the cop's revolver in his belt, Kurtz went around the back of the restaurant and peered out into the east parking lot. The Stooge called Curly was pacing back and forth behind the few parked cars, flapping his arms to stay warm. He was carrying a Colt .45 semiauto in one hand. Kurtz waited for Curly to make his turn and then walked silently out behind the short man and clubbed him over the head with the lead-weighted baton. He cuffed Curly with his hands behind his back, left him lying in the snow and walked around the front of the restaurant.

Moe looked up, recognized Kurtz, and started fumbling a weapon out from under his thick goosedown jacket even as he began to run. Kurtz caught up to him and clubbed him down into the snow. He kicked the pistol out of Moe's hand and looked through the glass doors of Ted's Hot Dogs. None of the workers at the empty service counter had noticed anything and the avenue was free of traffic at the moment.

Throwing Moe over his shoulder and pulling the .38 from his belt, the baton dangling from his wrist by its leather strap, Kurtz walked around to the west side of the building.

Larry must have sensed something. He was standing by Kurtz's Volvo and peering anxiously through the windows. He had a Mac-10 in his hands. According to other people Kurtz had known inside, Larry had always sung the praises of serious firepower.

With Moe still on his shoulder, Kurtz raised the .38 and shot Larry three times—body mass, head, and body mass again. The third Stooge went down quickly, the Mac-10 skittering away on ice and ending up under a parked SUV. The shots had been somewhat muffled by the falling snow. No one came to the door or window to check.

Still carrying Moe and dragging Larry's body, Kurtz tossed both men into the back seat of his Volvo, started the car, and drove around to the east side of the parking lot. Curly was moaning and beginning to come to, flopping around listlessly with his hands cuffed behind his back. No one had seen him.

Kurtz stopped the car, got out, lifted Curly, and tossed the moaning Stooge into the back seat with his dead and unconscious pals. He closed Curly's door, went around and unlatched the door behind the driver's position, got in, and drove away down Sheridan to the Youngman Expressway.

The Expressway was slick and icy, but Kurtz got the Volvo up to sixty-five miles per hour before glancing around. Larry's body was slumped up against the cracked-open door, Moe was still unconscious and leaning against Curly, and Curly was playing possum.

Kurtz cocked the service revolver with an audible click. "Open your eyes or I'll shoot you now," he said softly.

Curly's eyes flew open. He opened his mouth to say something.

"Shut up." Kurtz nodded toward Larry. "Kick him out."

The pale ex-con's face paled even further. "JesusfuckingChrist. I can't just—"

"Kick him out," said Kurtz, glancing back at the road and then turning around to aim the .38 at Curly's face.

His wrists handcuffed behind him, Curly shoved Moe aside with his shoulder, lifted his legs, and kicked Larry out the door. He had to kick twice to get him out. Cold air whirled inside the car. Possibly because of the storm, traffic on the Youngman was light.

"Who hired you to kill me?" asked Kurtz. "Be careful . . . you don't get many chances at the right answer."

"Jesus Christ," moaned Curly. "No one hired us. I don't even fucking know who you are. I don't even—"

"Wrong answer," said Kurtz. He nodded at Moe and then at the open door. Icy pavement was roaring by.

"Jesus Christ, I can't . . . he's still alive . . . listen to me, please . . ."

The Volvo tried to slide a bit as they came around a curve on the ice. Keeping one eye on the rearview mirror, Kurtz corrected the slide, turned back, and aimed the pistol at Curly's crotch. "Now," he said.

Moe started to gain consciousness as Curly kicked him across the seat to the open door. The icy air revived Moe enough that the bigger man reached up and grabbed the seat back and held on for dear life. Curly glanced at Kurtz's pistol and kicked Moe in the belly and face with both feet. Moe flew out into the night, striking the pavement with an audible wet noise.

Curly was panting, almost hyperventilating, as he looked up at Kurtz's weapon. His legs were up on the back seat, but he was obviously concocting a way to kick at Kurtz.

"Move those feet without permission and I put two into your belly," Kurtz said softly. "Let's try again. Who hired you? Remember, you don't have any wrong answers left."

"You're going to shoot me anyway," said Curly. His teeth were chattering in the blast of cold air from the open door.

"No," said Kurtz. "I won't. Not if you tell me the truth. Last chance."

Curly said, "A woman."

Kurtz glanced at the road and then back. That made no sense. The D-Block Mosque still had a $10,000 fatwa out on Kurtz as far as he knew. Little Skag Farino, still in the pen, had several reasons to see Kurtz dead, and Little Skag had always been a cheap son of a bitch, likely to hire skanks like the Stooges. An inner-city Crips gang called the Seneca Social Club had put out the word that Joe Kurtz should die. He had a few other enemies who might hire someone. But a woman?

"Not good enough," said Kurtz. He raised the aim toward Curly's belly.

"No, Jesus Christ, I'm telling the truth! Brunette. Drives a Lexus. Paid five thousand in cash up front—we get another five when she reads about you in the paper. She was the one who told us about you probably not carrying today because of your PO visit. Jesus Christ, Kurtz, you can't just—"

"What's her name?"

Curly shook his head wildly. Curly was bald. "Farino. She didn't say . . . but I'm sure of it . . . she's Little Skag's sister."

"Maria Farino is dead," said Kurtz. He had reason to know.

Curly began shouting, talking so fast that spittle flew. "Not Maria Farino. The other one. The older sister. I seen a family picture once that Skag had in stir. Whatshername, the fucking nun, Agelica, Angela, some fucking wop name—"

"Angelina," said Kurtz.

Curly's mouth twisted. "You're going to shoot me now. I told you the fucking truth, but you're going to—"

"Not necessarily," said Kurtz. It was snowing harder and this part of the Youngman was notorious for black ice, but he got the car up to seventy-five. Kurtz nodded toward the open car door.

Curly's eyes grew wide. "You're fucking joking . . . I can't—"

"You can take one in the head," said Kurtz. "Then I dump you. You can make your move, take a couple in the belly, maybe we crash. Or you can take a chance and tuck and roll. Plus, there's some snow out there. Probably as soft as a goosedown pillow."

Curly's wild eyes went to the door.

"It's your call," said Kurtz. "But you only have five seconds to decide. One. Two—"

Curly screamed something indecipherable, scooched over on the seat, and threw himself out the door.

Kurtz glanced at the mirror. Headlights swerved and spun as cars tried to take evasive action, tangled, bounced over the bundle in the road, and piled up behind Kurtz's Volvo.

He lowered his speed to a more sane forty-five miles per hour and exited at the Kensington Expressway, heading back west toward Buffalo's downtown. Passing Mt. Calvary Cemetery in the dark, Kurtz tossed the cop's pistol and baton out the window.

The snow was getting thicker and falling faster. Kurtz liked Buffalo in the winter. He always had. But this was shaping up to be an especially tough winter.

CHAPTER TWO

The offices of High School Sweetheart Search, Inc. were in the basement of a former X-rated video and magazine store close to the Buffalo bus station. The XXX store had never looked too classy and looked even less so now after it had been closed for three months and the entire block condemned by the city for demolition. A little before 7:30 A.M., Arlene parked in the alley behind the store, used her key to let herself in the back door, and was surprised to find Joe working at his computer. The long room was unfurnished except for the two desks, a coatrack, a clutter of servers and cables, and a sagging couch set against one wall.

Arlene hung up her coat, set her purse on her desk, removed a pack of Marlboros from the purse and lit one, then turned on her computer and the video monitor connected to the two cameras upstairs. The abandoned interior of the adult bookstore on the monitors looked as littered and empty as always. No one had ever bothered to clean the bloodstains off the linoleum floor up there. "You sleep here again last night, Joe?"

Kurtz shook his head. He called up the court file on Donald Lee Rafferty, age 42, 1016 Locus Lane, Lockport, NY. The file showed another DWI on Rafferty's record—the third this year. Rafferty's driver's license was one point away from being pulled.

"Goddamn it to hell," said Kurtz.

Arlene looked up. Joe rarely cursed. "What?"

"Nothing."

Kurtz's e-mail announcer chirped. It was a note from Pruno, replying to Kurtz's e-mail query sent at 4:00 that morning. Pruno was a homeless wino and heroin addict who just happened to have a laptop computer in the cardboard shack he sometimes shared with another homeless man named Soul Dad. Kurtz had wondered from time to time how it was that Pruno was able to keep his laptop when the very clothes the old man wore were constantly being stolen off his back. Kurtz opened the e-mail.

> **Joseph: Received your e-mail and I do indeed have some information on the surviving Ms. Farino and the three gentlemen in question. I would prefer to discuss this in private since I have a request to make of you in return. Could you stop by my winter residence at your earliest convenience? Cordially—P.**

"Goddamn it," Kurtz said again.

Arlene squinted at him through a haze of smoke. Her own computer monitor was filled with the day's requests for searches for former high-school boyfriends and girlfriends. She batted ashes into her ashtray but said nothing.

Kurtz sighed. It was inconvenient to go see the old man for this information, but Pruno rarely asked Kurtz for anything. Come to think of it, Pruno had *never* asked for anything.

The Rafferty thing, though . . .

"Goddamn it," whispered Kurtz.

"Anything I can help with?" asked Arlene.

"No."

"All right, Joe. But since you're here today, there are a few things you can help me with."

Kurtz turned off his computer.

"We need to find new office space," said Arlene. "This place gets demolished in a month and we get thrown out in two weeks, no matter what."

Kurtz nodded.

Arlene batted cigarette ashes again. "So are you going to have time to help me look for a new office today or tomorrow?"

"Probably not," said Kurtz.

"Then are you going to let me choose a place on my own?"

"No."

Arlene nodded. "Shall I scout some places? Let you look at them later?"

"Okay," said Kurtz.

"And you don't mind me looking during office hours?"

Kurtz just stared at his once and present secretary. She had come back to work for him the day he had gotten out of prison the previous autumn. After twelve years of hiatus. "Have I ever said anything to you about office hours or how you should spend your day?" he said at last. "You can come in and handle the on-line Sweetheart Search stuff in ten minutes for all I care. Take the rest of the day off."

"Uh-huh," said Arlene. Her look finished the sentence. Recently, the Sweetheart Search business had run to ten- and twelve-hour weekdays, most Saturdays, and the occasional Sunday. She stubbed out the cigarette and pulled out another but did not light it.

"What else do we need?" asked Kurtz.

"Thirty-five thousand dollars," said Arlene.

Kurtz reacted as he always did to surprise—with a poker face.

"It's for another server and some data-mining service," added Arlene.

"I thought this server and the data-mining we've already done would handle Sweetheart Search for the next couple of years," said Kurtz.

"They will," said Arlene. "This is for Wedding Bells."

"Wedding Bells?"

Arlene lit the next cigarette and took a long, slow drag. After exhaling, she said, "This high-school-sweetheart search was a great idea of yours, Joe, and it's making money, but we're reaching the point of diminishing returns with it."

"After four months?" said Kurtz.

Arlene moved her lacquered fingernails in a complex gesture. "What separates it from the other on-line school-sweetheart services is you tracking some of these people down on foot, delivering some of the love letters in person."

"Yeah?" said Kurtz. "So?" But he understood then. "You mean that there's only so much market share in this part of Western New York and Northern Pennsylvania and Ohio within range of my driving. Only so many old high-school yearbooks we can look through in the region. After that, we're just another on-line search agency. Yeah, I thought of that when I came up with this idea in prison, but I thought it would last longer than *four months.*"

Arlene smiled. "Don't worry, Joe. I didn't mean that we're going to run out of yearbook sources or clients for the next couple of years. I just mean we're reaching the point of diminishing returns—or at least for your door-to-door part of it."

"So . . . Wedding Bells," said Kurtz.

"Wedding Bells," agreed Arlene.

"I assume that's some sort of on-line wedding-planning service. Unless you're just going to offer it as a bonus package for our successful Sweetheart Search clients."

"Oh, we can do that," said Arlene, "but I see it as a full-service on-line wedding-planning dot com. Nationwide. Beyond nationwide."

"So I won't be delivering corsages to Erie, Pennsylvania, the way I'm doing now with the love letters?"

Arlene flicked ashes. "You don't have to be involved at all if you don't want to be, Joe. Besides putting up the seed money and owning the company . . . and finding us an office."

Kurtz ignored this last part. "Why thirty-five thousand? That's a lot of data-mining."

Arlene carried over a folder of spreadsheet pages and notes. She stood by Kurtz's desk as he looked through it. "See, Joe, I was just grabbing bits and pieces of data from the Internet and tossing it all into an Excel spreadsheet—more or less what the present on-line wedding services do—but then I used some of our income to build a new data warehouse on Oracle81 and paid Ergos Business Intelligence to begin mining the database of all these weddings that other individuals or services had planned."

She pointed to some columns on the spreadsheet. "And *voila!*"

Kurtz looked for patterns in the charts and columns. Finally he saw one. "Planning a fancy wedding takes two hundred and seventy to three hundred days," said

Kurtz. "Almost all of them fall in that range. So does everyone know this?"

Arlene shook her head. "Some individual wedding planners do, but not the few on-line wedding-service companies. The pattern really shows up when you look at a huge mass of data."

"So how does your . . . our . . . Wedding Bells dot com cash in on this?" asked Kurtz.

Arlene pulled out other pages. "We continue using the Ergos tool to analyze this two-hundred-seventy- to three-hundred-day period and nail down exactly when each step of the operation takes place."

"What operation?" asked Kurtz. Arlene was beginning to talk like some bank robbers he'd known. "Isn't a wedding just a wedding? Rent a place, dress up, get it over with?"

Arlene rolled her eyes. Exhaling smoke, she brought her ashtray over to Kurtz's desk and flicked ashes into it. "See, here, at this point early on? Here's the bride's search for a dress. *Every* bride has to search for a dress. We offer links to designers, seamstresses, even knock-off designer dress suppliers."

"But Wedding Bells wouldn't be just a bunch of hyperlinks, would it?" asked Kurtz, frowning slightly.

Arlene shook her head and stubbed out her cigarette. "Not at all. The clients give us a profile at the beginning and we offer everything from full service down. We can handle everything—absolutely everything. From sending out invitations to tipping the minister. Or the clients can have us plan some of it and just have us connect them to the right people for other decision points along the way—either way, we make money."

Arlene lit another cigarette and ruffled through the stack of papers. She pointed to a highlighted line on a 285-day chart. "See this point, Joe? Within the first month, they have to decide on locations for the wedding and the reception. We have the biggest database anywhere and provide links to restaurants, inns, picturesque parks, Hawaiian resorts, even churches. They give us their profile and we make suggestions, then connect them to the appropriate sites."

Kurtz had to grin. "And get a kickback from every one of those places . . . except maybe the churches."

"Hah!" said Arlene. "Weddings are important revenue sources for churches and synagogues. They want in Wedding Bells dot com, they give us a piece of the action. No negotiation there."

Kurtz nodded and looked at the rest of the spreadsheets. "Wedding consultants referred. Honeymoon locations recommended and discounts offered. Limos lined up. Even airline tickets reserved for relatives and the wedding couple. Flowers. Catering. You provide local sources and Web links to everything, and everyone pays Wedding Bells dot com. Nice." He closed the folder and handed it back to her. "When do you need the seed money?"

"This is Thursday," said Arlene. "Monday would be nice."

"All right. Thirty-five thousand on Monday." He grabbed his peacoat from the coatrack and slipped a semiauto pistol in his belt. The weapon was the relatively small and light .40 SW99—a licensed Smith & Wesson version of the Walther P99 double-action service pistol. Kurtz had ten rounds in the magazine and a second magazine in his coat pocket. Considering the fact that the SW99 fired fomidable .40 S&W loads rather than the more common 9mms, Kurtz trusted that twenty cartridges would do the trick.

"Will you be back in the office before the weekend?" asked Arlene as Kurtz opened the rear door.

"Probably not."

"Anywhere I can reach you?"

"You can try Pruno's e-mail in the next hour or so," said Kurtz. "After that, probably not. I'll give you a call here at the office before the weekend."

"Oh, you can call here Saturday or Sunday, too," said Arlene. "I'll be here."

But Kurtz was out the door and gone and the sarcasm was wasted.

CHAPTER
THREE

Kurtz liked Buffalo winters because the Buffalonians knew how to deal with winter. A few inches of snow—snow that would paralyze some wussy city such as Washington or Nashville—went all but unnoticed by Buffalo residents. Plows plowed, sidewalks got shoveled early, and people went on about their business. A foot of snow got people's attention in Buffalo, but only for as long as it took to push and plow it into the ten-foot-high heap of earlier-plowed snow.

But this winter had been a bitch. By January first, more snow had fallen than in the previous two winters combined, and by February, even stoic Buffalo had to shut down some schools and businesses when snow and consistently low temperatures kept blowing in off Lake Erie almost daily.

Kurtz had no idea how Pruno and some of the other winos who refused to stay in shelters more than a few of the worst nights managed to survive such winters.

But surviving the winter was Pruno's problem. Surviving the next few days and weeks was Kurtz's problem.

Pruno's "winter residence" was the packing-crate

hovel he and Soul Dad had cobbled together under the highway overpass near the rail yards. In the summer, Kurtz knew, fifty or sixty of the homeless congregated here in a sort of Bonus Army Village that was not totally without appeal. But most of the fair-weather bums had long since headed for shelters or Southern cities—Soul Dad favored Denver, for reasons known only to himself. Now only Pruno's shack remained, and snow had almost covered it.

Kurtz slid down the steep hill from the road above and postholed his way through the drifts to the shack. There was no real door—a section of corrugated, rusted tin slid into place across the opening of the nailed-together crates—so Kurtz knocked on the metal panel and waited. The freezing wind from Lake Erie cut right through the wool of his peacoat. After two or three more knocks, Kurtz heard a racking cough from the interior and took it as his permission to enter.

Pruno—Soul Dad had once mentioned that the old man's name was Frederick—sat against the concrete abutment that made up the far wall. Snow had drifted in through cracks and fissures. The long extension cord to the laptop still ran in from God knows where and a stack of Sterno cans provided both heat and cooking facilities. Pruno himself was almost lost in a cocoon of rags and filthy newspapers.

"Jesus," Kurtz said softly. "Why don't you go to a shelter, old man?"

Pruno coughed what might have been a laugh. "I refuse to render unto Caesar what is Caesar's."

"Money?" said Kurtz. "The shelters don't ask for money. Not even for work in trade for a bed at this time of year. So what would you be rendering unto Caesar— except maybe some frostbite?"

"Obeisance," said Pruno. He coughed and cleared his

throat. "Shall we get on with business, Joseph? What is it you would like to know about the redoubtable Ms. Farino?"

"First of all," said Kurtz, "what do you want in exchange for the information? Your e-mail mentioned getting something in return."

"Not really, Joseph. I said that I had a request to make of you in return. I assure you that I will be happy to give you the Farino information with no strings attached."

"Whatever," said Kurtz. "What's your request?"

Pruno coughed for a minute and pulled the newspapers and rags closer around him. The cold air coming in through the chinks and cracks in the packing-crate hovel was making Kurtz shiver and he was wearing a thick peacoat. "I wondered if you would be so kind as to meet with a friend of mine," said Pruno. "In your professional capacity."

"What professional capacity?"

"Investigator."

Kurtz shook his head. "You know I'm not a P.I. anymore."

"You investigated for the Farino family last year," said Pruno. The old man's wheezy, drug-addict's voice still carried more than a hint of a Bostonian accent.

"That was a scam I was part of," said Kurtz, "not an investigation."

"Nonetheless, Joseph, it would please me greatly if you would just meet with my friend. You can tell him yourself that you are no longer in the private investigation business."

Kurtz hesitated. "What's his name?"

"John Wellington Frears."

"And what's his problem?"

"I don't know precisely, Joseph. It is a private issue."

"All right," said Kurtz, imagining himself consulting with another wino. "Where should I find this John Wellington Frears?"

"Perhaps he could come to your office today? It would probably be better for my friend to come see you."

Kurtz thought of Arlene and the last time they'd had visitors at the office. "No," he said "I'll be at Blues Franklin tonight until midnight. Tell him to meet me there. How will I know him?"

"He likes to wear vests," said Pruno. "Now, about this Angelina Farino query. What would you like to know?"

"Everything," said Kurtz.

Donald Rafferty worked at the main post office down on William Street and liked to eat lunch at a little bar near Broadway Market. As a supervisor, Rafferty managed to take ninety-minute lunch hours. Sometimes he would forget to eat lunch.

This afternoon he came out of the bar and found a man leaning against his 1998 Honda Accord. The man was white—that's the first thing Rafferty checked—and was wearing a peacoat and a wool cap. He looked vaguely familiar, but Rafferty couldn't quite place the face. Actually, this had been an extra-long lunch hour and Donald Rafferty was having a little trouble finding his car keys in his pocket. He stopped twenty feet from the man and considered going back in the bar until the stranger left.

"Hey, Donnie," said the man. Rafferty had always hated the name Donnie.

"Kurtz," Rafferty said at last. "Kurtz."

Kurtz nodded.

"I thought you were in jail, asshole," said Rafferty.

"Not right now," said Kurtz.

Rafferty blinked to clear his vision. "Another state, you would have got the chair . . . or lethal injection," he said. "For murder."

Kurtz smiled. "Manslaughter." He had been leaning against the Accord's hood, but now he straightened and took a step closer.

Donald Rafferty took a step back on the slippery parking lot. It was snowing again. "What the fuck do you want, Kurtz?"

"I want you to stop drinking on days that you drive Rachel anywhere," Kurtz said. His voice was very soft but very firm.

Rafferty actually laughed, despite his nervousness. "Rachel? Don't tell me that you give a flying fuck about Rachel. Fourteen years and you never so much as sent the kid a fucking card."

"Twelve years," said Kurtz.

"She's mine," slurred Rafferty. "Courts said so. It's legal. I was Samantha's husband, ex-husband, and Samantha meant for me to have her."

"Sam didn't mean for anyone except Sam to take care of Rachel," said Kurtz, taking another step toward Rafferty.

Rafferty took three steps back toward the bar.

"Sam didn't plan on dying," said Kurtz.

Rafferty had to sneer at that. "She died because of you, Kurtz. You and that fucking job." He found his keys and threaded them through his fingers, making a fist. Anger was mixing with fear now. He could take this sonofabitch. "You here to cause trouble, Kurtz?"

Kurtz's gaze never left Rafferty's.

"Because if you are," continued Rafferty, his voice getting stronger and louder now, "I'll tell your parole officer that you're harassing me, threatening me, threatening Rachel . . . twelve years in Attica, who knows what filthy tastes you've acquired."

Something flickered in Joe Kurtz's eyes then, and Rafferty took four quick steps backward until he could almost touch the door to the bar. "You give me any shit, Kurtz, and I'll have you back in jail so fast that—"

"If you drive Rachel again when you're drunk," Kurtz interrupted softly, "I'll hurt you, Donnie." He took another step and Rafferty opened the bar's door in a hurry, ready to rush inside where the bartender—Carl—could pull the sawed-off shotgun out from under the counter.

Kurtz did not look at Donald Rafferty again. He brushed past him and walked down Broadway, disappearing in the heavily falling snow.

CHAPTER
FOUR

Kurtz sat in the smoky gloom of Blues Franklin and thought about Pruno's information on Angelina Farino and what it might mean. And he thought about the fact that he had been followed to the Blues Franklin by two homicide detectives in an unmarked car. It wasn't the first time they'd tailed him in recent weeks.

Blues Franklin, on Franklin Street just down from the Rue Franklin Coffeehouse, was the second-oldest blues/jazz dive in Buffalo. Promising talent tended to appear there on their way up and then reappear without much fanfare when they were serious headliners. This evening, a local jazz pianist named Coe Pierce and his quartet were playing, the place was half-filled and sleepy, and Kurtz had his usual small table, in the corner as far from the door as possible, his back to the wall. The nearby tables were empty. Occasionally the proprietor and chief bartender, Daddy Bruce Woles, or his granddaughter Ruby would come over to chat and see if Kurtz wanted another beer. He didn't. Kurtz came for the music, not for the booze.

Kurtz did not really expect Pruno's friend, Mr. John Wellington Frears, to show. Pruno seemed to know

everyone in Buffalo—of the dozen or so street inform-
ants Kurtz had used back when he was a P.I., Pruno had
been the gem of the lot—but Kurtz doubted if any friend
of Pruno's would be sober enough and presentable
enough to make it to Blues Franklin.

Angelina Farino. Other than Little Skag—Stephen or
Stevie to family members—she was the only surviving
child of the late Don Farino. Her older sister, the late
Maria Farino, had been a casualty of her own ambition.
Everyone Kurtz knew believed that older sister Angelina
had been so disgusted by the Family business that she
had removed herself to Italy more than five years earlier,
presumably to enter a convent. According to Pruno, this
was not quite accurate. It seems that the surviving Ms.
Farino was more ambitious than her brothers or sister
and had gone back to study crime with the family in
Sicily even while getting a master's degree in business
administration from a university in Rome. She also got
married twice while there, according to Pruno—first to
a young Sicilian from a prominent La Cosa Nostra family who managed to get himself killed, then to an elderly
Italian nobleman, Count Pietro Adolfo Ferrara. The information about Count Ferrara was sketchy—he may
have died, he may have retired, he may still be in seclu-
sion. He and Angelina may have divorced before she
returned here, but perhaps they had not.

"So our local mobster's kid is really Countess Angelina Farino Ferrara?" Kurtz had asked.

Pruno shook his head. "It appears that whatever her
marital status might be, she did not acquire that title."

"Too bad," said Kurtz. "It sounds funny."

Upon returning to the United States a few months
earlier, Angelina had worked as a liaison for Little Skag
in Attica, paying off politicians to ensure his parole in
the coming summer, selling the white elephant of the

family house in Orchard Park and buying new digs near the river, and—this was the part that floored Kurtz— opening negotiations with Emilio Gonzaga.

The Gonzagas were the other second-tier, has-been, wise-guy family in Western New York, and the relationship between the Gonzagas and the Farinos made Shakespeare's Capulets and Montagues look like kissing cousins.

Pruno had already known about the Three Stooges' contract on Kurtz. "I would have warned you, Joseph, but word hit the street late yesterday and it seems she met with the unlucky trio only the day before."

"Do you think she was acting on Little Skag's instructions?" asked Kurtz.

"That is the speculation I hear," said Pruno. "Rumor is that she was reluctant to pay for the contract . . . or at least reluctant to hire such inept workmen."

"Lucky for me she did," said Kurtz. "Skag was always cheap." Kurtz had sat in the windy packing crate, observing the ice crystals in the air for a silent minute. "Any word on who they'll send next?" he asked.

Pruno had shaken his oversized head on that grimy chicken neck of his. The old man's hands were shaking in a way that was obviously due more to need for an overdue injection of heroin than to the cold air. For the thousandth time, Kurtz wondered where Pruno found the money to support his habit.

"I suspect that the next time, they will invest more money," Pruno said glumly. "Angelina Farino is rebuilding the Farino Family's muscle base, bringing in talent from New Jersey and Brooklyn, but evidently they don't want to have the reemerging Family tied to this particular hit."

Kurtz said nothing. He was thinking about a European hit man known only as the Dane.

"Sooner or later, however, they will remember the old axiom," said Pruno.

"Which one's that?" Kurtz expected a torrent of Latin or Greek. On more than one occasion, he'd left the old man and his friend Soul Dad alone to hash out their arguments in classical languages.

" 'If you want a thing done right, do it yourself,' " said Pruno. He was glancing at the door of the shack, obviously eager for Kurtz to leave.

"One last question," said Kurtz. "I'm being followed off and on by two homicide cops—Brubaker and Myers. Know anything about them?"

"Detective Fred Brubaker has—in the argot of our time—a major hard-on for you, Joseph. He remains convinced that you were responsible for the demise of his friend and fellow shakedown artist, the late and totally unlamented Sergeant James Hathaway from Homicide."

"I know that," said Kurtz. "What I meant was, have you heard anything about Brubaker tying up with one of the families?"

"No, Joseph, but it should be just a matter of time. Such an association was a major source of income for Detective Hathaway, and Brubaker was always sort of a dull-witted understudy to Hathaway. I wish that I had more optimistic news for you."

Kurtz had said nothing to this. He'd patted the old man's quaking arm and left the shack.

Sitting in the Blues Franklin, waiting for the mysterious Mr. Frears, Kurtz wondered if it was coincidence that the two homicide cops were tailing him again this evening.

Coe Pierce's quartet was just wrapping up a fifteen-minute version of Miles Davis's "All Blues," filled with

Oscar Peterson–like solo riffs for Pierce to fool around with on the piano, when Kurtz saw the well-dressed, middle-aged black man coming toward him from across the room. Kurtz was still wearing his peacoat and now he slipped his hand into the right-side pocket and slid the safety off the .40-caliber S&W semiauto there.

The dignified-looking man came up to the opposite side of Kurtz's table. "Mr. Kurtz?"

Kurtz nodded. If the man made a move for a weapon, Kurtz would have to fire through his own coat, and he was not crazy about putting a hole in his only jacket.

"I am John Wellington Frears," said the man. "I believe that our mutual acquaintance, Dr. Frederick, told you that I would be meeting you tonight."

Dr. Frederick? thought Kurtz. He had once heard Soul Dad refer to Pruno as Frederick, but he'd thought it was the old wino's first name. "Sit down," said Kurtz. He kept his hand on the S&W and the pistol aimed under the table as the man took a chair across the table, his back to the quartet that had just taken a break. "What do you want, Mr. Frears?"

Frears sighed and rubbed his eyes as if weary. Kurtz noticed that the man was wearing a vest—as Pruno had said—but that it was part of a three-piece gray suit that must have cost several thousand dollars. Frears was a short man, with short, curly hair and a perfectly trimmed short, curly beard, all going gracefully to gray. His nails were manicured and his horn-rimmed glasses were classic Armani. His watch was subtle, classic and understated, but expensive. He wore no jewelry. He had the kind of intelligent gaze Kurtz had seen in photographs of Frederick Douglass and W.E.B. DuBois, and in person only with Pruno's friend Soul Dad.

"I want you to find the man who murdered my little girl," said John Wellington Frears.

"Why talk to me?" asked Kurtz.

"You're an investigator."

"I'm not. I'm a convicted felon, on parole. I have no private investigator's license, nor will I ever have one again."

"But you're a trained investigator, Mr. Kurtz."

"Not anymore."

"Dr. Frederick says—"

"Pruno has a hard time telling what day it is," said Kurtz.

"He assures me that you and your partner, Ms. Fielding, were the finest—"

"That was more than twelve years ago," Kurtz said. "I can't help you."

Frears rubbed his eyes again and reached into his inside jacket pocket. Kurtz's right hand had never left his pistol. His finger remained on the trigger.

Frears pulled out a small color photograph and slid it across the table toward Kurtz: a black girl, thirteen or fourteen, wearing a black sweater and silver necklace. The girl was attractive and sweet looking, her eyes alive with a more vital version of John Wellington Frears's intelligence. "My daughter Crystal," said Frears. "She was murdered twenty years ago next month. May I tell you the story?"

Kurtz said nothing.

"She was our darling," said Frears. "Marcia's and mine. Crystal was smart and talented. She played the viola . . . I'm a concert violinist, Mr. Kurtz, and I know that Crystal was gifted enough to become a professional musician, but that was not even her primary interest. She was a poet—not an adolescent poet, Mr. Kurtz, but a true poet. Dr. Frederick confirmed that, and as you know, Dr. Frederick was not only a philosopher, but a gifted literary critic. . . ."

Kurtz remained silent.

"Twenty years ago next month, Crystal was killed by a man we all knew and trusted, a fellow faculty member—I was teaching at the University of Chicago then, we lived in Evanston. The man was a professor of psychology. His name was James B. Hansen, and he had a family—a wife, and a daughter Rachel's age. The two girls rode horses together. We had bought Crystal a gelding—Dusty was its name—and we boarded it at a stable outside of town where Crystal and Denise, that was Hansen's daughter's name, would ride every Saturday during clement weather. Hansen and I took turns driving Crystal and Denise to the stable and we would wait while they took lessons and rode, Hansen one weekend, me the next."

Frears stopped and took a breath. There was a noise behind him and he glanced over his shoulder. Coe and the quartet were returning to the stage. They began a slow, Patricia Barberish rendition of "Inchworm."

Frears looked back at Kurtz, who had clicked on the safety of the .40 Smith & Wesson, left it in his pocket, and brought both hands up onto the table. He did not lift the photograph of the girl or look at it.

"One weekend," continued Frears, "James B. Hansen picked up Crystal saying that Denise was sick with a cold but that it was his turn to drive and he wanted to do so. But instead of driving her to the stable, he took her to a forest preserve on the outskirts of Chicago, raped our daughter, tortured her, killed her, and left her naked body to be found by hikers."

Frears's tone had remained cool and level, as if reciting a story that meant nothing to him, but now he paused for a minute. When he resumed, there was an undercurrent, if not a quaver, in his voice. "You may wonder, Mr. Kurtz, how we know for sure that James

B. Hansen was the perpetrator of this crime. Well, he called me, Mr. Kurtz. After killing Crystal, he called me from a pay phone—this was before cell phones were common—and told me what he had done. And he told me that he was going home to kill his wife and daughter."

The Coe Pierce Quartet shifted from the wandering "Inchworm" to a stylized "Flamenco Sketches" that would feature the young black trumpeter, Billy Eversol.

"I called the police, of course," said Frears. "They rushed to Hansen's home in Oak Park. He had arrived there first. His Range Rover was parked outside. The house was on fire. When the flames were extinguished, they found the bodies of Mrs. Hansen and Denise—they had each been shot in the back of the head by a large-caliber pistol—and the charred body of James. B. Hansen. They identified his body via dental records. The police determined that he had used the same pistol on himself."

Kurtz sipped his beer, set the glass down and said, "Twenty years ago."

"Next month."

"But your James B. Hansen isn't really dead."

John Wellington Frears blinked behind his round Armanis. "How did you know that?"

"Why would you need an investigator if he was?"

"Ah, precisely," said Frears. He licked his lips and took another breath. Kurtz realized that the man was in pain—not just existential or emotional pain, but serious physical pain, as if from a disease that made it hard for him to breathe. "He is not dead. I saw him ten days ago."

"Where?"

"Here in Buffalo."

"Where?"

"At the airport, Concourse Two to be precise. I was

leaving Buffalo—I had performed twice at Kleinhan's Music Hall—and was catching a flight to LaGuardia. I live in Manhattan. I had just passed through that metal-detector device when I saw him on the other side of the security area. He was carrying an expensive tan-leather satchel and heading for the doors. I cried out—I called his name—I tried to give chase, but the security people stopped me. I could not go through the metal detectors in the direction I had to in order to catch him. By the time the security people allowed me to go on, he was long gone."

"And you're sure it was Hansen?" said Kurtz. "He looked the same?"

"Not at all the same," said Frears. "He was twenty years older and thirty pounds heavier. Hansen was always a big man, he had played football back in Nebraska when he was in college, but now he seemed even larger, stronger. His hair had been long and he had worn a beard in Chicago—it was the early eighties, after all—and now he had short gray hair, a military sort of crew cut, and was clean-shaven. No, he looked nothing like the James B. Hansen of Chicago twenty years ago."

"But you're sure it was him?"

"Absolutely," said Frears.

"You contacted the Buffalo police?"

"Of course. I spent days talking with different people here. I think that one of the detectives actually believed me. But there is no James Hansen in any Buffalo-area directory. No Hansen or anyone fitting his description on the faculty of any of the local universities. No psychologists with that name in Buffalo. And my daughter's case file is officially closed. There was nothing they could do."

"And what did you want me to do?" said Kurtz, his voice low.

"Well, I want you to . . ."

"Kill him," said Kurtz.

John Wellington Frears blinked and his head snapped back as if he had been slapped. "Kill him? Good God, no. Why would you say that, Mr. Kurtz?"

"He raped and killed your daughter. You're a professional violinist, obviously well off. You could afford to hire any legitimate private investigator—hire an entire agency if you want. Why else would you come to me unless you wanted the man killed?"

Frears's mouth opened and then closed again. "No, Mr. Kurtz, you misunderstand. Dr. Frederick is the one person I know well in Buffalo—obviously he has fallen on hard times, but his sagacity abides beneath the sad circumstances—and he recommended you highly as an investigator who could find Hansen for me. And you are correct about my financial status. I will reward you very generously, Mr. Kurtz. Very generously indeed."

"And if I found him? What would you do, Mr. Frears?"

"Inform the police, of course. I'm staying at the Airport Sheraton until this nightmare is over."

Kurtz drank the last of his beer. Coe was playing a bluesy version of "Summertime."

"Mr. Frears," Kurtz said, "you're a very civilized man."

Frears adjusted his glasses. "So you'll take the case, Mr. Kurtz?"

"No."

Frears blinked again. "No?"

"No."

Frears sat in silence a moment and then stood. "Thank you for your time, Mr. Kurtz. I'm sorry to have bothered you."

Frears turned to go and had taken several steps when

Kurtz called his name. The man stopped and turned, his handsome, pained face showing something like hope. "Yes, Mr. Kurtz?"

"You forgot your photograph," Kurtz said. He held up the photo of the dead girl.

"You keep it, Mr. Kurtz. I no longer have Crystal and my wife left me three years after Crystal's death, but I have many photographs. You keep it, Mr. Kurtz." Frears crossed the room and went out the door of the Blues Franklin.

Big Daddy Bruce's granddaughter Ruby came over. "Daddy told me to tell you that those two cops parked down the street left."

"Thanks, Ruby."

"You want another beer, Joe?"

"Scotch."

"Any particular kind?"

"The cheapest kind," said Kurtz. When Ruby went back to the bar, Kurtz lifted the photograph, tore it into small pieces, and dropped the pieces into the ashtray.

CHAPTER
FIVE

Angelina Farino Ferrara jogged every morning at 6:00 A.M., even though 6:00 A.M. at this time of the winter in Buffalo meant she jogged in the dark. Most of her jogging route was lighted with streetlights or pedestrian-walkway streetlamps, but for the dark patches near the river she wore a backpacking headlamp held in place by elastic straps. It did not look all that elegant, Angelina supposed, but she didn't give a flying fuck how she looked when she ran.

Upon her return from Sicily in December, Angelina had sold the old Farino estate in Orchard Park and moved what was left of the Family operation to a pent-house condo overlooking the Buffalo Marina. Ribbons of expressways and an expanse of park separated the marina area from the city, but at night she could look east and north to what little skyline Buffalo offered, while the river and lake guarded her eastern flank. Since she had bought the place, the view westward was mostly of the ice and gray clouds above the river, although there was a glimpse of Canada, that Promised Land to her grandfather during Prohibition days and the earliest source of the family revenue. Staring at the ice and the dreary Buffalo skyline day after day, Angelina Farino Ferrara looked forward to spring, although she knew that summer would bring her brother Stephen's parole and the end of her days of being acting don.

Her jogging route took her a mile and a half north along the pathway following the marina parkway, down through a pedestrian tunnel to the frozen riverside—one could not call it a beach—for another half mile before looping around and returning along the Riverside Drive walkway. Even from behind bars in Attica, her brother Stevie—Angelina knew that everyone else thought of him as Little Skag—refused to allow her to go out alone, but although she was importing good talent from New Jersey and Brooklyn to replace the idiots her father had kept on retainer, none of these lasagna-fed mama's boys were in good enough shape to keep up with her when she ran. Angelina envied the new President of the United States; even though he didn't jog much, when he did, he had Secret Service men who could run with him.

For a few days, she had suffered the indignities of having Marco and Leo—the Boys, as she thought of them—follow along behind her on bicycles. Marco and Leo weren't very happy with that situation either, since neither had ridden a bike even when he was a kid and their fat asses hung over the saddles like so much un-leavened dough. But in recent weeks, they had compro-mised: Angelina jogging along the plowed walking path while Leo and Marco trolled alongside on the usually empty Riverside Drive in their Lincoln Town Car. Of course, after jogging through the pedestrian underpass, there were three or four minutes when she was techni-cally out of sight of the Boys—who waited at a turnout eating their doughnuts until she reappeared through the trees, now heading south—but Angelina figured she had those few minutes of privacy covered with the little

Italian-made .45-caliber Compact Witness semiauto she carried in a quick-release holster clipped to the waist of her jogging suit, under her loose sweatshirt. She also carried a tiny cell phone with the Boys' mobile number on speed-dial, but she knew she would reach for the Compact Witness before the phone.

This morning she was thinking about the ongoing discussions with the Gonzagas and did not even flick a see-you-later wave at the Boys when she followed the footpath west, away from the street, and jogged down through the underpass, careful as always not to slip on any ice there.

A man with a pistol was waiting for her at the far end of the underpass. It was a serious-caliber semiauto and he had it aimed right at her chest. He held the gun in one hand, the way her father and uncles used to do before an entire generation was trained to carry handguns two-handed, as if they weighed thirty pounds.

Angelina slid to a stop and raised her hands. She could always hope that it was just a robbery. If it was, she'd blow the motherfucker's head off as soon as he turned to go.

"Good morning, Signorita Farino," said the man in the peacoat. "Or is it Signora Ferrara?"

All right, she thought. *So much for the robbery hope.* But if it was a hit, it was the slowest goddamned hit in Mafia memory. This guy could have popped her and been gone by now. He must know about the Boys waiting just a few hundred meters away. Angelina caught her breath and looked at the man's face.

"Kurtz," she said. They'd never met, but she had studied the photograph Stevie had sent her to give to the Stooges.

The man neither smiled nor nodded. Nor did he lower his aim. "I know you're carrying," he said. "Keep your hands there and nothing dramatic's going to happen. Yet."

"You cannot imagine what a mistake you're making," Angelina Farino Ferrara said slowly and carefully.

"What are you going to do?" said Kurtz. "Put a contract out on me?"

Angelina had never met this man, but she knew enough about his history not to be coy with him. "That was Stevie's call," she said. "I was just the messenger."

"Why the Stooges?" asked Kurtz.

Angelina was surprised by the question, but only for a second. "Consider them an entrance exam," she said. She debated lowering her hands, looked at Kurtz's eyes, and kept them where they were.

"An exam for what?" asked Kurtz.

Keep talking, thought Angelina. Another two or three minutes and the Boys would come looking for her when she didn't appear on the return leg of the jog. *Or will they? It's cold this morning. The Lincoln is warm.* Perhaps four minutes. She kept herself from checking her big digital watch. "I thought you might be useful to us," she said. "Useful to me. Stevie ordered the contract, but I chose the idiots to see if you were any good."

"Why does Little Skag want me dead?" asked Kurtz. Angelina realized that the man must be very strong, since the .40-caliber pistol he was aiming was not light but his extended arm never wavered for a second.

"Stevie thinks you had something to do with my father and sister's deaths," she said.

"No he doesn't." Kurtz's voice was absolutely flat.

Knowing that if she argued with him, she might gain more time—or might just get shot in the heart more quickly—she decided to tell the truth. "He thinks you're dangerous, Kurtz. You know too much." *Such as the fact*

*that he hired you to hire the Dane to kill Maria and
Pop,* she thought, but did not say aloud.

"What's your angle?"

"My arms are getting tired. Can I just—"

"No," said Kurtz. The pistol's muzzle still did not
waver.

"I want some leverage when Stevie gets out," she
said, amazed to hear herself telling this ex-con what she
would tell no one else in the world. "I thought you
would be useful to me."

"How?"

"By killing Emilio Gonzaga and his top people."

"Why the hell would I do that?" asked Kurtz. His
voice did not even sound curious to Angelina, just
mildly bemused.

She took a breath. Now it was all or nothing. She
hadn't planned it this way. Actually, she'd planned to
have Kurtz on his knees in a few weeks, his hands
restraint-taped behind his back, and perhaps missing a
few teeth when she got to this part. Now all she could
do was go ahead and watch his face, his eyes, the muscles around his mouth, and his swallowing reflex—those
parts of a person that could not *not* react.

"Emilio Gonzaga ordered your little pal Samantha
killed twelve years ago," she said.

For a second, Angelina felt exactly like a duelist
whose only pistol shot has misfired. Nothing about Joe
Kurtz's hard face changed one iota—nothing. Looking
into his eyes was like looking at some Hieronymus
Bosch painting of a medieval executioner—if such a
painting existed, which she knew it did not. For a wild
instant, she considered throwing herself to the ground,
rolling, and pulling the .45 Compact Witness from her
belt, but the unwavering black muzzle aborted that
thought.

Another minute and the Boys will—She knew she did not have another minute. Angelina Farino Ferrara did not go in for self-delusion.

"No," Kurtz said at last.

"Yes," said Angelina. "I know you took care of Eddie Falco and Manny Levine twelve years ago, but they were on Gonzaga's leash at the time. He gave the word."

"I would have known that."

"No one knew that."

"Falco and Levine were small-time drug pushers," said Kurtz. "They were too stupid to . . ." He stopped, as if thinking of something.

"Yeah," said Angelina. "The little girl. The missing teenage girl—Elizabeth Connors—that your partner Samantha was hunting for. The high-school girl who later turned up dead. The trail led through Falco and Levine because the kidnapping was a Gonzaga gig; Connors owed him almost a quarter of a million dollars and the girl was leverage—just leverage—and those two idiots had been Elizabeth's friendly schoolyard pushers. After your partner stumbled across the connection, Emilio gave the word to Eddie and Manny to get rid of her and then he got rid of the kid. And then you got rid of Falco and Levine for him."

Kurtz shook his head slightly, but his gaze never left Angelina. The gun was still aimed at her chest. Angelina knew that the .40-caliber slug would smash her heart to a pulp before blasting it out through her spine.

"You were stupid, Kurtz," she said. "You even did time to help throw investigators off Gonzaga's track. It must amuse the shit out of him."

"I would have heard," said Kurtz.

"You didn't," said Angelina, knowing that time was up now—his and hers. It had to go one way or the other. "No one heard. But I can prove it. Give me a chance.

Call me and we'll set up a meeting. I'll show you the proof and tell you how I can buy you indemnity from Stevie. And more important, how you can get to the Gonzagas."

There was a long pause of silence, broken only by the wind blowing in from the lake. It was very cold. Angelina felt her legs threatening to quiver—from the cold, she hoped—and forced them not to. Finally, Joe Kurtz said, "Take that top off."

She had to raise her eyebrows at that. "Not getting enough, Joe? Been hard to score since you screwed my sister?"

Kurtz said nothing, but gestured with the muzzle of the pistol.

Keeping her hands in sight, she tugged off the straps of the tiny headlamp and pulled the loose sweatshirt over her head, dropping it on the black pavement. She stood there only in her jogging bra, knowing that her nipples were more than visible as they pressed through the thin cotton. She hoped it distracted the hell out of Kurtz.

It didn't. With his free hand, Kurtz pointed to the wall of the underpass. "Assume the position." When she spreadeagled against the wall with her hands on the cold concrete, he approached warily and kicked her feet farther apart. He tugged her Compact Witness .45 out of its holster and ran his hands quickly, professionally, down her front and thighs, pulling the cell phone from her pocket. He smashed the phone and put the Compact Witness in his peacoat pocket.

"I want that forty-five back," she said, speaking to the cold breath of the wall. "It has sentimental value. I shot my first husband in Sicily with it."

For the first time, there came something that might have been a human sound—a dry chuckle?—from Kurtz. Or maybe he was just clearing his throat. He handed her a cell phone over her shoulder. "Keep this. If I want to talk to you, I'll call you."

"Can I turn around?" said Angelina.

"No."

She heard him backing away and then there came the sound of a car starting. Angelina rushed to the opening of the tunnel in time to see an old Volvo disappearing along the footpath into the trees to the north.

She had time to put on her sweatshirt, tug on her headlamp, and slip the cell phone under her shirt before Marco and Leo came panting down the path, pistols drawn.

"What? What? Why'd you stop?" wheezed Leo while Marco swept the area with his pistol.

I should fire these shitheads, thought Angelina. She said, "Charley horse."

"We heard a car," panted Leo.

"Yeah, me too," said Angelina. "Big help you two would've been if it had been an assassin."

Leo blanched. Marco shot her a pissed look. *Maybe I'll just fire Leo,* she thought.

"You want a ride back?" asked Leo. "Or you gonna keep running?"

"With a charley horse?" said Angelina. "I'll be lucky to hobble to the car."

CHAPTER
SIX

It was just getting light—predawn Buffalo grayness bleeding into even dimmer Buffalo morning gray—when Kurtz got back to his flophouse hotel, only to find that Detectives Brubaker and Myers had come to roust him.

Kurtz had various telltales in his hotel to tell him if visitors were waiting, but these weren't called for this morning. The hotel was in a rough neighborhood and the local kids had already spray-painted Brubaker's unmarked Plymouth with the tag UNMRACKED CAR on the driver's side—spelling was not the local hoodlums' strong suit—and PIGMOBI^{LE}—they had not planned their spacing well—on the passenger side. Something about the sound of "pigmobi" amused Kurtz.

The rest of the situation did not amuse him all that much. Brubaker and Myers rousted him about once every three weeks and, so far, they'd not caught him with a weapon, but when they did—and the law of averages suggested they would have to—he'd be back in prison within twenty-four hours. Paroled felons in New York State were exempt from the God-given, Constitution-guaranteed, and redneck-worshiped right of every American to carry as much firepower as he wanted.

With his .40 S&W in one pocket and Angelina Farino Ferrara's cute but heavy little Compact Witness in the other, Kurtz went into the alley in back of his hotel and stashed both weapons behind some masonry he'd loosened himself two weeks earlier. The alley's resident winos and druggies were at the shelter or protecting their benches at this time of day, so Kurtz guessed that he might have a few hours before some scavenger would find his stash. If this roust took more than a few hours, he was screwed anyway and probably would not need the weapons.

Kurtz's residence hotel, the Royal Delaware Arms, had been a fancy place about the time President McKinley had been shot in Buffalo two turns of the century ago. McKinley may have stayed here the night before he was shot as far as Kurtz knew. The hotel had been going downhill for the past ninety years and seemed to have reached a balance point somewhere between total decay and imminent collapse. The Royal Delaware Arms was ten stories tall and boasted a sixty-foot radio-transmission tower on its roof, pouring out microwave radiation day and night, lethal doses according to many of the hotel's more paranoid inhabitants. The tower was about the only thing on the premises that worked. Over the preceding decades, the hotel part of the building, the lower five floors, had gone from a workingman's hotel to flophouse to low-income housing center, and then back to residential flophouse. Most of the residents were on welfare, lithium, and/or Thorazine. Kurtz had convinced the manager to let him live on the eighth floor, even though the top three floors had been effectively abandoned since the 1970s. A loophole in the fire and building codes had not specifically *prohibited* the rooms from being rented or some idiot from renting one—living up there amidst the peeling wallpaper, exposed lathing, and dripping pipes—and that is exactly what Kurtz was doing. The room still had a door and a refrigerator and running water, and that was all Kurtz really needed.

His room—two large, connected rooms, actually—was on the alley-side corner and served not by one but by two rusting fire escapes. The elevator doors above the fifth floor had been sealed off, so Kurtz had to walk the last three floors every time he came or went. That was a small trade-off for the security of knowing when anyone had visited him and for the warning he would get when someone *tried* to visit him. Both Petie, the manager and day man on the counter, and Gloria, the night man on the counter, were paid enough each month to be trustworthy about ringing Kurtz on his cell phone if anyone unknown to them headed toward the elevator or stairs.

Now Kurtz let himself in the alley entrance in case Brubaker had left his sidekick Myers in the lobby—unlikely, since plainclothes cops were like snakes or nuns and always traveled in pairs. He took the back stairs up to the third floor from the abandoned kitchen in back and then walked up the smelly main staircase to the eighth floor. At the sixth-floor level, Kurtz could see the two sets of footprints in the plaster dust he'd left covering the center of the stairs. Brubaker, who had the larger feet—Kurtz had noticed before—had a hole in his sole. That sounded about right to Kurtz.

The footprints led down the center of the dusty and dark corridor—Kurtz kept to the walls when he came and went—and ended at the open door to his room. The two detectives had kicked his door in, splintering the lock and knocking the door off the hinges. Kurtz braced himself, made his stomach muscles rigid, and walked into his home.

Myers came out from behind the door and hit him in the belly with what felt like brass knuckles. Kurtz went down and tried to roll against the wall, but Brubaker had time to step in from the opposite side of the door and give Kurtz a kick to the head that landed on his shoulder as he tucked and rolled again.

Myers kicked him in the back of his left leg, paralyzing the calf muscle, while Brubaker—the taller, uglier, smarter one of the pair—pulled his Glock-9mm and pressed it to the soft spot behind Kurtz's left ear.

"Give us a reason," hissed Detective Brubaker.

Kurtz did not move. He could not breathe yet, but he knew from experience that his stunned belly muscles and diaphragm would relax from the blow before he passed out from lack of oxygen.

"Give me a fucking *reason*!" shouted Brubaker, cocking the piece. It didn't need cocking of course, since it was a single-action, but it looked and sounded dramatic.

"Hey, hey, Fred," said Myers, sounding sincerely alarmed.

"Fuck hey, hey, Tommy," said Brubaker, spraying Kurtz's cheek with saliva. "This miserable fuck—" He slapped Kurtz hard on the neck with the cocked pistol and then kicked him in the small of the back.

Kurtz grunted and did not move.

"Pat him down," snapped Brubaker.

With Brubaker's Glock against his temple now, Kurtz lay still while Myers frisked him roughly, ripping buttons off his peacoat as he pulled it open, turning his pockets inside out.

"He's clean, Fred."

"Fuck!" The muzzle quit pressing into the flesh next

to Kurtz's left eye. "Sit up, asshole, hands behind your back, back against the wall."

Kurtz did as he was told. Myers was lounging on the arm of the sprung sofa Kurtz had dragged up to serve as both furniture and bed. Brubaker was standing five feet away with the 9mm still aimed at Kurtz's head.

"I ought to kill you right now, you miserable cock-sucker," Brubaker said conversationally. He patted the pocket of his cheap suit. "I've got a throwdown right here. Leave you here. The rats would have you three-fourths eaten before anyone fucking found you."

They'd have all *of me eaten before anyone found me up here,* thought Kurtz. He did not share the opinion aloud.

"Jimmy Hathaway's ghost would rest easy," said Brubaker, voice tense again, finger also tense on the trigger.

"Fred, Fred," said Myers, playing the good cop. Or at least the semi-sane cop. The non–rogue killer cop.

"Fuck it," said Brubaker, lowering the weapon. "You're not worth it, you piece of ratshit. Not when we'll get to do you legally soon enough. You're not worth the fucking paperwork this way." He stepped forward and kicked Kurtz in the belly.

Kurtz sagged against the wall and began the count-down to a point where he could breathe again.

Brubaker walked out. Myers paused for a moment, looking down at the gasping Kurtz. "You shouldn't have killed Hathaway," the fat man said softly. "Fred knows you did it, and someday he's going to prove it. Then there won't be any warnings."

Myers walked out too, and Kurtz listened to their footfalls and cursing about the elevator as they de-scended the echoing staircase. He made a mental note to sprinkle more plaster dust on the steps. He hoped they wouldn't tear his Volvo apart when they searched it.

It could have been much worse. Brubaker and Hathaway had been friends, of sorts, and both were crooked cops, but Hathaway had been on the Farino pad and on the personal payroll of Maria Farino during her short-lived bid to take over her father's business. Hathaway had seen a chance to take out Kurtz and curry favor with Maria Farino, and it had almost worked for him. Almost. If Brubaker and Myers had been working directly for the Farinos or Gonzagas now, it could have been a short, bad morning for Joe Kurtz. At least now he knew for sure that the cops weren't totally in Ms. Angelina Farino Ferrara's pocket.

When Kurtz could finally stand, he staggered a few steps, opened the window, and vomited out into the alley. No reason to get his bathroom all messy. He'd cleaned it just a week or two before.

When he could breathe a little better and his stomach muscles had quit their spasms, Kurtz went to the refrigerator to get breakfast, carrying the Miller Lite with him as he sprawled on the couch. He knew he had to get down to the alley to retrieve the two pistols, but he thought he'd rest a bit before doing that.

Ten minutes later, he flipped open his phone and called Arlene at the office.

"What's new, Joe? You're up early."

"I want you to do a deep data search for me," said Kurtz. "James B. Hansen." He spelled the last name. "He was a psychologist in Chicago in the early eighties. You'll find some newspaper articles and police reports from that period. I want everything you can get—everything—and a search of all James Hansens since then."

"*All?*"

"All," said Kurtz. "Cross-referenced to psychology journals, university faculties, crime database, marriage licenses, drivers' licenses, property transactions, the whole smash. And there's a triple murder and suicide involved in Chicago. Cross-check against all similar murder-suicides since then, using the crime database. Have the software search for common names, anagrams, factors, whatever."

"Do you know how much time and money this is going to cost us, Joe?"

"No."

"Do you care?"

"No."

"Should I use *all* of our computer resources?" Arlene's son and husband had been expert computer hackers and she had most of their tools at her disposal, including unauthorized e-mail drops and authority from her previous jobs as legal secretary—including one stint working for the Erie County district attorney. She was asking Kurtz whether she should break the law in requesting files.

"Yes," said Kurtz.

He could hear Arlene sigh and then exhale cigarette smoke. "All right. Is this urgent? Should I push it ahead of today's Sweetheart Search?"

"No," said Kurtz. "It'll keep. Get to it when you can."

"I presume this isn't a Sweetheart Search client we're talking about, is it, Joe?"

Kurtz sipped the last of his beer.

"Is this James B. Hansen in Buffalo now?" asked Arlene.

"I don't know," he said. "Also, I need another check."

"Listening," said Arlene. He could imagine her with her pen and pad poised.

"John Wellington Frears," said Kurtz. "Concert violinist. He lives in New York, probably Manhattan, probably the Upper East Side. He probably doesn't have a criminal record, but I want everything you can get on his medical records."

"Shall I use all possible—"

"Yes," said Kurtz. Medical records were among the most closely guarded secrets in America, but Arlene's last job while Kurtz was in prison had been with a nest of ambulance chasers. She could ferret out medical records that the patient's doctor did not know existed.

"Okay. Are you coming in today? We could look at some office space I marked in the paper."

"I don't know if I'll be in," said Kurtz. "How's Wedding Bells coming?"

"Data-mining services are all lined up," said Arlene. "Kevin's waiting to get us incorporated. I've got the Website designed and ready to go. All I need is the money in the bank so I can write the check."

"Yeah," said Kurtz and clicked off. He lay on the couch for a while and gazed at the twelve-foot-wide waterstain on the ceiling. Sometimes it looked like some fractal imagery or a medieval tapestry design to Kurtz. Other times it just looked like a fucking waterstain. Today it was a stain.

CHAPTER
SEVEN

Angelina Farino Ferrara hated eating shit for the Gonzagas. The "negotiations" all took place at the creepy old Gonzaga compound on Grand Island in the center of the Niagara River. This meant that Angelina and the Boys were picked up in one of Emilio Gonzaga's tacky white stretch limousines—the Gonzagas controlled most of the limousine services in Western New York—and driven across the bridge and through various checkpoints into the Grand Island fortress under the careful watch of Mickey Kee, Gonzaga's toughest killer. Once at the compound, more of Emilio's goons would pat them down and check them for wires before sitting the Boys down in a windowless vestibule and marching Angelina into one of the manse's many rooms as if she were a prisoner of war, which, in a real sense, she was.

The war hadn't been her doing, of course—nothing in the family business had been her doing for the past six years—but was a result of her brother Stephen's bizarre machinations to seize control of his own family business from behind bars in Attica. The housecleaning that Stevie had instigated—involving, Angelina knew, the murder of her conniving sister and useless father, although Stevie did not know that she knew—had also brought the Gonzagas into the Farino family business to the tune of a half-million dollars, most of it going to a hit man known only as the Dane, who had carried out the Hamlet-like last act for the don, Maria, and their double-dealing family consigliere at the time. The Gonzaga money had bought a sort of peace between the families—or at least a cease-fire with Stevie and the surviving members of the Farino family—but it also meant that tacit control of the Farino family was currently in the hands of their traditional enemies. When Angelina thought of the fat, fish-faced, blubbery-lipped, sweating pig-hemorrhoid that was Emilio Gonzaga determining the Farinos' destiny, she wanted to rip both his and her brother's heads off and piss down their necks.

"A pleasure to see you again, Angelina," said Emilio Gonzaga, showing his cigar-stained pig's teeth in what he undoubtedly thought was a seductive, debonair smile.

"So nice to see you, Emilio," said Angelina with a shy, self-effacing half-smile she had borrowed from a Carmelite nun she used to drink with in Rome. If she and Emilio had been alone at that moment, with none of Gonzaga's bodyguards around, especially the dangerous Mickey Kee, she would have happily shot the fat don in the testicles. One at a time.

"I hope it is not too early for lunch," said Emilio, leading her into a dark-beamed, dark-paneled, windowless dining room. The interior furnishings looked as if they had been designed by Lucretia Borgia on a down day. "Something light," said Emilio, gesturing grandly to a table and a dark-wood sideboard groaning under the weight of large bowls of pasta, haunches of beef, fish whose eyes stared up plaintively, a stack of lobsters glowing pink, three types of potatoes, entire loaves of

Italian bread, and half a dozen bottles of heavy wine.

"Wonderful," said Angelina. Emilio Gonzaga held the black, high-backed chair for her while she took her place. As always, the fat man smelled of sweat, cigars, halitosis, and something faintly Cloroxy, like stale semen. She gave him her coyest smile again while one of his pigboy bodyguards pulled out his chair as he took his place at the head of the table, to her left.

They talked business while they ate. Emilio was one of those men—like former President Clinton—who liked to grin and talk and laugh with his mouth full. Another reason Angelina had fled to Europe for six years. But now she ignored the display, nodded attentively, and tried to sound smart but not too smart, agreeable but not a total pushover, and—when Emilio flirted—appropriately slutty but not a complete roundheels.

"So," he said, segueing smoothly from the business side of the new merger and acquisition he was arranging, in which the Farino family would merge into oblivion and the Gonzagas would acquire everything, "this power-sharing thing, this idea of the three of us running things—" Emilio's veneer of education slipped as he pronounced the word *tings* "—it's what the old guys, the Romans, our ancestors, used to call a *troika*."

"Triumvirate," said Angelina. She immediately wished she'd kept her mouth shut. *Suffer fools,* Count Ferrara had taught her. *Then make them suffer.*

"What's that?" Emilio Gonzaga was picking at something in his side teeth.

"Triumvirate," repeated Angelina. "That's what the Romans used to call it when they had three leaders at one time. A *troika* is the Russian phrase for three leaders . . . or three anything. It was what they called three horses hitched to a sleigh."

Emilio grunted and glanced over his shoulder. The two white-jacketed goons he had left in the room to act as waiters stood with their hands over their crotches and their stares focused on nothing. Mickey Kee and the other bodyguard stared at the ceiling. No one wanted to be paying attention when the don was corrected.

"Whatever," said Emilio. "The point is that you benefit, I benefit, and Little Ska . . . Stephen . . . he benefits the most. Like old times, only without the rancor." Gonzaga pronounced the last word *rain-core.*

It's like old times, only this time with you elected God, me elected your whore, and Stevie elected to die within a few months after he gets out, thought Angelina. She lifted the glass of bilious cabernet. "To new beginnings," she said brightly.

The cell phone Kurtz had given her rang. Emilio stopped his chewing and frowned at her breach of etiquette.

"I'm sorry, Emilio," she said. "Only Stevie, his lawyer, and a few other people use this private line. I should take it." She rose from the table and turned her back to the pig on his throne. "Yes?"

"The Sabres are playing tonight," came Joe Kurtz's voice. "Go to the game."

"All right."

"After the first serious injury, go to the women's rest room near the main doors." He disconnected.

Angelina put the phone back in her tiny purse and sat down again. Emilio was sloshing after-dinner liqueur around in his cheeks as if it were mouthwash.

"That was short," he said.

"But sweet," said Angelina.

The goons brought coffee in a silver urn and five types of pastry.

• • •

It was late afternoon, snowing harder and almost dark when Kurtz drove thirty minutes north to the suburban village of Lockport. The house on Locust Street looked comfortable, middle-class, and safe—lights burning on both floors—when Kurtz drove past, turned left, and parked halfway down the next street in front of a ranch house for sale. Donald Rafferty didn't know Kurtz's Volvo, but this wasn't the kind of neighborhood that wouldn't notice if a car with someone in it kept parking along a residential street for long periods of time.

Kurtz had an electronic device the size of a compact boom box on the passenger seat, and now he plugged in earphones. To anyone passing by, he would look like someone waiting for a realtor late on a Friday afternoon, someone enjoying his Discman.

The boom box was a short-range radio receiver tuned to the five bugs he had planted in Rafferty and Rachel's home three months earlier. The electronic gear had cost him what savings he'd had at the time, and Kurtz had not chosen to get a stronger transmitter or tape equipment—he didn't have the time or personnel to pour through tapes anyway—but this way, he could eavesdrop when he was in the neighborhood, which was often. The evening sampling told him quite a bit.

Rachel, Sam's fourteen-year-old daughter, was an intelligent, quiet, sensitive and lonely child. She made daughterly overtures to Rafferty, her adoptive father, but the man was either too busy, too distracted by his gambling, or too drunk to pay any attention. He wasn't abusive to Rachel, unless one counted absolute indifference as abuse.

Sam had been married to Rafferty for only ten months—and that four years previous to Rachel's birth, which owed nothing to Donnie Rafferty—but Sam had left no other family behind when she was murdered twelve years ago, so his appointment as the girl's guardian had seemed to make sense at the time. Her insurance and family inheritance must have been attractive to Rafferty when he petitioned to adopt Rachel; the money had paid for his house and car and settled more than a few of his gambling debts. But now Rafferty had started losing heavily again, which meant that he was drinking heavily again as well. Rafferty had three regular girlfriends, two of whom spent nights with him in Lockport on a well-scheduled basis, so that each of the two would not find evidence of the other. The third girlfriend was a coke-pushing whore on Seneca Street who didn't know or care where Rafferty lived.

Kurtz tuned in the bugs. Donald Rafferty had just hung up after promising his bookie, a sleazo that Kurtz had known professionally, that he would have the next payment to him by Monday. Now Rafferty called DeeDee, his Number Two girlfriend, and started making plans for the weekend. This time, they were going away together, up to Toronto, which meant that Rachel was being left home alone again.

Kurtz had not bugged Rachel's bedroom, but he quickly checked the family room and kitchen taps. There came the soft sounds of plates being rinsed and set in the dishwasher.

Rafferty finished his phone conversation after telling DeeDee to "bring the little leather thing along this weekend" and walked into the kitchen—Kurtz could hear the footsteps. A cupboard was opened and closed; Kurtz knew that Rafferty kept his booze in the kitchen and his cocaine in the top drawer of his dresser. Another cupboard. The sensitive microphone picked up the sound of the drink—Rafferty stocked more bourbon than anything else—being poured.

"Goddamn snow. Walk'll need shoveling again in the morning." His voice was slurred.

"Okay, Dad."

"I've got a business trip again this weekend. I'll be back Sunday or Monday."

During the interval of silence, Kurtz tried to imagine what kind of weekend business trip a U.S. Postal Service clerk would have to take.

Rachel's voice. "Could Melissa come over tomorrow night to watch a video with me?"

"No."

"Could I go over to their house to watch one if I was back by nine?"

"No." The cupboard was opened and closed again. The dishwasher began running.

"Rache?" Kurtz knew from his sampling of her phone conversations with Melissa—her only real friend—that Rachel hated that nickname.

"Yes, Daddy?"

"That's really a pretty thing you're wearing."

For a time, the only noise was the dishwasher.

"This sweatshirt?"

"Yeah. It looks . . . different."

"It's not. It's the one I got at the Falls last summer."

"Yeah, well . . . you look pretty is all."

The dishwasher kicked into the rinse cycle.

"I'm going to take the garbage out," said Rachel.

It was full dark now. Kurtz left his earphones on as he drove around the block, slowing as he passed the house. He saw the girl at the side of the house. Her hair was longer now, and even in the dim glow from the porch light, he could see that it looked more the color of Sam's red hair than it had when it was shorter in the fall. Rachel pressed the garbage bag down in the trash can and stood for a minute in the side yard, turned mostly away from Kurtz and the street, holding her face up to the falling snow.

CHAPTER
EIGHT

At the same time, in the suburb of Tonawanda, a thirty-minute drive from Lockport, James B. Hansen—aka Robert Millworth aka Howard G. Lane aka Stanley Steiner aka half a dozen other names, none of which shared the same initials—was celebrating his fiftieth birthday.

Hansen—his current name was Robert Gaines Millworth—was surrounded by friends and loving family, including his wife of three years, Donna, his stepson Jason, and his eight-year-old Irish setter, Dickson. The long driveway to his modernist home facing Elicott Creek was filled with moderately expensive sedans and SUVs belonging to his friends and colleagues, who had braved yet another snowstorm to join him at his well-planned surprise party.

Hansen was relaxed and jovial. He'd returned from an extended business trip to Miami only a week and a half earlier and his tan was the envy of everyone. Hansen had indeed put on almost thirty pounds since his University of Chicago psychologist days, but he was six-feet-four, much of the extra weight was muscle, and even the fat was toned up and useful when push came to shove.

Now Hansen moved among his guests, stopping to chat with clusters of friends, grinning at the inevitable fiftieth-birthday-over-the-hill jokes, and generally patting everyone on the shoulder or shaking their hands. Occasionally Hansen would think about that hand of his, where it had been, about what he'd buried in an Everglades hummock twelve days earlier, and what that hand had touched, and he had to smile. Stepping out onto the modern concrete-and-industrial-wire terrace above the front door, James Hansen breathed in the cold night air, blinked snowflakes off his eyelashes, and sniffed his hand. After two weeks, he knew the smell of lime and blood could not still be there, but the memory of it made something hard stir in him.

When James B. Hansen had been twelve years old—living under his real name, which he had all but forgotten by now—and growing up in Kearney, Nebraska, he had seen the Tony Curtis movie *The Great Imposter*. Based on a true story, the film was about a man who went from job to job and identity to identity—at one point impersonating a doctor and actually carrying out lifesaving surgery. Since then, almost forty years ago, the idea had been used countless times in films and television and so-called "reality programming," but to young James B. Hansen, the movie was an epiphany comparable to Saul's being-knocked-off-his-ass revelation on the road to Damascus.

Hansen had immediately begun re-creating himself, first by lying to friends, teachers, and his mother—his father had died in a car accident when Hansen was six. Hansen's mother then died when he was a freshman at the University of Nebraska; within days he dropped out of the university, moved to Indianapolis, and changed his name and history. It was so easy. Identity in the United States was essentially a matter of choice and acquiring the proper birth certificates, driver's licenses, credit cards, college and graduate-school transcripts, and so forth was child's play.

Child's play for James B. Hansen as a child had been pulling the wings off flies and vivisecting kittens. Hansen knew that this was a sure early sign of a sociopathic and dangerous psychotic personality—he had earned his living for two years as a professor of psychology and taught those things in his abnormal-psych courses—but this did not bother him. What the conformity-straitjacketed mediocrities labeled as sociopathology, he knew to be liberation—liberation from social constraints that the weak millions never thought to challenge. And Hansen had unsentimentally known of his own superiority for decades: the only good thing his Nebraska high school had ever done for him was to administer a full battery of intelligence tests to him—he was being staffed for possible emotional and learning problems at the time—and the amazed school psychologist had told his mother that Jimmy (not his name at the time) had an IQ of 168, effectively in the genius category and as high as that battery of tests could measure intelligence. This was no news to Jimmy, who had always known that he was far more intelligent than his classmates and teachers (he had no real friends or playmates). This was not arrogance, merely astute observation. The school psychologist had said that a gifted/talented program or special school for the gifted would have been appropriate for young Hansen, but of course no such thing existed in 1960s Kearney, Nebraska. Besides, by that time, Hansen's teacher had become aware—through Jimmy's creative-writing essays—of the sixteen-year-old student's penchant for torturing dogs and cats, and Jimmy came close to being expelled. Only his ailing mother's intervention and his own stonewalling had kept him in school.

Those creative-writing papers had been the last time Hansen had told the truth about anything important.

At an early age, James B. Hansen had learned a profound truth: namely, that almost all experts and specialists and professionals are absolutely full of shit. The great bulk of each of their so-called professions is language, jargon, specialized babble. Given that, and some deep reading in the field, and the proper attire, anyone smart enough could do damned near anything. In his last thirty-two years of liberation from truth and imposed identity, Hansen had never impersonated an airline pilot or a neurosurgeon, but he suspected that he could if he put his mind to it. During those years, however, he had made his living as an English professor, a senior editor at a major publishing house, a handler of heavy construction equipment, a NASCAR driver, a Park Avenue psychiatrist, a professor of psychology, a herpetologist specializing in extracting venom, an MRI specialist, a computer designer, an award-winning realtor, a political consultant, an air traffic controller, a firefighter, and half a dozen other specialties. He had never studied for any of these fields beyond visits to the library.

Money did not run the world, James B. Hansen knew. Bullshit and gullibility did.

Hansen had lived in more than two dozen major American cities and spent two years in France. He did not like Europe. The adults were arrogant and the little girls there were too worldly. Handguns were too hard to find. But the fliks were as stupid there as cops were in America, and God knows, the food was better.

His career as serial killer did not begin until he was twenty-three years old, although he had murdered before that. Hansen's father had left no insurance, no savings, nothing but debts and his illegally obtained, Korean-era

M1 carbine and three clips of ammunition. The day after his ninth-grade English teacher, Mrs. Berkstrom, ran to the principal with Hansen's animal-torturing essays, Hansen had loaded the carbine, put it in his father's old golf bag with the clubs, and dragged the whole thing to school. There were no metal detectors in those days. Hansen's plan had been elegant—to kill Mrs. Berkstrom, the principal, the school psychologist who had turned traitor—going from recommending him for a gifted school to recommending intensive counseling—and then every classmate he could track down until he ran out of ammunition. James B. Hansen could have started the Columbine mass-murder fad thirty-five years before it finally caught on. But Hansen would never have committed suicide during or after the act. His plan had been to kill as many people as possible—including his coughing, wheezing, useless mother—and then, like Huck Finn, light out for the territory.

But a combination of his genius-level IQ and the fact that first period had been gym—Hansen did not want to go on his killing rampage wearing silly gym trunks—made him think twice. He hauled the stowed golf bag home during his lunch break and put the M1 back in its basement storage spot. He would have time to settle scores later, he knew, when it would not require going on the run for the rest of his life, with the cops chasing what he already thought of as his "larval identity."

So two months after his mother's funeral and the sale of their Kearney house, and one month after he had dropped out of the university with no forwarding address, Hansen had returned to his hometown in the middle of the night, waited for Mrs. Berkstrom to come out to her station wagon in the dim light of the Nebraska winter morning, and shot her twice in the head with the

M1, dumping the carbine in the Platte River on his way east.

He had discovered his taste for raping and killing young girls when he was twenty-three, after the failure—through no fault of his own—of his first marriage. Since then, James B. Hansen had been married seven times, although he saved real sexual satisfaction for his episodes with the young, teenage girls. Wives were good cover and part of whatever identity he was inhabiting at any given time, but their middle-aged flab and used, tired bodies held no excitement for Hansen. He considered himself a connoisseur of virgins. And terrorized virginity was precisely the bouquet and aroma of the fine wine he most enjoyed. James B. Hansen knew that the cultural revulsion from pedophilia was just another example of people pulling away furthest from what they wanted most. From time immemorial, men had wanted the youngest and freshest girls in which to plant their seed—although Hansen never planted his seed anywhere, being careful to wear condoms and latex gloves since DNA typing had become so prevalent. But where other men fantasized and masturbated, James B. Hansen acted and enjoyed.

More than once, Hansen could have found it convenient to add "gay" to his repertoire of chameleon identities, but he drew the line at that. He was no pervert.

Knowing the psychopathology of his own preferences, Hansen avoided stereotypical—and criminal "typable"—behaviors. He was now out of the age range of the average serial killer. He resisted the urge to harvest more than one kill a year. He could afford to fly whenever he wanted and took great care in spreading the victims around the country, with no geographical connection to his home location at any given time. He took no souvenirs except for photographs, and these were sealed away in his locked titanium case inside an expensive safe in his locked gun room in the basement of this house. Only he was allowed to go there. If the police found his souvenir case, then his current identity was long since blown. If his current wife or son somehow got into the room and got into the safe and found the case and somehow opened it . . . well, they were always expendable.

But that would not happen.

Hansen knew now that John Wellington Frears, the African-American violinist from his Chicago days two decades ago and father of Number Nine, was in Buffalo. He knew now that Frears had thought he'd seen him at the airport—which at first amazed and disturbed Hansen since he had undergone five plastic-surgery operations since Chicago and would not have recognized himself from those days—but he also knew that no one at police headquarters had given any credence at all to Frears's flutterings and sputterings. James B. Hansen was officially as dead as little Crystal Frears, and the Chicago P.D. had the dental records and photos of the charred corpse—complete with a partially identifiable Marine Corps tattoo James B. Hansen had sported—to prove it. And there was no question in his mind that others could not see any physical resemblance between the current iteration of James B. Hansen and that of his old Chicago-era persona.

Hansen had not heard the hullabaloo behind him at the airport—his hearing had been damaged slightly by too many years of practice shooting without ear protection—and did not learn about it right away at work because he had taken two days of vacation after his Florida business trip. It was always Hansen's practice to spend a day or two away from work and family after his annual Special Visit.

When Hansen did hear about Frears, his first impulse was to drive to the Airport Sheraton and blow the overrated fiddler away. He had driven to the Sheraton, but once again the cool, analytical part of his genius-level intellect prevailed. Any murder of Frears in Buffalo would lead to a homicide investigation, which would bring up the man's crank report of his airport spotting, which might involve the Chicago P.D. and some reopening of the Crystal Frears case.

Hansen considered waiting for the old black man to go back to his lonely life in New York and to his upcoming concert tour. Hansen had already downloaded the full itinerary of that tour and he thought that Denver would be a good place for a botched mugging to occur. A fatal shooting. A modest obituary in *The New York Times*. But that plan had problems: Hansen would have to travel to follow Frears on tour, and travel always left records; a murder in another town would mean that Hansen could have no connection with the homicide investigation. Finally, Hansen simply did not want to wait. He wanted Frears dead. Soon. But he needed someone else to be the obvious suspect—someone else not only to take the fall, but to take a bullet while resisting arrest.

Now Hansen went back into the house and moved from guest to guest, laughing, telling easy stories, chuckling at his own mortality looming at the age of fifty— in truth, he had never felt stronger or smarter or more alive—all the while moving toward the kitchen and Donna.

His pager vibrated.

Hansen looked at the number. "Shit." He didn't need these clowns screwing up his birthday. He went up to his bedroom to retrieve his cell phone—his son was on the computer and tying up the house line—and punched in the number.

"Where are you?" he asked. "What's up?"

"We're right outside your house, sir. We were in the area and have some news but didn't want to interrupt your birthday party."

"Good thinking," said Hansen. "Stay where you are." He pulled on a cashmere blazer and went down and out through a gauntlet of backslappings and well wishes. The two were waiting by their car at the end of the drive, hunkered against the falling snow and stamping their feet to stay warm.

"What happened to your vehicle?" asked Hansen. Even with only the glow from his distant porch lights, Hansen could make out the vandalism.

"Fucking homeboys tagged us when we—" began Detective Brubaker.

"Hey," said Hansen. "Watch the language." He detested obscenity and vulgarity.

"Sorry, Captain," said Brubaker. "Myers and me were following down a lead this morning when the locals spray-painted the car. We—"

"What is this important news that couldn't wait until Monday?" interrupted Hansen. Brubaker and Myers were dishonest, venial cops, associates of that murdered, crooked cop Hathaway, whom the entire department shed crocodile tears for the previous fall. Hansen detested crooked cops even more than he detested obscene language.

"Curly died," said Myers.

Hansen had to think for a second. "Henry Pruitt," he said. One of the three Attica ex-cons found on the I-90. "Did he ever regain consciousness?"

"No, sir," said Brubaker.

"Then what are you bothering me for?" There had been no real evidence on the triple killing, and none of the witnesses' descriptions from the restaurant had matched any of the other's. The uniformed cop who had been sapped remembered nothing and had become the laughingstock of his division.

"We had a thought," said Detective Myers.

Hansen restrained himself from making the obvious comment. He waited.

"A guy we had a run-in with today is an Attica ex-con," said Brubaker.

"A fourth of the population of our fair city has either been in Attica or is related to someone in Attica," said Hansen.

"Yeah, but this perp probably knew the Stooges," said Myers. "And he had a motive for offing them."

Hansen stood in the snow and waited. Some of his guests were beginning to drive off. The cocktail party had been a casual buffet affair, and only a few of his closest friends were staying for dinner.

"The Cell Block–D Mosque gang had put a fatwa out on our guy," said Brubaker. "Ten thousand dollars. A fatwa is—"

"I know what a fatwa is," said Hansen. "I'm probably the only officer in the division who's *read* Salman Rushdie."

"Yes, sir," said Myers, apologizing for his partner. Click and Clack.

"What's your point?" said Hansen. "That Pruitt, Tyler and Banes—" he never used nicknames or disrespectful terms for the dead "—were trying to cash in on the D-Block Mosque's bounty and your perp got them first?"

"Yes, sir," said Detective Brubaker.

"What's his name?"

"Kurtz," said Myers. "Joe Kurtz. He's an ex-con himself. Served eleven years on an eighteen-year sentence for—"

"Yes, yes," Hansen said impatiently. "I've seen his

sheet. He was on the list of suspects for the Farino massacre last November. But there was no evidence to tie him to the scene."

"There never is with this Kurtz," Brubaker said bitterly. Hansen knew Brubaker was talking about the death of his pal Jimmy Hathaway. Hansen had not been in Buffalo long when Hathaway was killed, but Hansen had met the man and thought he was possibly the dumbest cop he'd ever encountered, which was saying a lot. It had been Hansen's professional opinion—shared by most of the senior officers, including those who had been in the division for years—that Hathaway's ties to the Farino mob had gotten him killed.

"Word on the street has it that Kurtz tossed that drug dealer, Malcolm Kibunte, over Niagara Falls right after he got out of Attica," offered Myers. "Just threw him right over the fucking . . . sorry, Captain."

"I'm getting cold," said Hansen. "What do you want?"

"We been following this Kurtz some on our own time," said Brubaker. "We'd like to make the surveillance official. Three teams can do it. Woltz and Farrell aren't assigned to anything right now and—"

Hansen shook his head. "You're it. You want surveillance on this guy, do it on department time for a few days. But don't put in for overtime."

"Aw, Chri . . . cripes, Captain," said Myers. "We've put in twelve hours today already and—"

Hansen cut him off with a glance. "Anything else?"

"No, sir," said Brubaker.

"Then please move this piece of junk out of my driveway," said Hansen, turning back toward his lighted house.

CHAPTER NINE

Angelina Farino Ferrara sat in her expensive rink-side seat at the Sabres game and waited impatiently for someone to get hurt. She did not have to wait long. Eleven minutes and nine seconds into the first period, Sabres defenseman Rhett Warrener got Vancouver Canucks captain Markus Naslund against the boards in the corner, threw him down and fractured his tibia. The crowd went wild.

Angelina hated ice hockey. Of course, she hated all organized sports, but hockey bored her the most. The potential of watching these toothless apes skate for an hour with the possibility of no score—no score at all!—made her want to scream. But then again, she had been dragged to Sabres games for almost fourteen years by her late hockey-loving father. The new arena was called HSBC, which stood for some banking thing, but everyone in Buffalo knew that it meant either "Hot Sauce, Blue Cheese" or "Holy Shit, Buffalo's Cold!"

Angelina did remember one game she had enjoyed immensely, many years ago when she was young. It was a Stanley Cup play-off game in the old Coliseum, and the season had run later than usual, deep into May. The

temperature was in the low nineties when the game began, the ice was melting and setting off a thick fog, and
the fog awakened scores of bats that had been hanging
amidst the wooden rafters of the ancient Coliseum for
years. Angelina remembered her father cursing as the
fog grew so thick that even the expensive-seat holders
could see almost nothing of the action, merely hear the
grunts and shouts and curses from the rink as the players
collided and battled in the fog, all the while the bats
darted in and out of the mist, swooping among the
stands, making women shriek and men curse all the
louder.

Angelina had enjoyed that particular game.

Now, as trainers and medics and hulking teammates
on skates huddled around the fallen Naslund, Angelina
headed for the ladies' rest room.

The Boys, Marco and Leo, knuckled along beside her,
squinting suspiciously at the crowd. Angelina knew that
these two were decent bodyguards and button men—at
least Marco seemed to be—but she also knew that they
had been chosen by Stevie and that their first job was to
report her actions and behavior to her brother-behind-
bars. Angelina Farino Ferrara was all too familiar with
public figures—Prime Minister Indira Gandhi, for one—
who had been gunned down by their own turncoat security detail. She did not plan to check out that way.

At the entrance to the women's rest room, Marco and
Leo continued to hulk. "Oh, for God's sake," said Angelina. "No one's lurking in the john. Go get us some
beer and Cracker Jack and a hot dog. Three hot dogs."
Marco nodded at Leo to go but seemed intent on staying
around the women's rest room. "Go help Leo carry," she
ordered.

Marco frowned but followed the other huge man
around the corner toward the refreshment stand. Ange-

lina stepped into the crowded rest room, did not see Joe Kurtz standing around in drag, and quickly stepped back out into the corridor.

Kurtz was leaning against the wall at the opening to a side hallway across the way. Angelina walked over to join him.

Kurtz kept his right hand in his peacoat pocket and nodded for her to walk down the narrow service corridor.

"Is that a pistol in your pocket," said Angelina, "or are you just happy to—"

"It's a pistol." Kurtz nodded for her to open the door marked AUTHORIZED PERSONNEL ONLY at the end of the hall.

Angelina took a breath and went through the door, noticing that the latch had been taped Watergate-style. A metal stairway led down to a wildly cluttered underground filled with boilers and countless pipes and valves running to the rink above. Kurtz pointed down one of the narrow walkways through the machinery, and Angelina led the way. Halfway across the space, a black man looked through the window of his office, nodded at Kurtz, and went back to his business.

"A friend of yours?" asked Angelina.

"A friend of Ben Franklin's," said Kurtz. "Up that way." Another long, metal staircase led to a side door.

They emerged at the dark end of the parking lot behind the huge heating and air-conditioning blowers.

"Spread against the wall," said Kurtz. He had removed his .40-caliber semiauto and held it steady.

"Oh, for God's sake—" began Angelina.

Kurtz moved very, very quickly, spinning her around and shoving her toward the wall so fast that she had to raise her hands or plant her face in the brick. He kicked her legs farther apart, and she thanked the gods that she had changed out of her dress into wool slacks after visiting Gonzaga earlier in the day.

Once again, Kurtz's frisk was fast and effective and impersonal, if you can call having someone's hands moving across your breasts, buttocks, thighs, and crotch impersonal. He pulled the little .45 from its holster in the small of her back and slid it into his pocket while he pawed through her purse.

"I want that pistol back as well," she said.

"Why? Did you shoot your second husband with it?"

Angelina let out a breath. Comedians. They all thought they were comedians. "I know its maker," she said. "Fratelli Tanfoglio of the Gardone Tanfoglios." He ignored her and tossed her purse back to her as she turned toward him. "In Italy," she added uselessly.

"Let's go," said Kurtz.

"Go where?" asked Angelina, feeling a surge of alarm for the first time. "I was just supposed to tell you how to find the evidence that Emilio Gonzaga whacked your old partner. I don't have to go anywhere to—" She looked at Joe Kurtz's face and fell silent.

"Let's go," repeated Kurtz.

They walked through the dark and icy parking lot. "My Jaguar's parked on the other side," said Angelina. "In the VIP lot near—"

"We're not taking your car," said Kurtz.

"When Marco and Leo find me gone—with my car still there—they're going to go so totally apeshit that—"

"Shut up," said Kurtz.

Kurtz had the woman drive his Volvo. He sat with his back to the passenger door and the pistol propped on his left forearm. They were taking back streets through the snowy night, driving slowly because he had told her that if she drove over forty miles per hour, he would kill her. Kurtz had been in the driver's seat when someone was holding a gun on him, and he'd discovered that getting the car up to eighty-five or ninety miles per hour was a serious disincentive to the shooter.

"Tell me about Gonzaga and this guy," he said.

Angelina glanced at him. The yellow light from the sodium-vapor anticrime lamps was painting both their faces dead yellow. "You were in love with her, weren't you, Kurtz? Your partner. The woman Emilio ordered murdered. I'd thought it was just a Maltese Falcon sort of thing . . . you know, you can't let your partner get killed. That sort of macho shit."

"Tell me about Gonzaga and the guy we're going to see," said Kurtz.

"Gonzaga's man who brought the order down to the two punks you wasted—Falco and Levine—is named Johnny Norse. I was going to give you his name and address tonight. But there's no reason for me to go along. It's just going to cause a world of trouble when Marco and Leo—"

"Tell me about Johnny Norse," said Kurtz.

Angelina Farino Ferrara took a breath. She did not look nervous to Kurtz. He had considered settling this whole thing back in the darkened parking lot. But he needed information and right now she was the only conduit.

"Norse was Emilio Gonzaga's favorite button man back in the late eighties and early nineties," Angelina said. "A real Dapper Dan type. Always wore Armani. Thought he was Richard Gere. Ladies' man. Man's man. Swung both ways. Now he's dying of AIDS. He's dead, really, he just doesn't know it yet—"

"For your sake," said Kurtz, "he'd better not be dead."

Angelina shook her head. "He's in this hospice in Williamsville." She glanced at Kurtz in the yellow light. "Look, we can avoid the shitstorm that'll blow in if I'm out of the Boys' sight any longer. Let me go back to the game. I'll make up some bullshit story about where I was. Check out Norse on your own. He'll confirm what I told you about Gonzaga ordering the hit."

Kurtz smiled ever so slightly. "It sounds like a good plan," he said. "Except for the part where I go off to some address you give me and find ten of your boys— or Gonzaga's—waiting there. No, I think we'll do this together. Tonight. Now."

"What's to insure that you don't kill me anyway?" asked Angelina. "After I bring you to Norse. Even if he tells the truth?"

Kurtz's silence answered that question.

The hospice was in a tasteful, Georgian-style building at the end of a cul-de-sac in the expensive part of Williamsville. It might have been a private home had it not been for the "Exit" signs at the doors, the white-clothed aides pushing wheelchairs in the halls, and the receptionist behind the tiger-maple desk in the foyer. Kurtz wondered for a bemused second or so whether this was a home for aged and dying button men, whether the mob ran a chain of these places across the country—Wiseguy Manors. He suspected not. The receptionist told them quietly that visiting hours were over, but when Angelina said that they had come to see Mr. Norse, the receptionist was obviously surprised.

"No one has come to see Mr. Norse while he has been under our care," she said. "Are you family?"

"Gonzaga family," Kurtz said, but the woman showed no reaction. So much for the mob-franchise theory.

"Well . . ." The woman hesitated. "You are aware that Mr. Norse is very near the end?"

"That's why we've come," said Angelina Farino Ferrara.

The receptionist nodded and summoned a woman in white to take them to Mr. Norse.

The dying thing in the bed was no Dapper Dan. The remnants of Johnny Norse now weighed ninety pounds at the most, showed emaciated arms that reminded Kurtz of a baby bird's bended wings tipped with yellowed nails, and had flesh mottled with sores and the lesions of Kaposi's sarcoma. Most of the mobster's hair had fallen out. Oxygen tubes ran up under the man's gaping nostrils. Norse's lips were cracked and already pulled back over his teeth like a corpse's and his eyes had sunken, the corners radiating small white webs as if spiders had already laid claim there.

Pruno had given Kurtz a reading list before he left for prison, and the first book Kurtz had read was *Madame Bovary*. He was reminded now of how Emma Bovary's corpse had looked after the arsenic had killed her.

Norse stirred in his bed and turned unblinking eyes in their direction. Kurtz stepped closer to the bed.

"Who are you?" whispered Norse. There was a pathetic eagerness in that whisper. "Did Emilio send you?"

"Sort of," said Kurtz. "Do you remember Emilio Gonzaga having you pass down an order twelve years ago to kill a woman named Samantha Fielding?"

Norse frowned up at Kurtz and reached for the call button on a beige wire. Kurtz moved the button out of the man's trembling grasp. "Samantha Fielding," repeated Kurtz. "A private investigator. It was during the

Elizabeth Connors kidnapping. You were the go-between with Eddie Falco and Manny Levine."

"Who the fuck are you?" whispered Johnny Norse. The lusterless eyes flicked toward Angelina and then came back to Kurtz. "Fuck you."

"Wrong answer," said Kurtz. He leaned over with both arms extended as if to hug Norse, but instead, he closed his thumbs over the two oxygen lines and squeezed them shut.

Norse began gasping and rasping. Angelina closed the door and set her back against it.

Kurtz released the hoses. "Samantha Fielding?"

Johnny Norse's eyes were flicking back and forth like cornered rodents. He shook his head and Kurtz kinked the oxygen lines again, holding them kinked this time until Norse's gasps were as loud as Cheyne-Stokes death rattles.

"Samantha Fielding?" repeated Kurtz. "About twelve years ago."

The corpse in the bed nodded wildly. "The Connors kid . . . Emilio was . . . squeezing Connors . . . just wanted . . . the money."

Kurtz waited.

"Some . . . cunt . . . of a P.I. . . . found the connection . . . between Falco and Levine . . . and us snatching the kid. Emilio—" He stopped and looked up at Kurtz, his corpse mouth twitching in what might have been an attempt at an ingratiating Johnny Norse smile. "I didn't have . . . nothing to do with it. I didn't even know who they were talking about. I didn't—"

Kurtz reached for the oxygen hose.

"Jesus . . . fuck . . . all right. Emilio put the word out. I . . . delivered it . . . to the drug dealers . . . Falco and . . . Levine. You got what you want, asshole?"

"Yes," said Kurtz. He took the .40 S&W semiautomatic from his belt, thumbed back the hammer, and set the muzzle in Johnny Norse's mouth. The man's teeth chattered against the cold steel. Something like wild relief flickered behind the clouded eyes.

Kurtz removed the muzzle and lowered the hammer. There was a bottle of medical disinfectant on the expensive nightstand, and Kurtz sprayed the barrel of the S&W with it before wiping it with the hem of Norse's hospital gown and sliding it back in his belt. He nodded at the woman and they left.

CHAPTER
TEN

Kurtz had her drive farther east to an industrial park along the Thruway behind Erie Community College. They followed empty lanes and crossed empty parking lots to a silent loading-dock area. "Here," said Kurtz. The .40 S&W was steady, propped on his forearm.

Angelina Farino Ferrara set the emergency brake, left the engine running, and put her hands on top of the steering wheel. "Is this the end of the line?"

"Could be."

"What are my options?"

"Truth."

She nodded. Her lips were white but her eyes were defiant and Kurtz could see that her pulse, visible at the base of her throat, was slow and regular.

"Word on the street today," said Kurtz, "is that you put out another contract on me."

"Same contract. Different contractor."

"Who?"

"Big Bore Redhawk. He's—"

"An Indian," said Kurtz. "What is this? Hire the Attica Handicapped Month?"

Angelina shrugged slightly. "Stevie likes to deal with people he knows."

"Little Skag is a cheap fuck," said Kurtz. "When is Big Bore supposed to do this?"

"Any time in the next week."

"And if he fails?"

"Stevie has me look for real talent. And raises the price from ten thousand to twenty-five."

Kurtz sat in silence for a minute. The headlights were off. Snow fell steadily past the yellow lamps beyond the loading dock. The only sounds were the rough idle of the old Volvo engine and the distant hiss of traffic on the I-90 Thruway behind them.

"You don't want to kill me tonight," said Angelina.

"No?"

"No. We need each other."

Kurtz sat in silence for another short spell. Finally, he said, "Turn off the engine. Get out."

She did. Kurtz gestured toward the far end of the loading dock, near the Dumpsters. He had her walk ahead of him to the end of the asphalt there. Her Bally shoes made small tracks in the snow.

"Stop here."

Angelina turned to face him. "I said the wrong thing. You know it's bullshit. We don't need each other. I just need you—need to *use* you. And Joe Kurtz isn't a man who likes to be used."

Kurtz bent his arm, keeping it close to his body, aiming the pistol from his waist.

"Not in the face, please," said Angelina Farino Farrera.

Traffic passed on the Thruway, out of sight to their right.

"Why?" said Kurtz. "Why goad me and set me up this way and then meet me without backup? What did you expect?"

"I expected you to be more stupid."

"Sorry to disappoint you."

"You haven't so far, Kurtz. It's all been very amusing up to this point. Perhaps Big Bore Redhawk will avenge me."

"I doubt it."

"You're probably right. But my brother will."

"Maybe."

Two semis roared by on the Thruway, throwing slush into the cones of yellow light there. Kurtz did not glance that way. "I have most of it figured," he said. "How you were going to use me against both Little Skag and Gonzaga. But why me? You're planning to become don in reality if not in name—you've had all this time to plan—why not bring people you trust to do your work?"

"I'm getting cold," said Angelina. "Can we go back to your car now?"

"No."

"I'm going to raise my hands just to rub my arms, all right?"

Kurtz said nothing.

Angelina briskly massaged her arms through the thin jacket she was wearing. "I had more than six years to plan what I had to do, but the little bloodbath you were part of last November ruined those plans. If I was going to act, I had to act now, but all of a sudden my father's dead, my whore-sister Maria is dead, even Leonard Miles, the crooked consigliere, is dead. Stevie explains how you set it all up, hired the Dane. Revenge for something my father had done to you."

Kurtz said nothing.

"I know that's not true," said Angelina, speaking slowly and clearly. "Stevie set up the hit, borrowing money from the Gonzagas to do it. But you helped get Stevie's deal to the Dane, Kurtz. You were part of it."

"I just passed it along," said Kurtz.

"Just like Johnny Norse," said Angelina with an audible sneer. "Innocent. Just a messenger. I hope you end up in the ninth circle of hell, just like Norse."

Kurtz waited.

"Six years, Kurtz. You know what that sort of time is like—waiting, planning? I married two men to get in the right position, acquire the right sort of power and knowledge. All for nothing. I come back to chaos and the whole plan is shot to shit."

Red and blue police flashers reflected from the Thruway, but the cop car was out of sight, rushing somewhere else. Neither of them turned to look.

"Stevie sold what was left of the Family to Emilio Gonzaga," said Angelina. "He had to."

"Gonzaga controls the judges and the swing vote on the parole board," said Kurtz. "But why don't you just wait for Skag to get out? Rewrite the script. Run your game later, when he trusts you?"

"Stevie will be dead before autumn," Angelina said with a sharp little laugh. "Do you think that Emilio Gonzaga is going to keep the Farino heir apparent around? Emilio will be running both families then. He doesn't need Stephen Farino."

"Or you?"

"He needs me as his whore."

"Not a bad position to plot from," said Kurtz.

Angelina Farino Ferrara took half a step forward, as if she was going to slap Kurtz's face. She caught herself and stopped. "Want to know why I went to Sicily and the Boot?"

"A sudden interest in Renaissance art?" said Kurtz.

"Emilio Gonzaga raped me seven years ago," she said, voice flat and hard. "My father knew about it. Stevie knew about it. Instead of castrating that Gonzaga fuck with bolt cutters, they decided to send me away. I was pregnant. Twenty-five years old and pregnant with Emilio Gonzaga's love child. Daddy wanted me to have the baby. He wanted leverage for a merger. So I went to Sicily. Married an idiot don-in-waiting our family knew there."

"But you didn't have the baby," said Kurtz.

"Oh, but I did," said Angelina and laughed that hard, short laugh again. "I did. A boy. A beautiful baby boy with Emilio's fat, rubbery lips, lovely brown eyes, and the Gonzaga chin and forehead. I drowned him in the Belice River in Sicily."

Kurtz said nothing.

"You'll have a hard time killing Emilio Gonzaga, Kurtz. His compound on Grand Island isn't *like* a fortress, it *is* a fortress. The older Emilio gets, the more paranoid he becomes. And he was born paranoid. He rarely goes out anymore. Lets no one near him. Keeps twenty-five of the best killers in New York State on his payroll, rotting away out there on the island."

"How did you plan to kill him?" asked Kurtz.

Angelina smiled. "Well, I sort of hoped you'd take care of that detail for me, now that you know what you know."

"How did you find out about that? About Gonzaga authorizing the hit on Sam?"

"Stevie told me when he told me about you."

Kurtz nodded. His hair was wet with the falling snow. Three years in the same cell block with Little Skag, saving his ass—literally—from a black rapist named Ali. And all the while, Little Skag knew who had really been behind Sam's death. It must have amused Skag. Kurtz almost had to smile at the irony. Almost.

"Can we get out of this fucking snow now?" asked Angelina.

They walked back to the car. Kurtz nodded her to the

driver's seat. She was shaking from the cold when she turned the ignition and lights on.

"Are you in this with me, Kurtz?"

"No."

She let out a breath. "Are we going back to the HSBC arena?"

"No," said Kurtz. "But we'll stop somewhere you can find a cab."

"My absence is going to be hard to explain to the Boys and Stevie," said Angelina, driving across the parking lot and back onto the empty industrial service road.

"Tell them you were fucking Emilio," said Kurtz.

She looked at him then and it was good for Kurtz that he had the gun at that moment. "Yes," she said at last. "I might say just that."

They drove in silence for a few minutes. Finally Angelina Farino Ferrara said, "You really loved her, didn't you? Your ex-partner Sam, I mean."

Kurtz gestured with the pistol, explaining that she should shut up and drive.

CHAPTER
ELEVEN

Kurtz let himself into the office about ten the next morning, only to find Arlene taking a coffee-and-cigarette break at her desk while reading a detective novel. Kurtz tossed his peacoat onto the coatrack and settled into the old chair behind his desk. Three new files on his desktop were labeled "Frears," "Hansen," and "Other Murder-Suicides/Common Factors."

"How's the book?" asked Kurtz. He squinted at the title. "Isn't that the same guy you were reading twelve years ago, before I got sent away?"

"Yeah. His detective fought in the Korean War, which makes the old fart in his late sixties at least, but he still kicks ass. A new book comes out every year, if not sooner."

"Good, huh?"

"Not anymore," said Arlene. "The P.I.'s got a girl-friend who's a real bitch. An arrogant piece of work. And she's got a dog."

"So?"

"A dog who eats on the table and sleeps in their bed. And the P.I. loves them both to bits."

"Then why do you keep reading him?"

"I keep hoping the P.I. will wake up and cap both the girlfriend and that ratty dog," said Arlene. She put the book down. "To what do I owe this Saturday-morning pleasure, Joe?"

He patted the three files on the desk. He started thumbing through the Frears folder. It was quite a biography—born to upper-class parents in 1945, John Wellington Frears was one of those rarest of anomalies— an African-American in mid-twentieth-century America who had been a child of privilege. Something of a musical prodigy, Frears had gone to Princeton as an undergraduate but had transferred to Juilliard for his junior year. Then something truly strange: after graduation from Juilliard, with offers from several prestigious city symphonic groups, John Wellington Frears had volunteered for the U.S. Army and had gone to Vietnam in 1967. The note said that he had been with the Army Engineers, a sergeant in charge of demolition and disarming booby traps. He'd served two tours in Vietnam and one year in the States before returning to civilian life and beginning his professional music career.

"Now that is truly weird," Kurtz said aloud. "Him joining the army. And demolitions, no less."

"I thought that violinists wouldn't even play catch, they were so protective of their hands," said Arlene.

"What's this thick stack of medical stuff?"

"Mr. Frears is dying of cancer," said Arlene, stubbing out her cigarette and lighting another. "Colon cancer."

Kurtz was looking at the information from Sloan-Kettering Hospital.

"He's undergone every form of treatment, chemotherapy literally up the wazoo," continued Arlene, "but it's terminal. But look at the concert schedule he's been keeping during all of this."

Kurtz flipped to a separate printout. "Two hundred

and ten days a year on the road," he said. "And except for the last couple of weeks, he's honored almost all of them."

"Tough guy," said Arlene.

Kurtz nodded and opened the James B. Hansen file.

"Dead guy there," said Arlene.

"So they say."

"A long time ago," said Arlene.

Kurtz nodded, reading the police report of young Crystal Frears's murder and the subsequent murder-suicide of Hansen and his family. The details matched what John Wellington Frears had told him.

"I couldn't help but notice the connection there," said Arlene. "Does Mr. Frears think that this Hansen is still alive?"

Kurtz looked up. Even when he was a practicing P.I., he'd shared only the necessary details of cases with Arlene, not seeing a need to dump such facts on her. But her husband and son had been alive then, and she'd probably had more important things on her mind. "Yeah," said Kurtz, "that's exactly what Frears thinks. He was leaving Buffalo a couple of weeks ago . . ."

"I saw the concert booking on his itinerary," said Arlene, motioning with her coffee cup for Kurtz to go on.

"He thought he saw Hansen at the airport."

"Our airport?"

"Yeah."

"Do you think he did, Joe? See Hansen, I mean."

Kurtz shrugged.

"Where is Mr. Frears now?"

"Still out at the Airport Sheraton. Waiting."

"For what?"

"I'm not sure," said Kurtz. "It sounds like Buffalo Homicide isn't looking into anything for him. Maybe Frears can't leave town while there's a chance he could find Hansen here, but he's too sick to look."

"So he's waiting here to die at the Airport Sheraton."

"I think it's more than that," said Kurtz. "Mr. Frears has made a big stink with the police, got a little sidebar in the *Buffalo News* about seeing his daughter's murderer at the airport, even got an interview on a local talk-radio station. And he always mentions that he's staying at the Sheraton."

"He wants Hansen—if Hansen exists—to find him," Arlene said softly. "He wants Hansen to come out of hiding to kill him. *Make* the police take it all seriously."

Kurtz closed the Hansen file and picked up the "Other Murder-Suicides/Common Factors" folder. In the last twenty years there had been 5,638 murders of children and wives followed by the suicide of the male killer. There had been 1,220 male suicides before the police could arrest the suspect after child molestation and/or murder of a female child or teenager.

"Oy," said Kurtz.

"Yeah," agreed Arlene. She had finished her coffee break, lit another cigarette, and was working at her computer again. Now she lifted another, thinner, folder and carried it over to Kurtz's desk. "So I narrowed the parameters to include just perps who raped and murdered a teenage girl about Crystal Frears's age and who then went home and killed either themselves or their own family, after burning the house down around themselves."

"There can't be too many of those," said Kurtz. There were 235 cases resembling that scenario, but only thirty-one of them involved men about the age of James B. Hansen at that time. It took only a minute for Kurtz to go through the photographs and compare them to the photo in the Hansen file from the Chicago P.D.

"Bingo," said Kurtz. Atlanta, Georgia, five years after

the murder of Crystal Frears. A white man who looked
very little like psychologist James B. Hansen—bald
rather than long-haired, clean-shaven rather than
bearded, brown eyes rather than blue, thick glasses
where Hansen had worn none—but who was the same
man. Lawrence Greenberg, age thirty-five, a certified
public accountant, married three years, three children by
his wife's former marriage, had kidnapped a neighbor
girl, white, age thirteen, named Charlotte Hays, raped
her repeatedly in a deserted farmhouse outside of Atlanta, and had then driven home, had dinner with his
family, shot all four of them, and reportedly shot himself
in the head after setting fire to his home. Police had
identified him according to dental records and a charred
Rolex that Mr. Greenberg had always worn.

"Dental records," said Kurtz.

"Yeah, but to look at those details, we'll need the
printouts of the full reports," said Arlene. "The Chicago
P.D. file hadn't been fully digitized—just the overview
you have there—so we'd have to make an official request."

"Erie County District Attorney's Office at our third
P.O. box," said Kurtz.

"Mail fraud as well as everything else," said Arlene.
"At least three federal laws broken if we do it."

"Do it," said Kurtz.

"I called yesterday," said Arlene. "Requested the files
from both Chicago and Atlanta. I had them Express
Mailed since FedEx won't deliver to P.O. boxes. We'll
get the reports on Monday."

"How did you pay?"

"Charged it to the D.A.'s office," said Arlene. "I still
have their billing code."

"Won't they notice it?"

Arlene laughed and went back to her computer. "We

could charge a fleet of Lexuses to that office, Joe. No one would notice. Do you have time to look at some possible office space with me today?"

"No, I've got things to do. But I do need your help on something."

Kurtz drove alone to the bar near Broadway Market, where he'd braced Donnie Rafferty. Detectives Brubaker and Myers had been driving a different unmarked car that morning when they had followed him from the Royal Delaware Arms to his office, and they had stayed several cars back and attempted a serious tail rather than just harassing him, but Kurtz had made them immediately. If they stopped him now with the two guns he was carrying, it would be bad news, but he suspected that they were actually on surveillance. He pulled into the parking lot, grabbed the camera bag he'd brought from the office, and went into the bar. He noticed that Brubaker and Myers parked across the street to watch the parking lot and the bar's only entrance. When he'd been waiting for Donald Rafferty here, Kurtz had noticed the alley running behind the row of buildings and the high board fence concealing the alley from the parking lot.

"Back door?" Kurtz said to the bartender in the dark, hops-smelling space within. Only three or four committed regulars were celebrating Saturday morning there.

"It's for emergency use only," said the bartender. "Hey!"

Kurtz stepped into the alley, Arlene guided her blue Buick to a stop, and he got in. They drove a block, turned north, then turned west on a street parallel to where the detectives were parked.

"Where to?" asked Arlene.

"Back to the office for you," said Kurtz. "I have to borrow your car for a few hours."

Arlene sighed. "We're not that far from Chippewa Street. We could check out an office space there."

"I bet it's over a Starbucks," said Kurtz.

"How did you know?"

"Every third store on Chippewa is a Starbucks these days," said Kurtz. "I don't have time today. And we don't want to pay yuppie leases. Let's find an office somewhere less gentrified."

Arlene sighed again. "It would be nice to have windows."

Kurtz said nothing on the ride back to the office.

The Tuscarora Indian Reservation was northeast of the city of Niagara Falls, curled around half of the big Power Reservoir that stored water to run through the Power Project's giant turbines. Big Bore Redhawk was not a Tuscarora, and quite possibly wasn't an Indian—word was that Big Bore had discovered his Native American ancestry when he was trying to fence stolen jewelry and learned that he would be tax-exempt as an Indian jewelry salesperson—but his trailer was on the reservation property. Kurtz knew so much about Redhawk's personal life because the big man had been one of the most talkative morons in C-Block.

Kurtz took Walmore Road into the reservation and turned left onto the third gravel road. Big Bore's rusted-out trailer squatted in the deep snow just short of where Garlow Road ran along the reservoir. A clapped-out Dodge Powerwagon with a blade sat in the Indian's driveway and snow was heaped eight feet high on either side. Big Bore earned his drinking money from plowing the reservation's private roads during the winter. Kurtz pulled the Buick back behind one of these snowpiles so he could see the door to Redhawk's trailer. Snow was falling, stopping, then falling harder.

Twenty-five minutes later, all six-feet-five-inches of Big Bore came stumbling out the door wearing only jeans and a loose plaid shirt—he did not seem aware of Kurtz's car—climbed one of the higher drifts, and urinated toward the line of trees.

Kurtz drove the Buick up, slid to a stop, and got out quickly with the .40 Smith & Wesson in his hand. "Good morning, B.B."

Redhawk turned with mouth and fly agape. His bloodshot eyes flickered toward the trailer, and Kurtz guessed that the half-breed's gun was still inside. Big Bore had always been a shank man.

"Kurtz? Hey, man, fucking good to see you, man. You out on parole too?"

Kurtz smiled. "You drinking the advance on my hit, B.B.?"

Big Bore worked his face into a puzzled frown, glanced down, and zipped up his fly. "Huh?" he said. "What's the piece for? We were friends, man."

"Yeah," said Kurtz.

"Fuck, man," said Big Bore. "I don't know what you heard, but we can talk it out, man. Come on inside." He took a half step toward his trailer.

Kurtz raised the semiauto's aim slightly and shook his head.

Big Bore raised his hands and squinted. "You're a big man with that gun, aren't you, Kurtz?"

Kurtz said nothing.

"You put that fucking piece down and fight me like a fucking man, we'll see who's hot shit," slurred Big Bore.

"I beat you in a fair fight, you tell me who hired you?" said Kurtz.

The Indian jumped down from the drift, landing lightly for three hundred pounds of muscled fat, and raised his huge arms, flexing his fingers. "Whatever," he said, showing prison dentistry.

Kurtz thought about it, nodded, and tossed his pistol onto the hood of the Buick, out of reach. He turned back to Redhawk.

"Fucking moron," said Big Bore, pulling an eight inch hunting knife from a scabbard under his shirt. "Easiest fucking ten grand I ever earned." He grinned more broadly and took two crouched steps forward, flicking the fingers of his huge left hand in an invitation. "Let's see what you got, Kurtz."

"I've got a forty-five," said Kurtz. He pulled Angelina's Compact Witness from his coat pocket and shot Big Bore in the left knee.

The hunting knife went flying over the drift, blood and cartilage doing a Jackson Pollock on the snow, and Big Bore went down heavily.

Kurtz retrieved his S&W and walked over to the moaning, cursing Indian.

"I'm going to fucking kill your fucking ass, Kurtz, you fucking . . ." began Big Bore, then trailed away into a groan.

Kurtz waited for the monologue to continue.

"And fucking call the cops and fucking send you away until I'm motherfucking ready to kill your fucking ass," gasped the big man, wanting to hold his shattered knee together but unwilling to touch the mess.

"No," said Kurtz. "Remember telling everyone in the exercise yard how you killed your first two wives and where they're buried?"

"Aww, fuck, man," moaned Big Bore.

"Yeah," said Kurtz. He went into the trailer and rummaged through the mess there a bit, finding $1,410 in small bills hidden under a hardcase holding a shiny new .45 Colt. Kurtz was no thief, but this was a down payment on his own death, so he took the money and went back to the Buick. Big Bore had begun the crawl to the trailer and was leaving an unpleasant trail in the snow.

CHAPTER
TWELVE

Chief of Detectives Captain Robert Gaines Millworth, aka James B. Hansen, went into his office on Saturday morning at the main precinct station on Elmwood, just across from the courthouse. It was snowing.

The sergeant at the desk and a few duty officers were surprised to see Captain Millworth, since he had the rest of his weekend off for the last of his vacation. "Paperwork," said the captain, and went into his office.

Hansen called up the file on the ex-con that Brubaker and Myers were tailing. He'd run across Joe Kurtz's name before, but had never paid much attention to it. Rereading the previous arrest file and the man's thin dossier, Hansen realized that this lowlife Kurtz represented everything Hansen despised—a thug who had parlayed a short stint as a military policeman into a private detective's license in civilian life, had been tried for aggravated assault fifteen years earlier—dismissed on a technicality—and then plea-bargained out of a Murder Two charge into a Man One twelve years ago because of the laziness and sloppiness of the district attorney's office. The penultimate entry in the file was an interrogation by the late Detective James Hathaway the previous autumn, relating to an illegal weapons charge that was dropped when Kurtz's parole officer, Margaret O'Toole, had intervened to report to the watch commander that despite Hathaway's report, the perp had not been armed when arrested by the detective in her office. Hansen made a mental note to make life miserable for Miss O'Toole when he got the chance . . . and he would make sure that he got the chance.

There were several pages in the file speculating on Mr. Joe Kurtz's connections with the Farino crime family, specifically with his prison connections with Stephen "Little Skag" Farino in Attica, and the brief report of an interview with Kurtz the previous November after the gangland killings of Don Farino, Maria Farino, their lawyer, and several bodyguards. Kurtz had an alibi for the evening of the murders, and no forensic evidence had connected him to what the New York City TV stations and papers had called "The Buffalo Massacre."

Kurtz was perfect for a role that Hansen had in mind: a loner, no family or friends, an ex-con, a suspected cop-killer, probable mob connections, a history of violence. There would be no problem convincing a jury that Kurtz was also a thief, someone who would murder a visiting violinist just for his wallet. Of course it should never come before a jury. Send the right detectives to arrest this Kurtz—say, those clowns Brubaker and Myers— and the state would be saved the cost of an execution.

But there would have to be evidence—preferably DNA evidence at the scene of the crime.

Hansen shut off the computer, swiveled his chair, and looked out through the blinds at the gray heap that was the courthouse. As he often did when events seemed confusing, Hansen closed his eyes and gave a brief prayer to his Lord and Savior, Jesus Christ. James B. Hansen had been saved and born again in Christ at the age of eight—the one thing his miserable excuse for a mother had ever done for him was to connect him to the Evangelical Church of Repentance in Kearney. He never took that for granted. And although he knew that his special needs might be looked upon by others as an abomination in the eyes of the Lord, Hansen's own special relationship with Jesus reassured him that the Lord God Christ used James Hansen as His instrument, Culling only those souls whom Jesus Christ Almighty wished Culled. It was why Hansen prayed almost ceaselessly in the weeks leading up to his Special Visits. So far, he had been a true and faithful servant to the will of Jesus.

Finished with his prayer, the captain turned back to his desk and dialed a private number, choosing not to make a radio call.

"Brubaker here."

"This is Captain Millworth. Are you on the Kurtz surveillance now?"

"Yes, sir."

"Where is he?"

"The Red Door Tavern on Broadway, Captain. He's been in there about an hour."

"Good. There may be something to your idea that Kurtz murdered those three Attica ex-cons, and something may turn up that might connect him to the death of Detective Hathaway. I'm authorizing your continued surveillance until further notice."

"Yes, sir," came Brubaker's voice. "Do we get at least one more team?"

"Negative on that," said Hansen. "We're short on people right now. But I can okay overtime pay for you and Myers."

"Yes, sir."

"And Brubaker," said James B. Hansen, "you report

directly to me on this matter, understand? If this Kurtz is really the cop-killer you think he is, we're not going to leave a paper trail for Internal Affairs, or for the bleeding-heart Public Defenders' Office, or for anyone else to follow, even if we have to bend the rules with this punk."

There was a silence on the line. Neither Brubaker nor Myers nor anyone else in the division had ever heard Captain Robert Gaines Millworth talk about bending rules. "Yes, sir," Brubaker said at last.

Hansen broke the connection. As long as John Wellington Frears was sitting out at the Airport Sheraton, James B. Hansen did not feel comfortable or in total control of events. And James B. Hansen did not like feeling uncomfortable or out of control. This unimportant loose end called Joe Kurtz might prove to be very, very useful.

It was snowing harder when Kurtz took the toll bridge from the city of Niagara Falls onto Grand Island. The Niagara Section of the New York Thruway was a short-cut that ran north and south across the island from Buffalo to Niagara Falls. Grand Island itself was larger in size than metro Buffalo, but was mostly empty. Buckhorn Island State Park sat at its northern tip and Beaver Island State Park filled its southern end. Kurtz exited to West River Parkway and followed it along the Niagara River West, turning east again along Ferry Road, near the southern end of the island.

Kurtz pulled Arlene's Buick to the side of the road and lifted the Nikon with the 300-mm lens attached. The Gonzaga compound was set back a quarter of a mile from the road, recognizable only by distant tile roofs just visible above a high wall that ran completely around the complex. The long access road was private and monitored by video cameras. Kurtz could see razor wire along Ferry Road and more lines of fence between the outer perimeter and the actual wall. The entrance to the compound was gated; there was a Mediterranean-style guardhouse at the gate, and with the long lens, Kurtz could see the silhouettes of three men inside. One of the men was lifting a pair of binoculars.

Kurtz put the Buick in gear and drove east, getting back on the highway and turning north toward Niagara Falls.

The helicopter tour usually cost $125 and included a swoop over Niagara Falls and the Whirlpool downriver.

"I've seen the Falls and the Whirlpool," Kurtz told the pilot. "Today I want to see this property I'm considering on Grand Island."

The pilot—an older, redheaded man who reminded Kurtz of the actor Ken Toby—said, "That would be charter. This is just tourist. Different rates. Plus the weather's pretty shitty with these snow squalls. FAA doesn't want us flying tourists if the visibility isn't great or if there's a real chance of icing."

Kurtz handed him the two hundred dollars he had borrowed from Arlene.

"Ready to go?" asked the pilot.

Kurtz grabbed his camera bag and nodded.

From a thousand feet up, the layout of the Gonzaga compound was pretty obvious. Kurtz shot two rolls of black-and-white film.

Driving back to Buffalo, he called Angelina Farino Ferrara on the private line.

"We need to talk privately," he said. "At length. In person."

"How do we do that?" said the woman. "I've got two extra assholes these days."

"Me too," said Kurtz without elaborating. "What do you do when you want to meet some guy to screw him?"

There was a silence on the line. Eventually she said, "I presume this is relevant."

Kurtz waited.

"I bring them here," she said at last. "To the marina penthouse."

"Where do you pick them up?"

"A bar I go to or the health club," she said.

"Which health club?"

She named it.

"Expensive," said Kurtz. "Use the phone I gave you to call and leave a guest pass for me tomorrow at one. Your goons haven't seen photos of me, have they?"

"No one has except me," said Angelina.

"You and the guys you hire to kill me."

"Yes," she said.

"When do your bodyguards report to Little Skag?" asked Kurtz.

"I'm pretty sure it's Wednesday and Saturday if nothing really unusual happens," she said.

"We have a few days then," said Kurtz. "Unless screwing a stranger would be considered unusual for you."

Angelina Farino Ferrara said nothing.

"Do Tweedledee and Tweedledum actually work out with you?" asked Kurtz.

"They stay in the weight room where they can see me through the glass," said Angelina. "But I don't allow them to get close." She was silent for a minute. "I take it that you and I are going to discover an instant attraction, Kurtz."

"We'll see. At least we'll be able to talk at the health club."

"I want my two pieces of property back."

"Well, one of them you might not want to keep," said Kurtz. "I donated part of it to a Native American today."

"Shit," said Angelina. "But I still want it back."

"Sentimental value," said Kurtz.

"Yes. So are we going to discover an immediate attraction when we meet at the health club?"

"Who knows?" said Kurtz, although he had no plans to return to the Farino headquarters at the marina tomorrow. But if she didn't have him killed at the health club, he might need to spend more time with her if his Gonzaga plan was going to work.

"Assuming we do hit it off in this alternate universe, when the time comes are you going to ride to the penthouse with the Boys and me or will you be driving yourself?"

"Driving," said Kurtz.

"You're going to need a better car and a much nicer wardrobe."

"Tell them you're slumming," said Kurtz, and broke the connection.

Late that evening, Arlene drove Kurtz back to the Red Door Tavern—he had to pound on the alley door of the place to get the bartender to let him in so he could walk through—only to find Brubaker and Myers gone from their surveillance and his Volvo scratched down the length of its driver's side. Evidently one or the other of the detectives had looked inside the bar, found Kurtz gone, and then vented his frustration in true professional form.

"To protect and serve," muttered Kurtz.

He drove out to Lockport carefully, checking for tails. No one was following him. *These cops have the stick-to-it quality of an old Post-it Note* was Kurtz's uncharitable thought.

Down the street and around the corner from Rachel's home, he used the electronic gear he'd brought and checked on the various bugs. Donnie was out of town, as promised. Rachel was home alone, and except for the sound of the TV—she was watching *Parent Trap,* the Hayley Mills version—and some humming to herself, and one call from her friend Melissa in which Rachel confirmed Rafferty's absence, there was nothing to hear. Kurtz took the humming as a good sign, shut down his equipment, dropped the electronic gear by the office, and drove back to the Royal Delaware Arms.

The plaster dust was undisturbed since that morning. The repairs to his door allowed him to get the police bar in place. Kurtz cooked a dinner of stir-fry on the hot plate and ate it with some cheap wine he'd bought on the way home. The apartment had no TV, but he owned an old grille-front FM radio that he tuned to Buffalo's best jazz/blues station and listened to that while he read a novel called *Ada.* The wind was cold and seemed to blow in through the plaster cracks and seep up through the floor. By 10:00 P.M., Kurtz was cold enough to check his locks and police bar, flip the big couch into a fold-out bed, brush his teeth, make sure his .40 S&W and Farino Ferrara's two .45s were in reach, and turn in for the night.

CHAPTER
THIRTEEN

"Come here often?" asked Kurtz.

"Fuck you."

He and Angelina Farino Ferrara were pacing on parallel treadmills in the mirrored and teak-floored sixth-story main room of the Buffalo Athletic Club. Her bodyguards were in the adjoining weight room, clearly visible through the glass wall as they pressed heavy weights and admired each other's sweat-oiled muscles, but out of earshot. No one was exercising near Kurtz and Angelina.

"Did you bring my property?" she asked. Kurtz was wearing a bulky sweat suit, seriously out of fashion based on what the few other patrons were wearing, but Angelina's fashionable skintight leotard showed that she was not armed.

Kurtz shrugged and set the treadmill for a faster pace. Angelina set hers to match. "I want those two items back." She was breathing and speaking easily, but she had broken a sweat.

"Noted." Kurtz glanced over at the bodyguards. "Are they any good?"

"The Boys? Marco's all right. Leo's a waste of Stevie's money."

"Is Leo the one with the cupid lips and con torso?"

"Right."

"Are these your main men?"

"The Boys? They're the only ones with me full time, but Stevie's brought in eight other new guys. They're all competent at what they do, but they don't hang out at the marina. Shouldn't you be asking about Gonzaga's protection rather than mine?"

"All right. What about Gonzaga's people? How many? Any good? And who else is usually in his compound? And how often does he come out of that compound?"

"These days, he almost never comes out. And it's never predictable when he does." Angelina cranked up the speed and angle of her machine. Kurtz matched it. They had to speak a bit more loudly to hear one another over the whir. "Emilio keeps twenty-eight people on his payroll at that fortress," she said. "Nineteen of them are muscle. Pretty good, although they must be getting rusty just sitting there guarding his fat ass. The rest are cooks, maids, butlers, sometimes his business manager, technicians . . ."

"How many with guns in the main house when you visit?"

"I usually see eight. Two baby-sit the Boys in the outer foyer. Emilio usually has four bodyguards playing servant during the lunch. A couple of others roam the house."

"And the rest of the guards?"

"Two in the guardhouse at the gate. About four in the outbuilding security center, where they keep the video monitors. Three more always roaming the grounds with guard dogs. And two with radios driving the perimeter in Jeeps."

"Other people there?"

"Just the servants I mentioned and occasional visits from his lawyer and other people. They've never been there when I go for lunch. No other family there. His wife died nine years ago. Emilio has a thirty-year-old son, Toma, who lives in Florida. The kid was supposed to take over the business, but got disinherited six years ago and knows that he'll be whacked if he ever shows up in New York State again. He's a fag. Emilio doesn't like fags."

"How do you know all this? I mean about the security setup."

"Emilio took me on a tour the first time I visited."

"Not very smart."

"I think he wanted to impress me with his impregnability." Angelina set the treadmill to its fastest pace. She began running in earnest.

Kurtz clicked in matching settings. For a few minutes they ran in silence.

"What's your plan?" she asked at last.

"Am I supposed to have a plan?"

She gave him a look that seemed Sicilian in its intensity. "Yes, you're supposed to have a fucking plan."

"I'm not an assassin," said Kurtz. "I hire out for other things."

"But you are planning to kill Gonzaga."

"Probably."

"But you're not seriously planning to try to get to him in his compound."

Kurtz concentrated on breathing and ran in silence.

"How could you get to him there?" Angelina flicked sweat out of her left eye.

"Hypothetically?" said Kurtz.

"Whatever."

"Have you noticed that roadwork being done about half a mile south of the compound?"

"Yeah."

"Those bulldozers and huge graders and haulers that are parked there half the time?"

"Yeah."

"If someone stole one of the biggest of those machines, he could drive over the guardhouse, smash his way into the main house, shoot all the guards there, and whack Gonzaga in the process."

Angelina hit the stop button and trotted to a halt as the treadmill slowed. "Are you really that stupid?"

Kurtz kept running.

She raised the towel from her shoulders and mopped her face. "Do you know how to drive one of those big Caterpillar things?"

"No."

"Do you know how to *start* one?"

"No."

"Do you know anyone who does?"

"Probably not."

"You got this from a fucking Jackie Chan movie," Angelina said, and stepped off her treadmill.

"I didn't know they had Jackie Chan movies in Sicily and Italy," said Kurtz, killing his machine.

"They have Jackie Chan movies everywhere." She was toweling the bare skin where the leotard cut across her cleavage. "You're not going to tell me your plan, are you?"

"No," said Kurtz. He looked over at the Boys, who had finished bench-pressing and were admiring each other as they curled dumbbells with each hand. "This has been real fun. And I can feel this attraction building to the point where you're going to invite me home soon. Shall we meet again tomorrow, same time, same place?"

"Fuck you."

On Sunday mornings, James B. Hansen attended early morning worship service with his wife Donna and stepson Jason, went out with them for a late breakfast at a favorite pancake house on Sheridan Drive, and stayed home in the afternoon while his wife took their son to her parents' place in Cheektowaga. It was his weekly time for private reflection and he rarely missed it.

No one was allowed in the basement except Hansen. He was the only one who had the key to his private gun room. Donna had never seen the inside of the room, not even when it was being renovated when they had first moved in almost a year earlier, and Jason knew that any attempt to trespass in his stepfather's private gun room would incur serious physical punishment. "Spare the rod and spoil the child" was a Biblical injunction that was taken seriously in the home of Homicide Captain Robert G. Millworth.

The gun room was guarded by a keypad working on a separate code from the rest of the house security system, a steel door, and a physical combination lock. The room itself was spartan, with a metal desk, a wall of bookshelves holding a law-enforcement officer's assortment of reference books, and a case behind locked, shatterproof Plexiglas doors in which Hansen's expensive gun collection hung under halogen lights. A large safe was built into the north wall.

Hansen disarmed the third security system, entered the proper combination, and took his titanium case out from where it was nestled with stocks, bonds, and his collection of silver Krugerrands. Returning to his desk, he opened the case and reviewed the contents in the soft glow of the gun-case lights.

The thirteen-year-old girl in Miami two weeks earlier—a Cuban whose name he'd never learned, picking her up at random in the neighborhood where little Elian Gonzalez had stayed a few years earlier—had been Number Twenty-eight. Hansen looked at the Polaroid photos he had taken of her while she was still alive—and later. He paused only briefly at the single photograph he had taken with himself in the frame with her—he always took only one such photo—and then went on to study the rest of his collection. In recent years, he noticed, the twelve- to fourteen-year-olds had developed earlier than the girls of his own childhood. Nutrition, the experts said, although James B. Hansen knew it to be the Devil's work, turning these children into sexual objects sooner than in previous decades and centuries in order to entice men.

But there were no children in his collection of the twenty-eight Culled, Hansen knew, only demonettes who were not the Children of God, but the Spawn of the Enemy. This realization when Hansen was in his twenties—that God had given him this special ability, this second sight to differentiate the human girls from the young demons in human form—was what allowed him to carry out his ordained task.

This last girl's eyes stared up toward the camera after strangulation with that same look of total surprise and terror—surprise at being found out and terror at knowing she had been chosen to be Culled, Hansen knew—as had the other twenty-seven.

He always allowed himself precisely one hour to review the photographs. Showing the self-discipline that separated him from the mindless psychopaths that stalked the world, Hansen never took any souvenirs other than the Polaroid photos. Nor did he masturbate or otherwise attempt to relive the excitement of the actual Culling. This hour of reflection and review every Sunday was to remind him of the seriousness of his mission on earth, nothing more.

At the end of the hour, Hansen locked away the titanium case, looked lovingly at his collection of firearms reflecting the halogen spotlights, and left his gun room, scrambling the combination and activating the special alarm system as he did so. It would be another two or three hours before Donna and Jason returned from her parents' place; Hansen planned to use the time reading his Bible.

Donald Rafferty returned to his Lockport home on Sunday evening, obviously tired from his weekend trip with DeeDee, his Number Two girlfriend. Kurtz was parked down the street and monitoring the bugs in the Rafferty house.

"Did that kid—whatshername, Melissa?—come over this weekend while I was gone?" Rafferty's voice sounded slurred and tired.

"No, Dad."

"You lying to me?"

"No." Kurtz could hear the alarm in Rachel's voice.

"What about boys?"

"Boys?"

"Which boys were here while I was gone, goddammit?"

Kurtz knew from his phone taps that Rachel really didn't talk to any boys, other than Clarence Kleigman, who was in orchestra with her. She would never invite a boy to the house.

"Which boys did you have over here? Tell me the goddamn truth or I'll get the yardstick out."

"No boys, Dad." Rachel's voice was quavering slightly. "Did you have a good business trip?"

"Don't change the fucking subject." Rafferty was still quite drunk.

A minute of ambient noise and hiss. From the crashing around in the kitchen, it sounded like Rafferty was hunting for one of his bottles.

"I have homework to finish," Rachel said. Kurtz knew that she had finished all of her homework by Saturday night. "I'll be upstairs." From the bug in the hall, Kurtz could hear the sound of Rachel slipping the lock shut on her door as Rafferty stamped upstairs and began throwing his clothes around the bathroom.

It was snowing hard. Kurtz let the snow blanket the windshield as he sat listening to random noises through his earphones.

It had not been a promising week. Kurtz followed few rules in life, but not leaving enemies behind him came close to a rule for him, and this week he had left two people around who wished to do him harm—Big Bore Redhawk and the dying man, Johnny Norse. In each case it had simply been more trouble to deal with them than to let them live; Big Bore had more reasons to stay silent in the hospital than to rat Kurtz out, and Johnny Norse had no idea who Kurtz and Angelina were or what Kurtz's relationship to Emilio Gonzaga might be. Kurtz remembered Norse's almost obscene eagerness to hang onto the last dregs of life and felt secure that the dying man would not be contacting Gonzaga about the visit. But Kurtz's motto had always been "Why play the odds when you can fix the race?" In these cases, though, it would be riskier to deal with bodies than with odds.

Still, it was a bad habit to leave loose ends behind him and Kurtz could not afford bad habits at the mo ment.

Joe Kurtz knew that his one strength over the past dozen years—besides patience—was his ability to survive. Beyond the minimal survival skills necessary for spending more than a decade in a maximum security prison without getting raped or shanked or both, Kurtz had avoided the fatwa of the D-Block Mosque gangs when they had come to believe that he had killed a black enforcer named Ali a year before Kurtz's parole. Once back in Buffalo last autumn, Kurtz had gained the enmity of another black gang—the Seneca Street Social Club—who actually believed that he had thrown their leader, a drug-dealing psychopath named Malcolm Kibunte, over Niagara Falls.

The cops who were tailing him—Brubaker and Myers—believed that Joe Kurtz had shot a crooked homicide detective named Hathaway, even though there was absolutely no evidence for that. Kurtz knew that Brubaker's suspicion had been fueled from Attica by Little Skag Furino, whose gratitude for Kurtz having literally saved his ass from Ali was now being shown by the third-rate hit men that Skag was hiring to kill him.

Kurtz doubted that Brubaker and Myers would try to kill him, but sooner or later they would roust him while he was carrying, which meant jail again, which meant all the current death sentences on Kurtz converging.

Then there were the Farino and Gonzaga families. You don't strike—much less kill—a made guy without paying for it; it was one of the last enforceable tenets of the weakening Mafia structure. And while Kurtz had not been involved—directly—in the shootings of Don Farino, his daughter, his lawyer, or his bodyguards the previous autumn, that fact would do him little good. Little Skag knew that Kurtz had not killed his family members, since Little Skag had ordered the hits on them himself, but he was also aware that Kurtz had been there during the denouement at the Farino compound. Joe Kurtz knew too much to stay alive.

Now Angelina Farino Ferrara was trying to use Kurtz to kill Gonzaga. Kurtz hated being used more than almost anything in the world, but in this situation, the woman had leverage over him. He had done his eleven and a half years in Attica for the killing of Sam's murderers with some patience because it had been worth it—Samantha Fielding had been his partner in every way—but now those years were shown to be worthless. If it had been Emilio Gonzaga who put the hit on Sam, then Gonzaga had to die. And die soon, since Gonzaga would be taking over the Farino Family by the end of summer, which would make him all but invulnerable.

If Angelina really wanted Kurtz dead now, all she had to do was tell Gonzaga. There would be fifty button men on the street in an hour.

But she had her own agenda and timeline. That's why Kurtz was allowing himself to be used by her. Gonzaga's death would suit both their purposes—but then what? A woman could not become don. Little Skag would still be the heir apparent of what was left of the once-formidable Farino family, although without the Gonzaga judge and parole-board connections, Little Skag might be cooling his heels in maximum security for more years to come.

Was that Angelina's plan? Just to keep Little Skag in prison while she eliminated her rapist, Emilio Gonzaga, and tried to consolidate some power? If so, it was a dangerous plan, not just because Gonzaga's wrath would be terrible if an assassination failed, but because the other families would intervene eventually—almost certainly at Angelina's expense—and Little Skag had already shown a willingness, actually an eagerness, to whack a sister.

But if she could blame Gonzaga's murder on this loose cannon, this non-made-guy, this madman Joe

Kurtz— This scenario seemed especially workable if Joe Kurtz was dead before Little Skag's killers or the Gonzaga Family or the New York families' people caught up to him.

Joe Kurtz's strength might be survival, but he was having increasing difficulty in seeing how he could do everything he had to do and still survive this mess.

And then there was this Frears and James B. Hansen thing. And Donald Rafferty. And Arlene's need for another $35,000 to expand their on-line business.

Suddenly, Kurtz had a headache.

CHAPTER
FOURTEEN

"Did you bring the thirty-five thousand for Wedding Bells dot com?" asked Arlene when Kurtz came in the door.

It was late morning. Brubaker and Myers had followed him from the Royal Delaware Arms and were out there now—Brubaker in the unmarked car at the end of the alley, watching the back door, Myers on the street in front, watching the entrance to the abandoned video store upstairs.

"Not yet," Kurtz said. "Did you have Greg bring Alan's old Harley down this morning?"

Arlene nodded and gestured with her right hand. Cigarette smoke spiraled. "I'm more interested in finding a new office anyway. Do you have time today?"

"We'll see." Kurtz looked at the stack of files and empty Express Mail packages on his desk.

"I got them about an hour ago," said Arlene. "The Hansen file from the Frears murder in Chicago, the Atlanta thing that had exactly the same M.O., and the ones from Houston, Jacksonville, Albany, and Columbus, Ohio. The other four haven't arrived yet."

"You read them?"

"Looked through."

"Find anything?"

"Yes," said Arlene. She batted ashes. "I bet we're the only ones ever to look at all these family murders together. Or any two of them together, for that matter."

Kurtz shrugged. "Sure. The local cops all saw it as a local nut-case family murder—and they had the killer's corpse in the burned house. Each case open and shut. Why compare it to other cases they don't even know about?"

Arlene smiled. Kurtz hung up his coat, shifted the holstered .40 S&W on his waistband, and settled in to read.

Five minutes later he had it.

"The dentist," he said. Arlene nodded.

In each of the murder-suicides, identification of the killer's burned body was made through tattoos, jewelry, an old scar in the Atlanta case—but primarily through dental records. In three of the cases—the Chicago Frears/Hansen case, the Atlanta Murchison/Cable murders, and the Albany Whittaker/Sessions killings—the killer's dentist was from Cleveland.

"Howard K. Conway," said Kurtz.

Arlene's eyes were bright. "Did you see the dentists' signatures in the other cases?"

It was Kurtz's turn to nod. Different names. But all from Cleveland. And the handwriting was the same. "Maybe our Dr. Conway is just the dentist to psychopaths around the country. Probably was Ted Bundy's dentist."

"Uh-huh." Arlene stubbed her cigarette out and came over to Kurtz's desk. "What about the other I.D. factors? The tattoo in the Hansen killings? The scar in the Whittaker case?"

"My guess is that Hansen finds his replacement for

the fire first—some street person or male hooker or something—kills him, stores the body, and then decorates himself accordingly. If they have a tattoo, he sports a fake one. Whatever. It's just a few months."

"Jesus."

"I'll need his current—" began Kurtz.

She handed him a three-by-five card with Dr. Howard K. Conway's business address on it. "I called this morning and tried to make an appointment, but Dr. Conway is semiretired and isn't accepting new patients. A younger man answered the phone and shooed me away. I found listings for Dr. Conway going back to the early fifties, so the guy must be ancient."

Kurtz was looking at the photographs of the murdered girls. "Why would Hansen leave Conway alive all these years?"

"I guess it's easier than getting a new dentist all the time. Plus, the dental records are probably all older than whatever identity Hansen—whatever his name is—is using at the time. It'd be weird, something even local cops would notice, if their killer only had dental records a few months old."

"And it's not weird that someone living in Houston or Albany or Atlanta goes to a Cleveland dentist?"

Arlene shrugged. "The nut cases all moved from Cleveland in the past year or two. No reason for local homicide cops to red-flag that."

"No."

"What are you going to do, Joe?" There was an edge to Arlene's voice that he had rarely heard when he had been a P.I.

He looked at her.

"Come here often?" said Kurtz.

Angelina Farino Ferrara just sighed. They were working in the weight room today, and the Boys were outside on the treadmills.

Kurtz and Arlene had chosen the video-store basement for their office because it was cheap and because it had several exits: back door to the alley, stairway door to the now-defunct video store upstairs, and side door to the condemned parking garage next door. The drug dealers who had owned the place when it was a real bookstore had liked all those exits. So did Kurtz. It had come in handy when he'd left half an hour ago.

Arlene's late husband's Harley had been parked on the dark lower level, just beyond the metal door. Greg had left a helmet on the handlebars and the keys in the ignition. Kurtz had straddled the machine, fired it up, and weaved his way up ramps and out of the basement of the empty parking garage, snaking by the permanent barricade on Market Street that kept cars out. Detective Brubaker presumably still had been on watch on the alley side, and Detective Myers on the street side, but no one was watching the Market Street garage exit. Taking care on the snowy and icy streets, reminding himself that he'd not been on a bike for fifteen years or more, Kurtz had ridden to the health club.

Now he was doing repetitions on the chest-press machine with two hundred pounds. He had done twenty-three reps when Angelina said, "You're showing off."

"Absolutely."

"You can stop now."

"Thank you." He lowered the bar and left it lowered. Angelina was doing curls with fifteen-pound weights. Her biceps were feminine but well-defined. No one was within earshot. "When do you have lunch with Gonzaga this week?"

"Tomorrow, Tuesday. Then again on Thursday. Did you bring my property?"

"No. Tell me the drill when you and the Boys go for lunch." There was a heavy bag and a speed bag in the room, and he put on gloves and began working on the heavy bag.

Angelina set down the dumbbells and went to a bench to do some pull-ups. "The car takes us to Grand Island—"

"Your car or Gonzaga's?"

"His."

"How many people other than the driver?"

"One. The Asian stone-killer called Mickey Kee. But the driver's carrying as well."

"What can you tell me about Kee?"

"He's from South Korea. He was trained in their Special Forces—sort of Green Berets by way of SMERSH. I think he got a lot of on-the-job experience assassinating North Korean infiltrators, people the regime didn't like, that sort of thing. He's probably the most efficient killer in New York State right now."

"When you go to lunch, they pick you up at the Marina Tower?"

"Yeah."

"Frisk you there?"

"No. They take the Boys' guns at the guardhouse. Then they drive us the rest of the way. There's a metal-detector at the entrance to the main house—it's subtle, but it's there—and then I get frisked again by a woman in a private room off the foyer before being allowed into Emilio's presence. I guess they're afraid I'll go at him with a hat pin or something."

"A hat pin," repeated Kurtz. "You're older than you look."

Angelina ignored him. "The Boys sit on a couch in the foyer while the Gonzaga goons watch them. The Boys get their guns back when we drive out."

"Okay," said Kurtz. He concentrated on hitting the big bag for a few minutes. When he looked up, Angelina handed him a towel and a water bottle.

"You looked like you meant it with the bag," she said.

Kurtz drank and wiped the sweat from his eyes. "I'm going with you to Gonzaga's place tomorrow."

Angelina Farino Ferrara's lips went pale. "Tomorrow? You're going to try to kill Emilio tomorrow? With me along? You're fucking crazy."

Kurtz shook his head. "I just want to go along as one of your bodyguards."

"Uh-uh." She was shaking her head hard enough to cause sweat to fly. "They only allow two guys to come with me. Marco and Leo, that's been the drill."

"I know. I'll take the place of one of them."

Angelina looked over her shoulder to where the Boys were sitting watching television. "Which one?"

"I don't know. We'll decide later."

"They'll be suspicious, new guard."

"That's why I want to go tomorrow. So they'll know me on Thursday."

"I—" She stopped. "Do you have a plan?"

"Maybe."

"Does it involve bulldozers and earthmovers?"

"Probably not."

She rubbed her lower lip with her fist. "We need to talk about this. You should come out to the penthouse this evening."

"Tomorrow morning," Kurtz said. "I'll be out of town this evening."

"Where the hell is he going?" asked Detective Myers. He and Brubaker had spent a cold and boring and useless afternoon watching Joe Kurtz's car and office, and when the son of a bitch finally emerged and started driving his scratched-up Volvo, the bastard had taken the 190 out to 90-South and seemed headed for the toll booths and the Thruway to Erie, Pennsylvania.

"How the fuck should I know where he's going?" said Brubaker. "But if he leaves the fucking state, he's in violation of his parole and we've got him." Five minutes later, Brubaker said, "Shit."

Kurtz had exited onto Highway 219, the last turnoff before the I-90 West Thruway toll booths. It was snowing and getting dark.

"What's out here?" whined Myers as they followed Kurtz toward the town of Orchard Park. "The Farino Family used to have their headquarters out here, but they moved it to town after that nun sister showed up, didn't they?"

Brubaker shrugged, although, he knew exactly where the new Farino Family digs were at Marina Towers since he took his weekly payoff from Little Skag via Skag's lawyer, Albert Bell, near there every Tuesday. Brubaker knew that Myers suspected him of being on the Farino payroll but wasn't sure. If Myers was certain, he'd want in himself, and Brubaker didn't like sharing.

"Why don't we just roust Kurtz tonight?" said Myers. "I got the throwdown if he's not armed."

Brubaker shook his head. Kurtz had turned right near Chestnut Ridge Park, and it was hard to follow the Volvo in the gloom and snow along these two-lane roads amidst all the construction cones and commuter traffic. "We're out of our jurisdiction here," he said. "His lawyer could call it harassment if we get him out here."

"Fuck that. We got probable cause."

Brubaker shook his head again.

"Then let's just forget this shit," Myers said. "It's a fucking waste of time."

"Tell that to Jimmy Hathaway," Brubaker said, invoking the name of the cop killed under mysterious circumstances four months earlier. The only link to Kurtz, Brubaker knew, was Little Skag Farino's comment to him that Hathaway—who had been the Farinos' bitch for years—had tapped a phone call and followed Kurtz nomewhere on the night of the detective's murder. Hathaway had been eager to earn a bounty on Joe Kurtz's head at the time.

"Fuck Jimmy Hathaway," said Myers. "I never liked the asshole."

Brubaker shot a glance at his partner. "Look, if Kurtz leaves the state, we've got him on parole violation."

Myers pointed two cars ahead of him. "Leave the state? The fucker's not even leaving the county. Look—he just turned back toward Hamburg."

Brubaker lit a cigarette. It was hard to follow Kurtz now that it was really dark.

"You want him," said Myers, "let's roust him tomorrow in the city. Use the throwdown. Beat the shit out of him and turn him over to County."

"Yeah," said Brubaker. "Yeah." He turned back to Highway 219 and the Thruway to Buffalo.

CHAPTER
FIFTEEN

When Kurtz was sure that the unmarked car had turned back, he took the back road from Hamburg to the Thruway, accepted a ticket at the toll booth, and drove the two hundred miles to Cleveland.

Dr. Howard K. Conway's office and home were in an old section not far from the downtown. It was a neighborhood of big old Victorian homes broken into apartments and large Catholic churches, either closed or locked tight against the night. As the Italian and Polish residents had been replaced by blacks in the old neighborhoods, the parishes had died or moved to the suburbs. Despite its new stadium and rock-and-roll museum, Cleveland was still, like Buffalo, an old industrial city with rot at its heart.

If Emilio Gonzaga's compound was a fortress, Conway's home was fortress-lite, circled by a black iron fence, its first-floor windows caged, the old house dark except for a single lighted window on the second floor. The sign outside read DR. H.K. CONWAY, DDS. Kurtz unlatched the iron gate—assuming that an alarm was being tripped in the house—and walked to the front door. There was a buzzer and an intercom, and he leaned on the former and moaned in the direction of the latter.

"What is it?" The voice was young—too young for Conway—and harsh.

"I 'ave a 'oothache," moaned Kurtz. "I 'eed a 'entis'."

"What?"

"I 'ave a 'errible 'oothache."

"Fuck off." The intercom went dead.

Kurtz leaned on the buzzer.

"What?"

"I 'ave a 'errible 'oothache," moaned Kurtz, louder now, audibly whining.

"Dr. Conway doesn't see patients." The intercom clicked off.

Kurtz hit the buzzer button eight times and then leaned his weight on it.

There came a thudding on bare stairs and the door jerked open to the length of a chain. The man standing there was so large that he blocked the light coming down the stairway—three hundred pounds at least, young, perhaps in his twenties, with cupid lips and curly hair. "Are you fucking deaf? I said Dr. Conway doesn't see patients. He's retired. Fuck off."

Kurtz held his jaw, keeping his head lowered so that his face was in shadow. "I 'eed to see a dentist. It 'urts."

The big man started to close the door. Kurtz got his boot in the opening. "P'ease."

"You fucking asked for this, pal," said the big man, jerking the chain off, flinging the door open, and reaching for Kurtz's collar.

Kurtz kicked him in the balls, took the big man's offered right hand, swung it around behind him, and broke his little finger. When the man screamed, Kurtz transferred his grip to his index finger and bent it far back, keeping the hand and arm pinned somewhere around where the big man's shoulder blades were buried under fat. "Let's go upstairs," Kurtz whispered, stepping into a foyer that smelled of cabbage. He kicked the door shut behind them and wheeled the man around, helping him up the first stairs by applying leverage to his finger.

"Timmy?" called a quavery voice from the second floor. "Is everything all right? Timmy?"

Kurtz looked at the blubbering, weeping mass of stumbling flesh ascending the stairs ahead of him. *Timmy?*

The second-floor landing opened onto a lighted parlor where an old man sat in a wheelchair. The man was bald and liver-spotted, his wasted legs were covered by a lap robe, and he was holding some sort of blue steel .32-caliber revolver.

"Timmy?" quavered the old man. He squinted at them through pop-bottle-thick lenses set in old-fashioned black frames.

Kurtz kept Timmy's mass between him and the muzzle of the .32.

"I'm sorry, Howard," Timmy gasped. "He surprised me. He . . . ahhhhh!" The last syllable erupted as Kurtz bent Timmy's finger back beyond design tolerances.

"Dr. Conway," said Kurtz, "we need to talk."

The old man thumbed the hammer back. "You're police?"

Kurtz thought that question was too stupid to dignify with an answer. Timmy was trying to lean far forward to reduce the pain in his arm and finger, so Kurtz had to knee him in his fat buttocks to get him upright in shield position again.

"You're from *him?*" said the old man, voice shaking almost as much as the gun's muzzle.

"Yes," said Kurtz. "James B. Hansen."

As if these were the magic words, Dr. Howard K. Conway squeezed the trigger of the .32 once, twice, three, four times. The reports sounded loud and flat in the wood-floored room. Suddenly the air smelled of cordite. The dentist stared at the pistol as if it had fired of its own volition.

"Aww, shit," Timmy said in a disappointed voice and pitched forward, his forehead hitting the hardwood floor with a hollow sound.

Kurtz moved fast, diving around Timmy, rolling once, and coming up fast to knock the pistol from Conway's hand before the crippled dentist could empty chambers five and six. He grabbed the old man by his flannel shirtfront and lifted him out of the chair, shaking him twice to make sure there were no more weapons hidden under the slipping lap robe.

French doors opened onto a narrow balcony at the far end of the room. Booting the wheelchair aside, Kurtz carried the struggling scarecrow across the room, kicked those doors open, and dangled the old man over the icy iron railing. Dr. Conway's glasses went flying into the night.

"Don't . . . don't . . . don't . . . don't." The dentist's mantra had lost its quaver.

"Tell me about Hansen."

"What . . . I don't know any . . . good Christ, *don't. Please don't!*"

With one hand, Kurtz had literally tossed the old man backward and caught him by the shirtfront. Flannel ripped.

Dr. Howard K. Conway's dentures had come loose and were clacking around in his mouth. If the old piece of shit hadn't been a silent accomplice to a dozen or more children's murders, Joe Kurtz might have felt a little bit sorry for him. Maybe.

"My hands are cold," whispered Kurtz. "I might miss

my grip next time." He shoved the dentist back over the railing.

"Anything . . . anything! I have money. I have lots of money!"

"James B. Hansen."

Conway nodded wildly.

"Other names," hissed Kurtz. "Records. Files."

"In my study. In the safe."

"Combination."

"Left thirty-two, right nineteen, left eleven, right forty-six. Please let me go. No! Not over the drop!"

Kurtz slammed the old man's bony and presumably unfeeling ass down hard on the railing. "Why didn't you tell someone, Conway? All these years. All those dead women and kids. Why didn't you tell someone?"

"He would have killed me." The old man's breath smelled of ether.

"Yeah," said Kurtz and had to stifle the immediate urge to throw the old man down onto the concrete terrace fifteen feet below. First the files.

"What will I do now?" Dr. Conway was sobbing, hiccuping. "Where will I go?"

"You can go to—" began Kurtz and saw the old man's rheumy eyes focus wildly, hopefully, on something low behind Kurtz.

He grabbed the dentist by his shirtfront and swung him around just as Timmy, who had left a bloody trail across the parquet floor, fired the last two bullets from the pistol he'd retrieved.

Conway's body was too thin and hollow to stop a .32 slug, but the first bullet missed and the second hit Conway in the center of his forehead. Kurtz ducked, but the spray of blood and brain matter was all from the entry wound; the bullet had not exited.

Kurtz dropped the dentist's body on the icy balcony

and walked over to Timmy, who was clicking away on empty chambers. Not wanting to touch the weapon even with his gloves on, he stepped on the man's hand until he dropped it and then rolled Timmy over with his boot. Two of the original .32 slugs had hit the big man in the chest, but one had caught him in the throat and another had entered below the left cheekbone. Timmy would bleed out in another minute or two unless he received immediate medical assistance.

Kurtz walked into what had to be Dr. Conway's study, ignored the row of locked filing cabinets, found the big wall safe behind a painting of a naked man, and tried the combination. He thought that Conway had rattled it off too quickly, under too much stress, to be lying, and he was right. The safe opened on the first try.

Lying in the safe were metal boxes holding $63,000 in cash, stacks of bonds, gold coins, a sheaf of stock certificates, and a thick file folder filled with dental X-rays, insurance forms, and newspaper clippings. Kurtz ignored the money and took the folder out into the light, slamming the safe door and scrambling the lock as he did so.

Timmy was no longer twitching and the viscous flow of blood ran out onto the cement balcony where it had pooled around Dr. Conway's ruined skull and was coagulating in the process of freezing. Kurtz set the folder on the round table next to the empty wheelchair and flipped through it. He didn't think that this was a neighborhood where people would dial 911 at the first sound of what could be a gunshot.

Twenty-three news clippings. Fifteen photocopies of letters to various urban police headquarters, dental X-rays attached. Fifteen different identities.

"Come on, come on," whispered Kurtz. If Hansen's current Buffalo identity wasn't here, this whole mess had been for nothing. But why would it be here? Why would Conway know Hansen's current alias before it was necessary to identify him to the next round of homicide detectives?

Because Hansen has to have the cover story ready in case the old dentist dies. Timmy would do the honors then. But there has to be a dentist of record.

The next-to-last paper in the folder had the record of an office visit the previous November—a cleaning and partial crown. No X-rays. There was no bill, but a handwritten note in the margin read "$50,000." No wonder Dr. Howard K. Conroy accepted no new patients. Beneath it was an address in the Buffalo suburb of Tonawanda, and a name.

"Holy shit," whispered Kurtz.

CHAPTER
SIXTEEN

"Where the hell is he?" Detective Myers asked Detective Brubaker. The two had requisitioned a much better surveillance vehicle—a gray floral-delivery van—and were parked on station near the Royal Delaware Arms at 7:30 A.M., just in case Kurtz took it in his head to go to his office early. They'd discussed where and how to interdict him—an observed traffic violation on Elicott Street would be the pretext—and then the fast roust, the discovery of a weapon—the throwdown, if Kurtz wasn't armed in violation of parole, which they guessed he would be—the attempted resisting arrest, the subduing, and the arrest.

Brubaker and Myers were ready. Besides wearing body armor, each man was carrying a telescoping, weighted baton in addition to his 9mm Glock, and Myers had a 10,000-volt Taser stun gun in his pocket.

"Where the fuck is he?" repeated Myers. Kurtz's Volvo was nowhere in sight.

"Maybe he left early for that shithole office of his," said Brubaker.

"Maybe he never came back from Orchard Park last night."

"Maybe he was kidnapped by fucking UFOs," snarled Brubaker. "Maybe we should quit speculating and go find him and get this over with."

"Maybe we should just skip it." Myers was not eager to do this thing. But then, Myers was not being paid $5,000 by Little Skag Farino to bust Kurtz and get him back into prison so he could be shanked. Brubaker had considered telling his partner about the payment and sharing the money. Considered it for about two milliseconds.

"Maybe you should shut up," said Brubaker, shifting the van into gear and driving away from the Royal Delaware Arms.

James B. Hansen had to wait for the two other homicide detectives to drive off before he could park his Cadillac SUV where their van had been, and then go in the back entrance of the fleabag hotel. He took the back stairs up all seven flights to the room number Brubaker and Myers had listed in their report. Hansen could have used his badge to get the passkey for Joe Kurtz's room, but that would have been terminally stupid. However legitimate his excuse for checking on Kurtz might sound later, Hansen wanted no connection between the ex-con and himself until the investigation of the murder of one John Wellington Frears.

Hansen noticed the plaster dust in the center of the stairs and hall leading to the eighth-floor room. Knowing that Kurtz had come and gone over the past few days, it had to be some sort of paranoid alarm system. Hansen kept to the walls, leaving no trace. The door to Kurtz's room was locked, but it was a cheap lock, and bringing out the small leather-bound kit of burglary tools he'd used for fifteen years, Hansen had the door open in ten seconds.

The suite of rooms was cold and drafty but strangely neat for such a loser. Wearing gloves but still touching nothing, Hansen peered into the adjoining room— weights, a heavy bag, no furniture—and looked around the big room where Kurtz appeared to spend his time. Books—a surprise. Serious titles, a bigger surprise. Hansen made a mental note not to underestimate the intelligence of this shabby ex-con. The rest of the room was predictable—a half-sized refrigerator, a hot plate for cooking, a toaster, no TV, no computer, no luxuries. Also no notes or diaries or loose papers. Hansen checked in the closet—a few well-worn dress shirts, some ties, a decent suit, one pair of well-polished black shoes. There was no dresser, but a box in the corner held folded jeans, clean underwear, more shirts, and some sweaters. Hansen looked in all the obvious hiding places but could find no guns or illegal knives. He went back to the box of sweaters and raveled a long thread from the top sweater on the pile, dropping it into a clean evidence bag.

In the sink was a rinsed coffee cup, a small plate, and a sharp kitchen knife. It looked as if Kurtz had used the knife to cut a slice of French bread and spread butter on it, then rinsed the blade. Lifting the knife gingerly, Hansen dropped it into a second evidence bag.

The bathroom was as neat as the main room, with nothing beyond basics in the medicine cabinet—not even prescription pills. Kurtz's hairbrush and shaving kit were lined up neatly on the old pedestal sink. Hansen had to stop himself from grinning. Lifting the brush, he found five hairs and transferred them to a third evidence bag.

Checking to make sure that he had left no trace, Hansen let himself out of the hotel room, locked the door behind him, and kept to the walls while descending the stairs.

Kurtz had returned late from Cleveland, driven to the office, used his computer to double-check Captain Robert Millworth's address in Tonawanda, and then, around 6:00 A.M., had driven to Arlene's small home in Cheektowaga. She was awake and dressed, drinking coffee in the kitchen and watching a network early morning show on a small TV on her counter.

"Don't come into the office today," Kurtz told her as he stepped past her into the kitchen.

"Why, Joe? I have more than fifty Sweetheart Searches to process today—"

He quickly explained about Dr. Conway's demise and the information he'd found in the dentist's safe. This was information Arlene had to know if she was going to be a help over the next few days. Kurtz glanced at the manila folder on the table. "Are those the photos I asked you to process?" Their old office on Chippewa Street years ago had been big enough to hold a darkroom in which Arlene had developed all the photos he and Sam had shot on the job. After her husband's death, Arlene had converted an extra bathroom into a darkroom at home.

She slid the folder across the table. "Shopping for property?"

Kurtz glanced through the blowups of the Gonzaga compound he'd taken from the helicopter. They'd all turned out.

"So what do I do from home today, Joe?"

"I'll be back in a while and someone may be with me. You have any problem entertaining a visitor?"

"Who?" said Arlene. "And for how long? And why?"

Kurtz let that go. "I'll be back in a while."

"Since we aren't going into the office, is there any chance we can look at new office space today after your visitor leaves?"

"Not today." He paused by the door, tapping the folder of photos against his free hand. "Keep your doors locked."

"The Hansen thing, you mean."

Kurtz shrugged. "I don't think it will be a problem. But if the cops get in touch, call me right away on the cell phone."

"The cops?" Arlene lit a cigarette. "I love it when you talk like that, Joe."

"Like what?"

"Like a private eye."

"So he's not at his fucking flophouse and he's not at his fucking office. Where the fuck is he?" said Detective Myers.

"Did anyone ever tell you that you use the F word too much, Tommy?"

Brubaker had given up smoking seven months earlier, but now he took a last drag on his cigarette and flipped the butt out the window of their surveillance van. It was almost 9:00 A.M., and not only was Kurtz's Volvo not parked in the alley behind his office, but the secretary's Buick wasn't there either.

"So now what?"

"How the fuck do I know?" said Brubaker.

"So we just sit on our asses and wait?"

"I sit on my ass," said Brubaker. "You sit on your *fat* ass."

CHAPTER
SEVENTEEN

It was just 8:00 A.M. when Kurtz knocked on the hotel-room door, but when it opened, John Wellington Frears was dressed in a three-piece suit, tie knotted perfectly. Although Frears's expression did not change when he saw Kurtz, he took a surprised half step back into the room. "Mr. Kurtz."

Kurtz stepped into the room and closed the door behind him. "You were expecting someone else." It was not a question.

"No. Please sit down." Frears gestured to a chair by the window, but Kurtz remained standing.

"You were expecting James B. Hansen," continued Kurtz. "With a gun."

Frears said nothing. His brown eyes, so expressive in the publicity photos Kurtz had seen, now suppressed even more pain than Kurtz had seen the previous week at Blues Franklin. The man was dying.

"That's one way to flush him out," said Kurtz. "But you'll never know if he's brought to justice for his crimes. You'll be dead."

Frears sat on the hard chair by the desk. "What do you want, Mr. Kurtz?"

"I'm here to tell you that your plan won't work, Mr. Frears. Hansen's in Buffalo, all right. He's lived here for about eight months, moving here from Miami with his new family. But he can kill you today and he'll never be accused of the crime."

Frears's eyes literally came alive. "You know where he is? What his name is here?"

Kurtz handed the man the dental bill.

"Captain Robert G. Millworth," read the violinist. "A police officer?"

"Homicide. I checked."

Frears's hands were shaking as he set the bill on the desktop. "How do you know this man is James Hansen? What does the bill—however high—from a Cleveland dentist prove?"

"It proves nothing," said Kurtz. "But this is the dentist who's provided dental records to police around the country after a dozen murder-suicides identical to the one in your daughter's case. Always different names. Always different records. But always involved in murders that Hansen committed." He handed across the folder.

Frears went through the pages, slowly, tears forming. "So many children." Looking up at Kurtz, he said, "And you can tie this Captain Millworth to these other names? You have dental records for him?"

"No. I don't think Conway kept any other records or X-rays on file for this office visit. I think he was going to use the standard X-rays when Millworth's corpse— whatever corpse Millworth provided—would need identification."

Frears blinked. "But we can make the dentist testify?"

"The dentist is dead. As of yesterday."

Frears started to speak, stopped. Perhaps he wondered if Kurtz had killed Conway, but perhaps it was not important to him to know right now. "I can present this folder to the FBI. The bill ties Millworth to the dentist. The payment is obviously extortion. Conway was blackmailing James Hansen."

"Sure. You can try to make that case. But there's no official record of Millworth's payment, just of an office visit."

"But I don't understand how the dental X-rays matched the teeth of the bodies Mr. Hansen left behind in these various murder-suicides."

"It looks as if Dr. Conway, DDS, had a clientele mostly of corpses."

Frears looked at the forms again. "Conway's office was in Cleveland. Many of these murder-suicides occurred in cities far away from there. Even if Hansen somehow harvested these other men to be future burned bodies for him, how did he get them to go to Cleveland to have dental X-rays taken?"

Kurtz shrugged. "Hansen is one smart son of a bitch. Maybe he offered these poor bastards dental care as part of an employment package. My guess is that he had Conway fly to whatever city he was living in at the time, X-ray the fall guys' teeth—maybe when they were already dead—and then have the dentist send the X-rays from Cleveland. It doesn't really matter, does it? What matters right now is getting you out of here."

Frears blinked again and a stubborn look appeared on his pain-ravaged face. "Out of Buffalo? I won't go. I have to—"

"Not out of Buffalo, just out of this hotel. I have a better way for you to nail our Captain Millworth than becoming just another unsolved homicide in the good captain's case file."

"I don't have anyplace to—"

"I've got somewhere for you to stay for a couple of days," said Kurtz. "It's not one-hundred-percent safe, but then, nowhere in Buffalo is really safe for you right now." Or for me either, he could have added. "Get packed," said Kurtz. "You're checking out."

Brubaker and Myers trolled the downtown streets, watching for a glimpse of Kurtz's blue Volvo, checking the sidewalks for a glimpse of him, and driving by the Royal Delaware Arms every orbit.

"Hey," said Myers, "what about his secretary's house? Whatshername? Arlene DeMarco."

"What about it?" said Brubaker. He was on his fifth cigarette.

Myers flipped through his grubby little notebook. "She lives out in Cheektowaga. We've got the address here. Her car's not there today. If she didn't come in, maybe Kurtz went out to her."

Brubaker shrugged, but then turned the car and headed for the Expressway. "What the fuck," he said. "Worth a try."

"Mr. Frears," said Kurtz, "this is my secretary, Mrs. DeMarco. She won't mind if you stay here for a day or two."

Arlene glanced at Kurtz but extended her hand. "A pleasure, Mr. Frears. I'm Arlene."

"John," said Frears, taking her hand in his, putting his feet together and bowing slightly in a way that made him look as if he was going to kiss her hand. He did not, but Arlene blushed with pleasure as if he had.

They were in Arlene's kitchen. When Frears's back was turned, Kurtz said, "Arlene, you still have your . . ." He opened his peacoat slightly to expose the pistol on his belt.

She shook her head. "It's at work, Joe. I don't keep one here."

Kurtz said to Frears, "Excuse us a moment," and led Arlene into her living room. He handed her Angelina Farino's gun—not the Compact Witness she had a sentimental thing for, but the little .45 he'd taken away from her at the hockey arena. Arlene slid the magazine out of the grip, made sure it was loaded, slapped the magazine back in, checked to make sure the safety was on, and slipped the small but heavy pistol into the pocket of her cardigan sweater. She nodded, and the two of them went back to the kitchen.

"I'm afraid this is going to be a terrible imposition," began Frears. "I'm perfectly capable of finding—"

"We may find you another place after a day or two," said Kurtz. "But you saw the situation with Hansen/Millworth. Right now I think you'd be safer here."

Frears looked at Arlene. "Mrs. DeMarco . . . Arlene . . . this will bring danger into your home."

Arlene lit a cigarette. "Actually, John, it will bring a little much-needed excitement into my life."

"Call me if anything comes up," said Kurtz. He went out to his Volvo.

"Got him!" said Detective Myers. They had been headed down Union Road in Cheektowaga when they saw Kurtz's Volvo pull out of a side street and head north toward the Kensington Expressway.

Brubaker made a U-turn through a Dunkin' Donuts' parking lot and pulled the floral-delivery van into northbound traffic.

"Keep way back," said Myers.

"Don't fucking tell me how to tail someone, Tommy."

"Well, just don't fucking get *made*," whined Myers.

"Kurtz doesn't know this van. We stay back, we got him."

Brubaker stayed back. Kurtz got onto the Kensington headed into town and the van followed six vehicles back.

"We should wait until he's into the city to take him," said Myers.

Brubaker nodded.

"Maybe near that flophouse hotel of his, if he's headed there. It would make sense that we'd have probable cause to roust him near there."

"Yeah," said Brubaker. "If he's headed to the hotel."

Kurtz was headed to the hotel. He parked in the crappy neighborhood nearby, and Brubaker drove the van a block farther and doubled back along side streets in time to see Kurtz locking his car and walking toward the Royal Delaware Arms. Brubaker parked the van in front of a hydrant. They could intercept Kurtz on foot before he got to the hotel. "We've fucking *got* him. You got your club and the throwdown?"

"Yeah, yeah," said Myers, anxiously patting his pockets. "Let's do this."

Kurtz had just turned the corner a block from the hotel. The two detectives jumped out of the van and began quick-walking to catch up. Brubaker pulled his Glock from its holster and carried it in his right hand. He clicked the safety off.

Myers's phone rang.

"Ignore it," said Brubaker.

"It might be important."

"Ignore it."

Myers ignored Brubaker instead. Answering the phone even as he ran, he said, "Yeah. Yeah? Yes, sir. Yes, but we're just going to . . . no . . . yeah . . . no . . . right." He folded the phone and stopped.

Brubaker whirled at him. *"What?"*

"It was Captain Millworth. We're to drop the surveillance on Kurtz."

"Too fucking *late!*"

Myers shook his head. "Uh-uh. The captain says that we're to drop the surveillance and get the hell over to Elmwood Avenue to help Prdzywsky with a fresh street killing. We're finished with Kurtz . . . his words."

"Fuck!" shouted Brubaker. An old woman in a black coat stopped to stare. Brubaker took three strides, rounded the corner, and looked at Kurtz approaching the hotel across the street. "We *have* the fucker."

"We go after him now, Millworth will have our balls for breakfast. He said not to mess with Kurtz. What's your hard-on for, Fred?"

Tell him about the money from Little Skag Farino? thought Brubaker. *No.* "That perp killed Jimmy Hathaway. And those Three Stooges from Attica, too."

"Bullshit," said Myers. He turned toward the van. "There's no proof for that and you know it."

Brubaker looked back toward the hotel and actually lifted his Glock as if he was going to shoot at Kurtz's retreating back a block away. "Fuck!" he said again.

Someone had been in Kurtz's room. Two of the tiny telltales on the door had been knocked free. Kurtz pulled his gun, unlocked the door, kicked it open, and went in fast. Nothing. He kept the S&W in his hand as he checked both rooms and the fire escape. He didn't see anything out of place at first inspection, but someone had been in here.

A knife was gone. Just a sharp kitchen knife. Kurtz went over everything else, but except for the fact that his shaving kit and brush had been moved slightly in the bathroom and some books set back on the shelf not quite as he had left them, nothing else was missing or out of place.

Kurtz showered, shaved, combed his hair, and dressed in his best white shirt, conservative tie, and dark suit. The black Bally dress shoes in the back of his closet needed only a buffing to be brought up to full shine. His trench coat hanging in the closet was old but well-made and clean. Slipping the .40 S&W into his belt and dropping Angelina's Compact Witness .45 into his coat pocket, he went out to the Volvo and drove to the Buffalo Athletic Club. On the way, he stopped at a Sees Candy, bought a medium-sized box of chocolates in a heart-shaped box, and tossed away most of the chocolates.

"You're late," said Angelina Farino Ferrara as he came into the exercise area. "And out of uniform." He was still wearing his suit and trench coat.

"No exercise for me today." He handed her the box of chocolates. The Boys looked over curiously from where they had just finished their work in the weight room.

Angelina untied the ribbon, opened the heart-shaped box, and looked at the Compact Witness nestled under the few loose chocolates. "My favorite," she said, eating a pecan cluster and closing the lid. "Did you still want to do lunch?"

"Yes."

"You're sure that today's the right day?"

"Yes."

"But nothing dramatic is going to happen there, right?"

Kurtz remained silent.

"We'll talk about this out at my penthouse," said Angelina. "I have to change before lunch. You can ride out with me. I'll have to introduce you to the Boys and anyone else who's interested. So far, you've just been the Man Hitting on Me at the Athletic Club. What did you say your name was?"

"Dr. Howard Conway."

Angelina raised an eyebrow and mopped her sweaty face. "*Dr.* Conway. How nice for you. Surgeon?"

"Dentist."

"Oh, too bad. I understand that dentists suffer from depression and suicide at an alarming rate. Are you armed today, Dr. Conway?"

"Yes."

"You know the Boys are going to relieve you of it as soon as we get in the car?"

"Yes."

Angelina Farino Ferrara's smile was predatory.

CHAPTER
EIGHTEEN

They rode out to the marina in silence. Marco and Leo
had shaken his hand in the parking garage and then
searched him well.

"Why does a dentist need a gun?" asked Leo, slipping
the S&W into his cashmere coat.

"I'm paranoid," said Kurtz.

"Aren't we all?" said Angelina.

Marina Towers rose twelve stories above an expanse
of snowy lawn that overlooked the Buffalo Marina and
the frozen Niagara River. From the parking garage beneath the complex, the four of them rode a private elevator to the eleventh floor, where the Boys lived—Kurtz
caught a glimpse of desks, computers, teletypes, a few
accountant types, and knew that this was where the Farino offices had been moved—and then Angelina took
him up the final flight on a separate elevator. They
stepped out into a marble-lined foyer, where she produced a key and let them into her penthouse.

The series of open rooms ran the full length of the
building and filled the entire floor so that Kurtz could
look northeast to downtown Buffalo and southwest toward the marina and the river. Even with low clouds on
a gray day, the view was impressive.

"Very nice—" began Kurtz and stopped as he turned. Angelina was aiming the Compact Witness .45 at him and had pulled a second, larger automatic from a drawer.

"Can you think of any reason I shouldn't gut-shoot you right now, Joe Kurtz?"

Kurtz did not move his hands. "It might ruin your plan to surprise Mr. Gonzaga."

The woman's lips looked very thin and bloodless. "I can make other plans."

Kurtz had no argument for that.

"You humiliated me twice," said Angelina. "Threatened to kill me."

Kurtz could have mentioned the four men she had hired to kill him, but he didn't think that would be the best argument to make in these circumstances. If she shot him now, she'd earn points with her brother.

"Tell me why I shouldn't get rid of you and get someone else to go after Gonzaga," said Angelina Farino Ferrara. "Give me one good reason."

"I'm thinking . . . I'm thinking," said Kurtz in his best Jack Benny voice.

Maybe Angelina was too young to get the joke. Her finger curled on the trigger. "Time's up."

"Can I reach slowly into my suit pocket?"

Angelina nodded. She was holding the larger .45 aimed steadily at his midsection and had set the Compact Witness on the maple table under a painting.

Kurtz took the cassette tape out of his pocket and tossed it to her.

"What is it?"

"Play it."

"I hate games," said Angelina, but she walked five paces to a stack of stereo components built into a bookcase, slipped the cassette in, and punched "Play."

Her voice came from the speakers. "Oh, but I did. I

did. A boy. A beautiful baby boy with Emilio's fat, rubbery lips, lovely brown eyes, and the Gonzaga chin and forehead. I drowned him in the Belice River in Sicily." Her voice went on for a minute, explaining how hard it would be to get to Emilio Gonzaga in his compound, and then came Kurtz's voice: "How did you plan to kill him?"

"Well, I sort of hoped you'd take care of that detail for me now that you know what you know," came Angelina's voice.

Angelina shut off the player and pocketed the cassette. She was actually smiling. "You miserable son of a bitch. You were wired that night out in Williamsville."

Kurtz said nothing.

"So," said Angelina, "in the event of your disappearance here, who gets copies of the tape? Emilio, of course."

"And your brother," said Kurtz.

"Not the cops?"

Kurtz shrugged.

"I should shoot you just on general principles," said Angelina. But she put the .45 back in its drawer. Then she hefted the smaller Compact Witness. "You gave it back to me loaded?"

"Yeah."

"You take chances, Joe Kurtz. Stay here. There's fruit juice in the refrigerator over there, liquor at the bar. I'm going to shower again and get dressed. Emilio's car will be here to pick me up in thirty minutes. I hope to God you have a plan."

Kurtz looked at his watch.

Fifteen minutes later, Angelina phoned down for the Boys to come up. She met them in the foyer and led them into the penthouse, where Kurtz was waiting with his S&W, now sporting a silencer she had loaned him. Angelina closed the door behind the Boys.

"What the fuck..." began Leo. Marco, the bigger man, simply raised his hands and watched both Kurtz and Angelina.

"Quiet," said Kurtz. "Unload the hardware. Carefully. Tips of fingers only. Good. Now kick the guns this way. Gently. Good." He sat on the edge of a couch, the pistol covering both of them.

"Ms. Farino?" said Leo. "You part of this bullshit?"

Kurtz shook his head and tapped one finger against his lips. "Gentlemen, we have a proposition for you. Do the smart thing and you live and make quite a bit of money. Do the stupid thing and... well, you don't want to do the stupid thing."

Marco and Leo stood with their hands half-raised, Marco vigilant, Leo twitchy, his eyes flicking back and forth as if gauging his chances for leaping at his revolver on the floor before Kurtz could fire.

"Are you listening, fellows?" said Kurtz.

"We're listening," said Marco. The big man sounded calm.

"I want to visit the Gonzagas today with Miss Ferrara," said Kurtz. "Since they only allow two bodyguards with her, one of you will have to stay behind. We thought the big bathroom up here would be a good place for the volunteer to stay until we get back. Miss Ferrara had a pair of handcuffs in her bedroom, I didn't ask why, and one of you will wear those, probably connected to the washbasin pedestal in there with your arms behind you, until we return. Then we'll find a more comfortable arrangement for the next couple of days."

"Next couple of days!" shouted Leo. "Are you fucking out of your fucking mind? You know what Little

Skag Farino is going to do with your sorry ass, cock-sucker?"

Kurtz said nothing.

Marco said, "Where does the money come in?"

Angelina answered. "When our negotiations with Emilio Gonzaga are completed, there's going to be more money coming in than the Farino Family has seen for decades. Anyone who helps me with this will get a lion's share."

"Helps *you*?" sneered Leo. "Who the fuck do you think you are, cunt? When Little Skag gets out, you're going to be —"

"My brother Stephen is not a part of this," said Angelina. Kurtz thought that she had spoken very politely for someone who had just been called the C word.

Marco nodded. Leo looked at him with a dumb-founded expression. He glanced at the weapons on the floor again.

"So which one of you volunteers is going to stay behind?" said Kurtz.

Neither man spoke for a minute. Kurtz could see Marco mulling it over. Leo's fingers were twitching.

"No volunteers?" said Kurtz. "I guess I'll just have to pick." He shot Leo through his left eye.

Marco did not move as Leo's body fell back onto the parquet floor, blood streaming from the back of his skull. Leo's legs twitched once and were still. Angelina gave Kurtz a startled look.

"You understand the drill?" Kurtz asked Marco.

"Yeah."

"My name's Howard Conway and I'm filling in for Leo, who has the flu."

"Yeah."

"You'll have your gun back, minus the bullets. Of

course, when we're at the Gonzagas', you can blow the whistle on us any time."

"What would that get me?"

Kurtz shrugged. "Probably the eternal appreciation of Emilio Gonzaga."

"I'd rather have the clap," said Marco. Angelina had picked up the bodyguards' guns and was thumbing the slugs out of the magazine in Marco's semiauto. "Can I ask a question of Ms. Farino?" said the bodyguard.

It was Angelina who nodded.

"Ma'am, is this your show or this . . . dentist's?"

"It's my show."

Marco nodded, accepted the now-empty pistol, and slid it back in his shoulder holster. "Can I move?"

Kurtz nodded.

Marco glanced at his watch. "The Gonzaga limo's going to be here in about three minutes. You want me to do something with this?" He inclined his head toward Leo.

"There are a couple of blankets in that first closet," said Angelina. "Store him in the back of the big walk-in freezer for now. I'll get the mop."

CHAPTER
NINETEEN

James B. Hansen left his office at police headquarters in late morning and drove to the Airport Sheraton. He had an absolutely untraceable .38-caliber pistol in his briefcase, right next to the clear evidence bags containing the knife, thread, and hairs he had picked up in Joe Kurtz's hotel room.

It might have been a slight problem finding John Frears's room number—Hansen was certainly not going to show his badge and ask at the desk—but the old violinist had left his phone number, complete with room extension, when he had spoken to a bored lieutenant in Homicide the week before about the unlikely sighting at the airport. Frears was making it almost too easy.

Hansen knew what the old man was up to, speaking to the *Buffalo News,* going on a radio talk show and all the rest. He was offering himself up like a staked-out goat, trying to flush the man he'd known as James B. Hansen out of hiding so the police would put two and two together and track down the killer. Hansen had to smile at that. Homicide detectives, under Hansen's supervision—after all, John Wellington Frears was an important man in his own little musical circles, and his murder would demand the A-team's presence—would put two and two together all right. And then the finger-prints on the knife and the DNA in the hair would lead them straight to an ex-con killer named Joe Kurtz.

Hansen entered by a side door, went up an empty staircase to the fifth floor, paused outside Frears's room, and readied the card key—programmed by Hansen him-self to open any door in the Sheraton—in his left hand and the .38 in his right. The pistol, of course, would later be found in Kurtz's flophouse room. The knife—which would not be the murder weapon, but which would draw blood as if the two men were fighting over it—would be found in the hotel room. Hansen had taken care to wait until the maids would be done with their housekeeping and the long hallway was empty as he keyed the door open. The chain lock was not on. Hansen had planned to hold his badge up to the peephole if it had been.

As soon as Hansen saw the sterile, empty room and neatly made bed, he knew that Frears had fled.

Damn it. Hansen immediately asked forgiveness from the Lord for his curse.

He closed the door, went out to his SUV, and used a disposable cell phone to call the Sheraton's front desk. "This is Detective Hathaway of the Buffalo Police De-partment, badge number . . ." He rattled off the retired number he'd looked up in the dead detective's file. "We're returning a call from one of your guests, ah . . ." He paused a few seconds as if looking up the name. "Mr. John Frears. Could you ring him for me, please?"

"I'm sorry, Detective Hathaway, Mr. Frears checked out this morning. About three hours ago."

"Really? He wanted to talk to us. Did he leave a for-warding address or number?"

"No, sir. I was the one who checked Mr. Frears out and he just paid his bill and left."

Hansen took a breath. "I'm sorry to bother you with all this, Mr.—"

"Paul Sirsika, Detective. I'm the day manager here."

"Sorry to bother you with all this detail, Mr. Sirsika, but it might be important. Was there someone with him when he checked out? Mr. Frears had some concerns for his safety, and I need to ascertain that he didn't leave under duress."

"Under duress? Good heavens," said the clerk. "No, I don't remember anyone at the counter with him or seeing him speak with anyone else, but there were other people in the lobby at the time."

"Did he leave alone?"

"I don't recall anyone going out with Mr. Frears, but I was busy with other guests checking out."

"Sure. Do you know if he called a cab or caught one outside? Or perhaps he mentioned something about the airport or catching a flight?"

"He didn't mention a flight to me or ask me to call a cab, Detective Hathaway. He might have hailed one outside. I could ask our bell captain."

"Would you do that, please? I'd appreciate it."

The clerk was back in a minute. "Detective Hathaway? Clark, our bell captain, remembers Mr. Frears leaving but noticed that he did not take a cab. Clark said that he was walking to the parking lot, carrying his suitcase in one hand and his violin case in the other when Clark last saw him."

"So Mr. Frears had a rental car?" asked Hansen. "The license number would be on your registration card and in the computer."

"Just a second, please, Detective." The clerk was sounding a bit peevish now. "Yes, sir. It says that the vehicle was a white Ford Contour. Mr. Frears did give us a tag number when he checked in. I have it here if you'd like it."

"Go ahead," said Hansen. He memorized the number rather than write it down.

"I wish I could help you more, Detective."

"You've been a big help, Mr. Sirsika. One last question. Did you or any of the other clerks or bellhops—or perhaps someone working in the restaurant or gift shop—notice anyone visiting Mr. Frears, dining with him, calling for him?"

"I would have to ask everyone," said Clerk Sirsika, sounding very put-upon now.

"Would you do that, please? And call and leave a message at this number?" said Hansen. He gave them his private line at work.

Hansen used his phone to have "Detective Hathaway" call all of the rental-car agencies at the airport. The white Contour was a Hertz vehicle, rented by Mr. Frears eight days ago upon his arrival in Buffalo, rental extended six days ago. It had not been returned. It was an open-ended rental. Hansen thanked the clerk and drove around the hotel parking lot, checking to make sure that the car was not there. His next step would be to check airlines to see if Frears had flown out without returning the car, but Hansen did not want Detective Hathaway to do more phoning than he had to.

The white Contour was parked near the far end of the lot. Hansen made sure no one was watching, slim-jimmed the driver's door open, checked the interior—nothing—and popped the trunk. No luggage. Frears had left with someone.

Driving his Cadillac SUV back toward police headquarters on the Kensington, Hansen mentally reviewed everything Frears had told Detective Pierceson when the violinist had made out his airport-sighting report. Frears had said that he knew no one in Buffalo other than some of the booking people at Kleinhan's Music Hall, where he had played his two concerts. Them and someone he had known years ago at Princeton.

Hansen couldn't close his eyes while driving, but he mentally did so in a trick he had used since he was a kid to recall entire pages of text with perfect recall. Even as he drove on the Kensington, he could see Pierceson's report on the interview with Frears the week before.

Dr. Paul Frederick. A former philosophy and ethics professor at Princeton. Frears thought he lived in Buffalo and was searching for him.

Well, that's an obvious place to start this investigation, thought Hansen. *Find this old Professor Frederick. Perhaps your old pal came to pick you up at the Sheraton and told you to leave your car.*

Hansen would join in the search for one Professor Paul Frederick. It shouldn't be hard to find him. Academics tended to hang around academia until they died.

But if Frears wasn't with his old friend?

Then where are you, Johnny boy? Whom did you leave with this morning?

Hansen was not happy with this development, but it was just a puzzle. He was very, very good at solving puzzles.

Angelina Farino Ferrara realized halfway through her meal with Emilio that Joe Kurtz was going to get himself killed, her killed, and everyone else in the house killed.

The drive over from Marina Towers had been uneventful enough. Mickey Kee, the killer who always rode shotgun with Gonzaga's driver, had stared at Kurtz standing next to Marco and asked where Leo was.

"Leo's doing other things," Angelina said. "Howard here is with Marco and me today."

"Howard?" Mickey Kee said dubiously. Gonzaga's button man had tiny eyes that missed nothing, short, black hair cropped to a widow's peak, and skin so smooth that he could be any age between twenty-five and sixty. "Where are you from, Howard?"

Kurtz, the perfect lackey, had glanced at Angelica for permission before answering. She nodded.

"Florida," said Kurtz.

"Which part of Florida?"

"Raiford, mostly," said Kurtz.

The driver had snorted at this, but Mickey Kee showed no amusement. "I know some guys serving time in Raiford. You know Tommy Lee Peters?"

"Nope."

"Sig Bender?"

"Nope."

"Alan Wu?"

"Nope."

"You don't know many people, do you, Howard?"

"When I was there," said Kurtz, "Raiford had five thousand–some guys doing time. Maybe your friends weren't in the general population. I seem to remember that Raiford had a special ward for kept bitches."

Mickey Kee squinted at that. The driver, Al, had tugged at the gunman's arm and held the limo door open for Angelina, Marco, and Kurtz to get in the back. The window was up between the front section and the passenger area, but Angelina assumed that the intercom was kept on, so the drive to Grand Island was made in silence.

Angelina's choice of Joe Kurtz to carry out the elimination of Emilio Gonzaga had been one of the most dangerous decisions she had ever made, but up to now she had not considered it totally reckless. She could have Kurtz eliminated at any time, she thought, and erase the record of her contacts with him at the same time. But now there was the problem of those tapes he'd made. For the first time since her return to the States, Angelina felt the way she had in her first chess games with the bedridden Count Ferrara, when she would be trading a few pawns, working on her attack, only to realize that the dying old man had set her up—that his apparently defensive and random movements had been part of an attack so subtle that she had no place to flee, no pieces to move in defense, the only response to tip over her king and smile graciously.

Well, thought Angelina, *fuck that.*

She'd known that Joe Kurtz was a stone-killer. Her brother Stevie . . . fuck it, Little Skag . . . had told her about Kurtz's past: the former detective's love for his dead partner, Samantha Fielding, that resulted in one of the probable killers disappearing and the other being thrown out of a six-story window onto the roof of an arriving squad car. Kurtz had done more than eleven years of hard time for that vengeance, and according to Little Skag, had never whined once about it. The day after Kurtz got out of Attica, he'd made a business proposition to Don Farino. That had been a bloody business and before it was over, Angelina's father and sister were dead. Kurtz hadn't killed them—Little Skag, Angelina's darling little brother, had arranged that—but Kurtz had left his own wake of bodies.

Angelina had been sure that she could control Kurtz or, if not control him exactly, *aim* him. Johnny Norse, the breathing corpse in the Williamsville hospice, had supplied Angelina and her sister with drugs from junior high on—Don Farino would have disowned his girls if he'd found them buying drugs from his own people—

and it had been from Norse that she had heard about Emilio's order to kill Samantha Fielding twelve years earlier. It had meant nothing to Angelica when she heard it, but using that information to aim Joe Kurtz at Emilio seemed like a good idea when her other plans had failed.

But Angelina was constantly being surprised by Joe Kurtz. Like other sociopaths she had known, Kurtz seemed contained, quiet, almost sleepy at times, but unlike the other stone-killers she'd been around, including her first husband in Sicily, Kurtz sometimes revealed a sense of humor bordering on real wit. And then, just as she began thinking that he would be too weak for this job . . . well, she remembered the way Kurtz had put a bullet through Leo's left eye without changing expression.

Kurtz seemed sleepy as they stopped at the gate to the Gonzaga compound. He gave up his pistol and submitted to a careful frisk without expression. He still seemed half-asleep as they drove up the long drive, but Angelina knew that Kurtz was looking at everything in the compound, making mental notes. Marco was his usual silent self and Angelina had no clue to what he was thinking.

Inside, they were frisked again. When Angelina was led in for lunch with Emilio, Mickey Kee took the unusual step of staying out in the foyer with the two guards watching Marco and "Howard." Kee seemed to see or sense something in Kurtz that focused his attention.

It was after the soup course with Emilio and after listening to the fat bastard sweet-talk her and explain the new split on drugs and prostitution after the two families "merged," and after the fish had been served, that Angelina suddenly realized what Joe Kurtz was going to do.

Kurtz wasn't here today to case the place or to let

Emilio's guards get used to him so he could return with her later, when the plans were made. *Today* was the day. She knew that Kurtz didn't have so much as a penknife with him but that he planned somehow to get a weapon out in the foyer—take a gun away from Mickey Kee?— kill Kee and the other two guards, shoot Marco, and come into the dining room with guns blazing.

Kurtz didn't care that there was no way out for him or Angelina. Kurtz's plan was simple—kill Emilio and everyone else in the room before he got gunned down himself. Maybe he'd grab Angelina and use her as a human shield while he was killing Emilio. Elegant.

"Whatsamatta?" said Emilio. "Fish bad or something?"

Angelina realized that she had quit eating with her fork still raised. "No. No, it's fine. I just remembered something I have to do." *Run. Get the hell out of here. Survive.*

But how? Tell Emilio Gonzaga that the new bodyguard she'd brought into the paranoid don's compound was here to shoot him? And that she knew about it because she'd set it up? Not a good plan.

Fake menstrual cramps? These Sicilian macho shits were so squeamish about a woman's period that they wouldn't ask questions if she requested a police escort in her retreat. Did she have time for this playacting?

Suddenly there was a commotion in the hallway and Joe Kurtz came into the dining room, his eyes looking wild.

CHAPTER
TWENTY

James B. Hansen parked his Cadillac Escalade beyond the overpass and followed a trodden path through the snow down toward the railroad yards. It was Captain Millworth's lunch hour.

Calls to the university showed no Dr. Paul Frederick on the staff. The Buffalo area phone directories did not list a Paul Frederick. The precinct showed only one record of a Paul Frederick being detained—no photographs, no fingerprints, no rap sheet, just a detention 326-B form mentioning a vagrant named Pruno, aka the Prof, aka P. Frederick, being picked up during a sweep to interrogate homeless people after a murder of a vagrant some two summers ago. Hansen had talked to the uniformed officer who handled the downtown homeless beat and was told that this Pruno wandered the streets, almost never went to shelters, but had favorite niches under the overpass and a shack near the tracks.

Hansen had no trouble finding the shack. The path through the snow led to it, and there were no other structures here in what must be a hobo jungle in the summer. *Why would this vagrant stay out here in weather like this?* wondered Hansen. It had stopped snowing but the temperature had dropped to the single digits and a cold wind came in off the river and Lake Erie.

"Hello?" Hansen did not expect a response from the shack, and he didn't get one. Actually, he thought, "shack" was too fancy a title for this miserable heap of corrugated steel and plywood and cardboard. He took out the .38 that was going to become the property of Mr. Joe Kurtz after the murder of John Wellington Frears, stooped low, and went into the shack, expecting to find it empty.

It was not empty. An old wino in an overcoat stinking of urine sat close to a small burner. The floor was plastic-tarp material, the walls whistled cold wind through, and the wino was so high on crack or heroin that he hardly noticed Hansen's entrance. Keeping the gun aimed at the man's chest, Hansen worked to make out the wino's features in the dim light. Gray stubble, grime-rimmed wrinkles, reddened eyes, wisps of gray hair left on his mottled skull, a chapped-looking chicken neck disappearing into the oversized raincoat—he matched the description of Pruno aka the Prof aka one P. Frederick that the uniformed officer had given Hansen. But then, what wino didn't?

"Hey!" shouted Hansen to get the nodding addict's attention. "Hey, old man!"

The homeless man's red, watery eyes turned in the police captain's direction. The grubby fingers were in plain sight, red and white from the cold, and shaking. Hansen watched the internal struggle as the old addict reluctantly tried to focus his attention.

"You Paul Frederick?" shouted Hansen. "Pruno? Paul Frederick?"

The wino blinked repeatedly and then nodded dubiously. Hansen felt physically sick. Nothing repulsed him more than one of these useless derelicts.

"Mr. Frederick," said Hansen, "have you seen John Wellington Frears? Has Frears been in touch with you?" The thought of this old heroin addict being a friend of the urbane Frears, much less the idea of Frears visiting him in this shack, was absurd. But Hansen waited for an answer.

The wino licked his cracked lips and tried to concentrate. He was looking at the .38. Hansen lowered the muzzle slightly.

As if seeing his chance, the old man's right hand shot into his raincoat, reaching for something.

Without thinking, Hansen lifted his aim and fired twice, hitting the wino once in the chest and once in the neck. The old man flopped backward like an empty bundle of rags. For a minute he continued to breathe, the laborious rasp sounding high and cracked and obscene in the cold dark of the shack, but then the breathing stopped and Hansen lowered the hammer on the .38. Then he stuck his head out the door of the shack and took a quick look around—there was no one to hear the shot, and trains were crashing and roaring in the yards just out of sight—and Hansen crouched by the body. He needed to search the corpse, but he wasn't going to touch those filthy, lice-ridden rags.

Hansen found a stick the old man had used for lifting his cooking pot and stirring soup, and pushing open the filthy raincoat, Hansen saw that the wino's hands had been reaching not for a weapon, but for a stubby pencil. The dead fingers were just touching it. A small yellow pad—empty of writing—had also tumbled out of the wino's vest pocket.

"Damn," whispered Hansen, saying a fast prayer asking forgiveness for his use of the obscenity. He'd not planned on killing the old man, and the fact that he'd asked the patrolman about him might raise suspicions.

Not at all, thought Hansen. *When Frears ends up dead, this will be just another killing connected to Joe Kurtz. We won't know why Kurtz killed both of them, but the .38 found in Kurtz's apartment will provide the connection.* Hansen slid the revolver into his coat pocket. He had never kept a murder weapon with him after the act—it was amateurish—but in this case, he would have to, at least until he found and killed Frears. Then he could plant the weapon in Kurtz's hotel room . . . or on Kurtz's body if the perp tried to resist arrest, which James B. Hansen fully anticipated.

Sitting in the little room thirty feet from Emilio Gonzaga's dining room, feeling the stares from Mickey Kee, Marco, and the two Gonzaga bodyguards, Joe Kurtz felt himself beginning to prepare for what was to come.

He would be leaving a lot of loose ends behind—the thing with Frears and Hansen, for instance, but that wasn't Kurtz's business. Arlene would take care of Frears, perhaps try to get the Conway-connection information to the police. It wasn't Kurtz's problem. Then there was Donald Rafferty and Rachel—that *was* Kurtz's business—but there was nothing for Kurtz to do there. Right now, Kurtz's business was Emilio Gonzaga, Samantha's real killer, and Emilio Gonzaga was only thirty feet away, down a short hallway and through an unlocked door.

When it happened, it would have to happen fast. And soon. Kurtz guessed that Gonzaga and the Farino woman were on their main course now, the three bodyguard-servants in there, standing by the wall.

Mickey Kee was very vigilant, but—like all bodyguards—he was also bored. Familiarity bred laxness. Even the past twenty minutes, when Marco did nothing but read a racing form and Kurtz did nothing but sit with his eyes half-closed, had lowered Mickey Kee's guard. The other two bodyguards were chimps—sloppy—their attention had already wandered to the small TV set on a buffet near the wall. Some soap opera rattled away and both of the guards were fascinated with it. They probably watched every day.

Mickey Kee was obviously troubled by Kurtz's presence. Like all good bodyguards, he was suspicious of anything out of the ordinary. But Kee was also thirsty and kept crossing to the inlaid-mahogany bar near Kurtz—walking within three feet of Kurtz—to refill his glass of club soda. And while he held the glass in his left hand—Kurtz had noticed that he was right-handed—it still occupied too much of his attention. It was almost time for Kee to refill his glass.

When it happens, it will have to happen fast. Kurtz had also noticed that Kee carried his primary weapon, a 9mm Beretta, in a quick-draw shoulder holster. All the better for Kurtz, who would use his left forearm to slam into Kee's windpipe, his right hand pulling the Beretta and firing into the two armed bodyguards at a distance of only six feet.

It would have to happen fast, but there was no way to do this without warning Gonzaga and his goons inside. Kurtz would need more weapons, more bullets, so he'd have to take another ten seconds to retrieve the bodyguards' guns after he shot them. Marco would have to be neutralized, although if he fled, Kurtz was prepared to let him go. He would not be a factor.

Then another twenty seconds to get down the hall and go through the dining room door, low, firing both weapons, the third one in his belt. Kurtz had only one target in that dining room, although he was prepared to kill everyone else there to get to that one target.

He thought he had a decent chance of getting into the dining room and getting to that target before it fled or called for reinforcements, but Kurtz didn't think he had much chance of surviving that exchange. The guards there would have gone for their guns at the first sound of gunfire. Still, they would be confused. Unlike expertly trained Secret Service operatives, they were cheap hoods, killers, and their first instinct would be self-preservation, not throwing themselves between Emilio Gonzaga and a fusillade of bullets.

Still, Kurtz would have to move fast, shoot fast. If he somehow survived the dining-room exchange, he would make sure that Gonzaga was dead—an extra bullet through the head should do that—and only then would Kurtz worry about getting out of the compound. His best bet would be the limo they'd arrived in, although even it couldn't crash that metal security gate out front. But Kurtz had studied the aerial photos, knew the service roads and back exits to the compound. There would be more than a dozen guards still loose on the grounds, TV monitors, the Jeep that patrolled the place, but they would be confused, reluctant to shoot at Gonzaga's personal limo, not ready for someone trying to break *out* of the compound. Kurtz might have a slim chance of survival, even if wounded.

No, I don't, he told himself. Emilio Gonzaga was one of the few made men in Western New York, head of his own sub-family. However unimportant Buffalo mob business might be, the real New York families weren't going to sit by and let a nobody kill one of their franchise boys without stepping in to reset the balance of pain in the universe. Even if Joe Kurtz killed everyone in the Gonzaga compound today and got away unscathed, the Mafia would find out who had done it and track him down if it took twenty years. Joe Kurtz was dead as soon as he raised a hand against Emilio Gonzaga.

C'est la vie, thought Kurtz and had to fight the impulse to smile. He didn't want to do anything right now that would make Mickey Kee pay more attention to him. Kurtz felt all other thought fade as he became an organ of watchfulness and preparation, an adrenaline engine with one purpose.

Mickey Kee sipped the last of his club soda. For a second, Kurtz was afraid that the man had drunk enough, but Kee was still thirsty. Vigilant, carrying the glass in his left hand—but not vigilant enough, Kurtz knew—Kee began crossing the room toward the bar again.

Kurtz had mentally rehearsed his next moves until they would require no further thought or preparation. Kee would be dead in five seconds, but it was necessary that Kurtz come away with the Beretta as the killer fell, Kurtz clicking the safety off even as he swung the pistol toward the startled bodyguards in front of their soap opera. . . .

Mickey Kee came within range.

Joe Kurtz's cell phone rang.

Kee paused and stepped back, his hand moving toward his shoulder holster. Kurtz let out the breath he'd been holding, held up one finger to remind Kee that he was unarmed, and answered his phone. There was nothing else to do at the moment.

"Joe?" Arlene's voice was more alarmed than he had ever heard it.

"What is it?"

"It's Rachel."

"What?" Kurtz had to come back from wherever he had gone in his preparation—most of his mind and body were still involved in shooting the bodyguards, breaking into the dining room, bringing the bead of the Beretta's gunsight in line with Emilio Gonzaga's fat, fish face. "What?" he said again.

"It's Rachel. She's in the hospital. She's hurt bad."

"What are you talking about? How do you know—"

"Alan's sister, remember? Gail. She's a nurse at Erie County. She knows about Rachel. She knew Sam, remember? She called me just now. Gail just came on-shift. Rachel was admitted this morning, about nine A.M."

"Rafferty hit her?" said Kurtz. Mickey Kee and the others were watching him with interest. Marco licked his lips, obviously wondering if this new wrinkle would affect his chances for surviving the next hour.

"No. They were in a car crash on the Kensington. Donald Rafferty was drunk. Gail says that he's got a broken arm and a possible concussion, but he'll be okay. Rachel's in really bad shape."

"How bad?" Kurtz heard his own voice as if it were miles away.

"They don't know yet. Rachel's been in surgery all morning. Gail said they've removed her spleen and one kidney. They'll know more in the next hour or so."

Kurtz said nothing. A red film descended over his vision, and he heard a noise that sounded like an elevated train rushing by.

"Joe?"

"Yeah," he said. He realized that if he did not relax his hand, he was going to snap the little phone in half.

"There's more," said Arlene. "Something worse."

Kurtz waited.

"Rachel was conscious when they cut her out of the car. The paramedics were talking to her to keep her conscious. She told them that she'd run away the night before and that her stepfather had come after her and found her near the bus station, made her get in the car, and that she'd run away because he'd been drinking and tried to rape her."

Kurtz clicked off the connection, folded the phone, and set it carefully in his suit's chest pocket.

"Whatsamatter?" said Mickey Kee. "Lose a big bet or something, Mr. Howard from Raiford? Somebody named Rafferty slapping around one of your bitches?"

Ignoring Kee and the other bodyguards, shaking off their restraining hands, Kurtz stood and walked down the hall and went into the dining room to get Angelina Farino Ferrara so they could get the hell out of there.

CHAPTER
TWENTY-ONE

"You wanted to see us, Captain?"

"Sit down," said Hansen.

Detectives Brubaker and Myers glanced at each other before taking their seats. Captain Millworth had called them into his office on occasion, but he'd never asked them to sit before.

Hansen came around his desk, sat on the edge of it, and handed Brubaker a photograph of John Wellington Frears. "You know this man?"

Brubaker took the photo and shook his head. Hansen hadn't expected them to have heard about Frears's appearance at the station when he made his report. He was going to tell them that Frears was missing and put them on special assignment—undercover—to track him down. Hansen planned on dealing later with the complications this would cause.

"Hey, I saw this guy," said Myers.

Hansen was surprised. "At the station?"

"At the station? No, uh-uh. Fred, we saw this guy go into Blues Franklin last week when we were tailing Kurtz, remember?"

Brubaker took the photo back. "Yeah, could be same guy."

"Could be? Shit, it *is*. Remember, he drove up in a white . . . Ford, I think, maybe a Contour . . . and parked right near us when we were staking out the Franklin when Kurtz was in there."

"Yeah."

If Hansen had not been sitting on the edge of his desk, he might have collapsed onto the floor. This was too perfect. "You're saying that this man was in the Blues Franklin at the same time as Joe Kurtz?"

"Absolutely, Captain," said Myers. Brubaker nodded.

Hansen felt his universe click back into focus. What had seemed chaos a moment before became a perfectly clear mosaic now. This coincidence was a gift from God, pure and simple. "I want you to find this man," he said. "His name is Mr. John Wellington Frears and we're concerned about his safety." He went through the whole report-to-me-only routine with the two idiots.

"Jesus," said Myers. "Sorry, Captain. But you think this guy's disappearance this morning has anything to do with Joe Kurtz?"

"You were on surveillance then," said Hansen. "Where was Kurtz?"

"He slipped out of sight last night and this morning," said Brubaker. "We picked up his tail out in Cheektowaga this morning. We were going to check out Kurtz's secretary's house there, but we saw Kurtz driving down Union . . ." He paused.

"Near the Airport Sheraton," said Hansen.

Myers nodded. "Not that far away."

"It looks like we're back on Kurtz surveillance," said Brubaker.

Hansen shook his head. "This is more important than that. This concert violinist, Frears, is a very important man. This could be a potential kidnapping situation."

Myers frowned. "You mean SWAT, FBI, all that shit?

Sorry, Captain, but you know what I mean."

Hansen went around his desk and sat in his leather executive chair. "Right now it's just you two, me, and a hunch. Just because you saw Frears go into the Blues Franklin at the same time Joe Kurtz was there doesn't mean there was a connection. Did either of you ever see Kurtz and Frears together during your surveillance?"

The two detectives shook their heads.

"So I want some careful surveillance done. Starting this afternoon. Round the clock."

"How can we do that?" said Brubaker, adding a "sir."

"Solo work," said Hansen.

"Twelve-hour shifts?" whined Myers. "Alone? This Kurtz bastard is dangerous."

"I'll pitch in," said Hansen. "We'll work out a schedule. And we're not talking weeks here, just a day or two. If Kurtz has something to do with Frears's disappearance, we'll know soon enough. Fred, you take the first shift. Check out that secretary's house in Cheektowaga. Tommy, you'll spend the next few hours looking for Kurtz at his home, office, and so forth. Fred, you stay here a minute. I want to talk to you."

Myers and Brubaker glanced at each other before Myers went out, closing the door behind him. Captain Millworth had never called either of them by his first name before.

Brubaker stood by the desk and waited.

"Internal Affairs was checking in with me about you last week," said Hansen.

Brubaker lifted a toothpick to his mouth, but said nothing.

"Granger and his boys think you have some connections with the Farinos," said Hansen, staring the other man in the eye. "They think you're on Little Skag's payroll, picking up where your pal Hathaway left off last November."

Brubaker's eyes showed nothing. He shifted the toothpick back and forth with his tongue.

Hansen moved some paperwork on his desk. "I'm mentioning this because I think you'll need someone to cover your back, Fred. Someone to let you know who's sniffing around and when. I could do that."

Brubaker removed the toothpick, looked at it, and set it in his pocket. "Why would you do that, Captain?"

"Because I need your best work and discretion for this project, Brubaker. You scratch my back and I'll protect yours."

Brubaker stood there, staring, obviously trying to understand this deal.

"That's all," said Hansen. "Go hunt for Kurtz. Relieve Tommy on stakeout in eight hours. Call me on my cell if anything comes up. But tell Myers . . . you two do *nothing* but observe without my permission. Understand? *Nothing*. You see Kurtz buggering the Mayor's son on Main Street at high noon, call me before you do anything. *Capische?*"

"Yeah."

Hansen nodded toward the door and Brubaker went out.

The homicide captain swiveled his chair and spent several minutes looking out at the gray pile of the old courthouse across the street. This was all going too far, too fast. It had to be resolved, but even if something happened to Detectives Brubaker and Myers—and anything could happen to a plainclothes officer when dealing with someone like Kurtz—there would still be too many loose ends around afterward.

Hansen sighed. He had enjoyed being a homicide detective. Heck, he was good at it. And he liked his wife

Donna and stepson Jason. This persona had only lasted fourteen months and James B. Hansen had thought it might go another year or two, perhaps longer.

He closed his eyes for a moment. *Thy will be done, Lord. Thy will be done.* Hansen opened his eyes and used his private line to dial the number of a certain dentist in Cleveland. It was time for Robert Gaines Millworth's dental records to be made ready.

CHAPTER
TWENTY-TWO

"Are you a member of the immediate family?" asked the nurse.

"I'm Donald Rafferty's brother," said Kurtz. He'd met Arlene's sister-in-law Gail and knew that she was a surgical nurse on the ninth floor, but he didn't want her to see him here.

The reception nurse grunted and glanced at one of the computer screens at her station. "Mr. Rafferty's in six-twenty-three. He was treated for a mild concussion and a broken wrist and is sleeping right now. The doctor who treated him, Dr. Singh, will be available in about twenty minutes if you want to talk to him."

"What about the girl?" said Kurtz.

"Girl?"

"Rachel . . . Rafferty. She was in the car with Donald. I understand she suffered more serious injuries."

The nurse frowned and tapped the keys again. "Yes. She's out of surgery."

"Can I see her?"

"Oh, no . . . the surgery went on for almost five hours. The girl will be in the ICU recovery for several hours."

"But the surgery went all right? She'll be all right?"

"You'd have to speak to the doctor."

"Dr. Singh?"

"No, no." The nurse frowned more deeply, her important time at the desk obviously being eaten up here on inconsequentials, and tapped more keys. "Dr. Fremont and Dr. Wiley were the primary surgeons."

"Two surgeons?"

"I just said that."

"Can I talk to them?"

The nurse rolled her eyes and played with the keyboard again. "Dr. Fremont has left the hospital and Dr. Wiley will be in surgery until after five o'clock."

"Where's the ICU?"

"You won't be allowed in there, Mr. . . . ah . . . Rafferty."

Kurtz leaned over close enough that the nurse had to turn away from the computer screen and look into his eyes. "Where is it?"

She told him.

Kurtz, Angelina, and Marco had left the Gonzaga compound in a hurry, Angelina explaining to an obviously irritated Emilio that something important had come up for her and that they would reschedule the luncheon. Arnie and Mickey Kee had driven the silent trio back to Marina Towers in the armored limo. They had taken the elevator straight to the penthouse before talking.

"What the hell is going on, Kurtz?" Angelina was pale with anger and fighting a backwash of adrenaline.

"I need a car."

"I'll take you back to the health club where you parked your—"

Kurtz shook his head. "I need a car *now*."

Angelina hesitated for a second. Acquiescing to Kurtz

now would change their relationship—whatever that was at the moment—forever. She looked at his face and then reached into her purse and tossed him a set of keys. "My silver Porsche Boxster, parked closest to the elevator in the garage."

Kurtz nodded and turned toward the elevator.

"What about him?" Angelina had brought out her .45 Compact Witness and was aiming it at Marco.

"He's not stupid," said Kurtz. "You can still use him. Offer him handcuffs in the john the way you offered Leo."

Angelina looked at Marco. "Sure. Why not?" said the big bodyguard. "Beats the alternative."

"All right," said Angelina. "What about . . ." She flicked her head toward the big walk-in freezer in the utility room off the kitchen.

"Tonight," said Kurtz. "I'll be back."

"This is not good," said Angelina, but Kurtz had already stepped into the elevator and closed the door.

Kurtz stepped out of the elevator and saw immediately how the Intensive Care Unit was set up with a nurses' station at the locus of a circle of single rooms with clear glass walls. The three nurses at the central station watched their own readouts but could look into any of the rooms and see the patients and their computer screens. An older nurse with a kind face looked up as Kurtz approached. "Can I help you, sir?"

"I'm Bob Rafferty, Rachel Rafferty's uncle. The nurse downstairs said she was in recovery here."

The nurse nodded and pointed toward one of the glass-walled rooms. Kurtz could see only Rachel's auburn hair, so much like Sam's. The rest was blankets, tubes, monitors, and a ventilating unit.

"I'm afraid you won't be able to visit her for a few days," said the nurse. "After such extensive surgery, the doctors are very concerned about infection and—"

"But she came out of surgery all right? She's going to live?"

The kind-faced nurse took a breath. "You really should talk to Dr. Fremont or Dr. Wiley."

"I was told they'd be unavailable all day."

"Yes. Well . . ." She looked at Kurtz. "Rachel had a very close thing this morning, Mr. Rafferty. Very close. But Dr. Wiley told me that the prognosis is good. We've given her eight units of blood—"

"Is that a lot?"

The woman nodded. "Essentially, we've replaced all the blood in her system, Mr. Rafferty. The Flight for Life helicopter saved her life."

"And they removed her spleen and a kidney?"

"Yes. Her left kidney. The damage was too extensive."

"That means that even if she recovers from this, she'll always be at risk, right?"

"It makes future illnesses or accidents more problematic, yes. And there will be a long recovery period. But your niece should be able to lead a normal life." She looked at where Kurtz was gripping the edge of the counter and lifted one hand as if she was going to touch him. She pulled back her hand. "Dr. Singh should be free very soon if you want to talk to him about your brother's injuries—"

"No," said Kurtz.

He took the elevator to the sixth floor and started down the corridor to Room 623. Kurtz had removed the .40 S&W in the elevator and now carried it in his right palm, letting the long sleeve of his open raincoat hang down over that hand. He paused three doors away from Rafferty's room.

A woman cop in plainclothes, probably a rape-contact officer, and a bored uniformed cop were sitting on folding chairs just outside the room. Kurtz stood there a minute, but when the woman plainclothes cop looked up at him, he stepped into the closest room. An ancient man lay asleep or in a coma on the only occupied bed. The old guy's eyes had sunken into his head in the way that Kurtz had seen in week-old corpses. Kurtz put his Smith & Wesson back in his belt holster and stood by the old man's bed for a minute. The geezer's gnarled hand was liver-spotted and bruised from IV punctures. The fingers were curled and the nails were long and yellow. Kurtz touched the hand once before going out the door and taking the elevator down to the parking garage.

The Boxster was a beautiful sports car, but it handled like shit on snow and ice. He had just headed south on the Kensington toward the downtown and Marina Towers when his cell phone rang again.

"Have you seen Rachel, Joe? How is she?"

Kurtz told Arlene what the nurse had said.

"And what about Donald Rafferty?"

"He's not going to survive the accident," said Kurtz.

Arelene was silent a minute. "I was heading down to the hospital, Mr. Frears said that he'd be all right here, but Mrs. Campbell, one of my older neighbors, called me and said that a suspicious-looking man in a gray Ford was parked in front of her house, half a block down the street."

"Shit," said Kurtz.

"Mrs. Campbell called the police."

"And?"

"And I was watching through the blinds. The squad car stopped, one of the uniformed officers got out, the man in the parked car showed him something, and the squad car left in a hurry."

"It's probably either Brubaker or Myers, one of the two homicide detectives who've been tailing me," said Kurtz. "But it could be Hansen . . . Captain Millworth. I don't know how he could've made the connection with Frears, but . . ."

"I used Alan's binoculars. It's a fat man, almost bald. Not very tall. Brown suit."

"That's Myers," said Kurtz. He pulled the Boxster off at the East Ferry exit and did a fast loop, getting back on the Expressway headed out toward Cheektowaga. "Arlene, we don't know that Brubaker and Myers aren't working directly for Hansen. Stay put. I'll be there in fifteen minutes."

"And do what, Joe? Why don't I take Mr. Frears and leave here for Gail's house?"

"Can you get out without being seen?"

"Sure. Through the carport and across the alley to the Dzwrjskys'. Mona will loan me her ex-husband's station wagon. Gail's at work, but I know where the extra key is. We'll leave Detective Myers sitting down the street all day."

Kurtz slowed the Boxster to below seventy. "I don't know . . ."

"Joe, there's something else. I checked our business e-mail from here and there's a message to you that was copied to my e-mail address. It was dated at one P.M., and it's signed just 'P.' "

Pruno, thought Kurtz. Likely checking up on whether he'd met with Frears. "It's probably not important," said Kurtz.

"The message says that it's urgent, Joe. Let me read

it to you—'*Joseph, absolutely imperative that you meet me as soon as possible at that place where the thing occurred on midsummer night's eve. This is urgent. P.*'"

"Oh, man," said Kurtz. "All right. Call me as soon as you get to Gail's place." He folded the phone away, took a high-speed exit onto Delavan Avenue, drove east a block, and accelerated south on Fillmore.

The main Buffalo train station was a dignified and imposing structure in its time; now, after being abandoned for a decade, it was a sad mess. The sprawling structure was dominated by a twenty-story tower built along the lines of one of the brooding, stepped-back skyscrapers in Fritz Lang's movie *Metropolis*. On the twelfth-story level of each corner of the tower, oversized clocks had stopped at different times. Some shards of glass remained in the hundreds of broken windows, which made the battered facade look all the more dismal. Besides the two main entrances on the tower building, four large, awninged and arched doorways that looked like entrances to blimp hangars had been situated along the five-story main structure to allow the thousands of passengers to enter and leave the huge complex without undue jostling.

There were no crowds jostling today. Even the hilly driveway to the expanse of the abandoned parking lot was drifted over with snow. Kurtz parked the Porsche Boxster on a side street and walked past the boulders placed in the drive to keep cars out of the lot. Trespassers and winos and kids intent on breaking the last of the windows had left a myriad of old and new footprints in the snow on the lot, so there was no way for Kurtz to tell who had passed here when. He followed some tracks across to the hurricane fence around the station itself and found a three-foot height of wire cut just under one of the yellow KEEP OUT. NO TRESPASSING signs. He passed under the massive overhang with its NEW YORK & BUFFALO RAILROAD legend just visible in the rusting metal and dimming light. The huge doors were firmly sealed with sheet metal and plywood, but the corner of one of the window coverings had been jimmied loose, and Kurtz squeezed his way in there.

It was much colder inside than out. And darker. The tall, high windows that had once sent down shafts of sunlight onto soldiers traveling off to World War II and onto the weeping families left behind were all dark and boarded up now. A few frightened pigeons took flight in the great, dim space as Kurtz crunched his way across the littered tile.

The old waiting areas and the ramps to the train platforms were empty. Kurtz climbed a short staircase to the tower building that had once housed the railroad offices, pried open a plywood barrier, and walked slowly through narrow corridors into the main hall. Rats scurried. Pigeons fluttered.

Kurtz slid his pistol out, racked a round into the chamber, and carried the gun by his side as he moved into the wide, dark space.

"Joseph." The whisper seemed to come from the far corner, forty feet from Kurtz, but there were only shadows and a tumble of old benches there.

He half-raised the gun.

"Up here, Joseph."

Kurtz stepped farther out into the hall and peered up at the mezzanines in the darkness. A shadow beckoned.

Kurtz found the staircase and climbed, leaving a trail through fallen plaster. The old man was waiting for him by the railing on the second mezzanine. He was carrying what looked to be a lumpy garment bag.

"Rather interesting acoustics," said Pruno. The old man's stubbled face seemed even more pale than usual in the dim light. "They accidentally constructed a whispering gallery when they built this hall. All sounds uttered up here seem to converge in that corner down there."

"Yeah," said Kurtz. "What's up, Pruno? You interested in Frears?"

"John?" said the old heroin addict. "Well, of course I'm interested in that, since I put you two in contact, but I assumed that you did not decide to help him. It's been almost a week. To be truthful, Joseph, I'd almost forgotten."

"What is it, then?" said Kurtz. "And why here?" He gestured at the dark hall and the darker mezzanines. "This is a long way from your usual haunts."

Pruno nodded. "It seems that there is a literal dead man in my usual haunt."

"A dead man. Who?"

"You wouldn't know him, Joseph. A homeless contemporary of mine. I believe his name was Clark Povitch, a former accountant, but the other addicts and street persons have known him as Typee for the last fifteen years or so."

"What did he die of?"

"A bullet," said Pruno. "Or two bullets, I believe, although I am no forensic expert."

"Someone shot your friend in your shack?"

"Not my friend, precisely, but in this inclement weather, Typee sometimes availed himself of my hospitality—specifically of my Sterno heater—when I was elsewhere."

"Do you know who killed him?"

"I do have a clue. But it does not seem to make any sense, Joseph."

"Tell me."

"An acquaintance of mine, a lady named Mrs. Tuella Dean—I believe you would refer to her as a bag lady—was on a grate today, under some newspapers and inadvertently concealed, on the corner of Elmwood and Market when she heard a patrolman outside his parked squad car speaking on either his radio telephone or a cell phone. The patrolman was giving directions to my domicile and mentioned my name . . . names, actually . . . and actually gave a description of me to his interlocutor. According to Mrs. Dean, the patrolman's tone was almost obsequious, as if speaking to a superior. She happened to mention this to me when I saw her near the HSBC arena just before I returned home and discovered Typee's body."

Kurtz took in a long, cold breath of air. "Did this Mrs. Dean catch the other guy's name?"

"She did, actually. A Captain Millworth. I would presume that this would mean a captain of police."

Kurtz let out the breath.

"There would seem to be no connection," said Pruno, "as police captains are not known for murdering the homeless, but it would be too much of a coincidence to think the events are unrelated. Also, there is another mild coincidence here that worries me."

"What's that?"

"To a stranger," said Pruno, "to someone who knew me only from another person's description, Typee might look a little bit like me. Quite a lot like me, actually."

Kurtz reached out and took his old friend's sharp elbow through the overcoat and other rags. "Come on," he said softly, hearing his whisper repeated in the darkness below. "We're getting out of here."

CHAPTER
TWENTY-THREE

Hansen could not get in touch with Dr. Howard Conway by phone and this bothered him. It bothered him a lot. He considered driving to Cleveland to check on Conway—make sure that the old fart hadn't died or finally run out on him—but there simply wasn't time. Too much was happening too fast, and too much had to happen even faster in the next twenty-four hours.

He canceled his meetings for the rest of the afternoon, called Donna to say that he'd be home soon, called Brubaker to make sure that he hadn't found Kurtz at his office or home, called Myers to make sure he was on surveillance at the secretary's house, and then he drove to a rotting industrial cold-storage facility near the Buffalo River. Behind an abandoned mill, a line of walk-in freezers—each with its own backup generator—had been rented to restaurateurs, meat wholesalers, and others needing overflow freezer storage. Hansen had kept a locker there since he'd driven a freezer truck up from Miami nine months ago.

Hansen unlocked the two expensive padlocks he kept on the unit and stepped into the frigid interior. Five halves of beef hung on hooks. Hansen had planned to use one of these during the July cookout he was going to throw at his Tonawanda home for his detectives and their wives, but it looked as if he would not be around Buffalo in July. Against the back wall were tall wire racks, and on these were four long, opaque plastic bags holding more frozen meat.

He unzipped the bag on the middle shelf. Mr. Gabriel Kendall, fifty years old, the same height, weight, and general build as James B. Hansen, stared up through a rim of frost covering his open eyes. The cadaver's lips were blue and pulled back, frozen into the position where Dr. Conway had X-rayed the teeth in Cleveland the previous summer. All four of the men's bodies stored here had a similar rictus. Kendall was the one Hansen had chosen for Captain Robert Gaines Millworth's suicide and the dental records should be on file, ready for the blanks to be filled in.

If he could get in touch with that miserable wretch Conway.

Satisfied that no one had been in the freezer or tampered with its contents, Hansen zipped the body bag shut, locked the freezer behind him, and drove back home in his Cadillac SUV. The sight of the hanging sides of beef had made him hungry. He used his cell phone to call Donna and tell her to set aside whatever else she had planned for dinner; they would grill steaks on the GrillAire Range tonight.

Arlene's sister-in-law Gail's home was the second floor of an old duplex on Colvin Avenue north of the park. Gail was divorced and was working a double shift at the Medical Center; Arlene had explained that Gail was sleeping at the hospital and wouldn't be home until late the following afternoon. *Good thing,* thought Kurtz as

Arlene unlocked the door and led Pruno and him up the side stairway. Upstairs, Kurtz looked at the herd of refugees he was collecting—Frears hugging Pruno affectionately as if the old addict didn't smell like a urinal—Arlene with the .45 still in her sweater pocket. For all the years that he had used Pruno as a street source when he was a P.I., Arlene had never met the old wino, and now the two were busy with their introductions and conversation. Kurtz, a loner all his life, was beginning to feel like Noah, and he suspected that he might need a bigger ark if this refugee crap kept up.

The four of them sat in the tiny living room. Cooking smells came from the adjoining kitchen, and occasionally she would stand and go in to check on something and the conversation would pause until she returned.

"What is going on, Mr. Kurtz?" asked John Wellington Frears when they were all gathered around like a happy chipmunk family again.

Kurtz slipped his peacoat off—it was hot in the little apartment—and explained what he could about James B. Hansen being the esteemed Homicide Captain Robert Millworth.

"This dentist . . . Conway . . . admitted this to you?" asked Pruno.

"Not in so many words," said Kurtz. "But let's say that I confirmed it with him."

"I would guess that this Dr. Conway's life wouldn't be worth much right now," said Frears.

Kurtz had to agree with that.

"So how do you think this Millworth . . . Hansen . . . made the connection between Mr. Frears and you, Joe?" asked Arlene.

"We're not certain that he has."

"But it would be dangerous to assume anything else," said Frears.

"It is folly," said Pruno, "to form policy based on assumptions of the enemy's intentions . . . judge his capabilities and prepare accordingly."

"Well," said Arlene, "a captain in Homicide is capable of using the entire police department to track down Mr. Frears and the rest of us."

Kurtz shook his head. "Not without blowing his cover. We have to remember that this Hansen isn't a real cop."

"No," Frears said evenly, "he is a serial rapist and child killer."

That stopped conversation for a while. Finally Arlene said, "Can he trace us here, Joe?"

"I doubt it. Not if Myers didn't follow you."

"No," said Arlene. "I made sure that we weren't followed. But they'll get suspicious when Mr. Frears and I don't leave my house tomorrow."

"Or when the lights don't come on tonight," said Pruno. It was getting dark outside.

"I left the lamps in the front room on a timer I use when on vacation," said Arlene. "They're on now and will go off at eleven."

Kurtz, who was suddenly feeling exhausted, looked up at that. "When have you ever taken a vacation?"

Arlene gave him a look. Kurtz took it as his cue to leave. "I have to return a car," he said, standing and tugging on his peacoat.

"Not until you eat," said Arlene.

"I'm not hungry."

"No? When was the last time you ate, Joe? Did you have lunch?"

Kurtz paused to think. His last meal had been a sweet roll he'd grabbed with coffee at a Thruway stop during his midnight drive back from Cleveland. He hadn't eaten all this Wednesday and hadn't slept since Tuesday night.

"We're all going to have a good meal," Arlene said in a tone that brooked no argument. "I've made lots of spaghetti, fresh bread, some roast beef. You all have about twenty minutes to wash up."

"I may need all of that time," said Pruno. Kurtz laughed but the old man shot him a glance, lifted the bundle of his garment bag, and disappeared into the bathroom with dignity.

The family of Robert Gaines Millworth—his wife Donna and fourteen-year-old stepson Jason—ate as a family every night because James Hansen knew it was important that a family eat together. This night they had steak and salad and rice. Donna had wine. Hansen did not drink alcohol, but he allowed his wives to, in moderation.

While they ate, Donna talked about her work at the library. Jason talked about basketball and about ice hockey. Hansen listened and thought about his next move in this rather interesting chess game he had become involved in. At one point, Hansen found himself looking around the dining room—the art, the glimpse of bookcases from the family room beyond, the expensive furniture and Delft china. It would be a shame, all this lost to the fire. But James B. Hansen had never been one to confuse material possessions with the more important things of the soul.

After dinner, he would go down to his office, keeping his cell phone with him in case Brubaker or Myers called, and contemplate what he had to do tomorrow and in the days to come.

It was a strange dinner for Kurtz—a good dinner, lots of spaghetti and roast beef and gravy and real bread and a good salad and coffee—but strange. It had been a while since his last home-cooked dinner eaten with other people. How long? Twelve years. Twelve years and a month. A dinner with Sam at her place, also spaghetti that night, with the baby, the toddler, in a tall chair—not a high chair, it didn't have a tray—what had Sam called it? A youth chair. With little Rachel in the youth chair at the table, chattering away, reaching over to tug at Kurtz's napkin, the child babbling even as Sam told him about this interesting case she was pursuing—a teenage runaway missing, drugs involved.

Kurtz stopped eating. Only Arlene noticed and she looked away after a second.

Pruno had come out of the bathroom showered, shaven, skin pink and scalded-looking, his fingernails still yellowed and cracked but no longer grimy, his thinning gray hair— which Kurtz had never seen except as a sort of nimbus floating around the old wino's head—slicked back. He was wearing a suit that might have been two decades out of style and no longer fit. Pruno's frail form was lost in it, but it also looked clean. *How?* wondered Kurtz. How could this old heroin addict keep a suit clean when he lived in a packing crate and in cubbies under the Thruway?

Pruno—or "Dr. Frederick," as Frears kept addressing him—looked older and frailer and more fragile without his protective crusts of grime and rags. But the old man sat very upright as he ate and drank and nodded his head to accept more food and addressed John Wellington Frears in measured tones. Frears had been his student at Princeton. One old man dying of cancer and his ancient teacher sitting there in his double-breasted, pinstripe suit—making conversation about Mozart as a prodigy and about the Palestinian situation and about global warming.

Kurtz shook his head. He'd not had any wine because he was so damned tired already and because he might have to keep his head clear for several hours more on this endless day, but enough was enough. This scene was not just unreal, it was surreal. He needed a drink.

Arlene followed him out to the kitchen.

"Doesn't your sister-in-law keep any booze in the house?" asked Kurtz.

"That top cupboard. Johnnie Walker Red."

"That'll do," said Kurtz. He poured himself three fingers' worth.

"What's the matter, Joe?"

"Nothing's the matter. Other than this serial-killer police captain after all of us, I mean. Everything's great."

"You're thinking about Rachel."

Kurtz shook his head and took a drink. The two old men in the dining room laughed at something.

"What are you going to do about that, Joe?"

"What do you mean?"

"You know what I mean. You can't let her go back to Donald Rafferty."

Kurtz shrugged. He remembered tearing up the photograph of Frears's dead daughter—Crystal. He remembered leaving the torn bits of the photograph on the scarred table at Blues Franklin.

Arlene lit a cigarette and pulled down a small bowl for an ashtray. "Gail won't let me smoke in her house. She'll be furious when she gets home tomorrow."

Kurtz studied the amber liquid in his glass.

"What if the police don't arrest Rafferty, Joe?"

He shrugged again.

"Or if they do?" said Arlene. "Either way, Rachel is going to be at risk. A foster home? Samantha had no other family. Just her ex-husband. Unless he has family who can take care of her."

Kurtz poured another finger of scotch. Rafferty's only living family was an alcoholic bitch of a mother who lived in Las Vegas and a younger brother who was doing time in an Indiana state prison for armed robbery. He'd listened to the phone conversations.

"But if she goes into some sort of temporary foster home . . ." began Arlene.

"Look," said Kurtz, slamming the empty glass down on the counter, "what the hell do you want me to do about it?"

Arlene blinked. Joe Kurtz had never yelled at her in all their years of working together. She exhaled smoke and batted ashes into the dainty little ceramic bowl. "DNA," she said.

"What?"

"DNA testing would show paternity, Joe. You could—"

"Are you fucking nuts? An ex-con who served time for manslaughter? A former P.I. who will never get his license back? Somebody with at least three death sentences out on him?" Kurtz laughed. "Yeah, I don't see why the courts wouldn't place the kid with someone like that. Besides, I don't know for sure that I'm the—"

"Don't," said Arlene, her finger raised and pointed. "Don't say that. Don't even pretend to me that you think it."

Kurtz went out into the tiny living room, retrieved his peacoat and the S&W .40 from where he'd left them and went down the stairs and out of the house. It was dark out and it had begun to snow again.

CHAPTER
TWENTY-FOUR

"I was just about to call and report a stolen Porsche," said Angelina Farino Ferrara.

"That little electronic-card thing is handy," said Kurtz. "It lets you into both the parking garage and the elevator. Useful."

"I hope you put the Boxster back in the same slot. And there had better not be any scratches."

Kurtz ignored her and walked over to the center of the penthouse's living room. Beyond the floor-to-ceiling window on the east side, the lights of downtown Buffalo glowed through the falling snow. To the west was the darkness of the river and lake, with only a few distant ship lights blinking against blackness.

"We have to get rid of Leo," said Angelina.

"I know. Any problems with Marco?"

"Not a peep. He's handcuffed in the bathroom. Seems to be mildly amused by all this. Marco may be smarter than I thought."

"Maybe so. You have anyone on the floor below us?"

"Five people work there—no muscle, just bookkeeper types—but they went home at six. Marco and Leo were the only ones using the living quarters there."

"I thought Little Skag brought in new muscle from the east."

"He did. Eight other new guys besides Marco and Leo. But they're all out doing what they do—running what's left of Stevie's crews, handling the whores and gambling. Day-to-day stuff. They don't come by here that much."

"Who does?"

"Albert Bell is the lawyer who acts as liaison between Little Stevie and me. I usually see Mr. Bell on Saturdays."

"But Marco and Leo check in with Little Skag by phone every Wednesday?"

"Right. Stevie calls his lawyer. The call is forwarded. I don't know where the Boys take the call."

"Marco will tell us," said Kurtz. He felt very tired. "You ready to transport the frozen goods?"

"I'll go down and back the Town Car right up to the elevator."

"I'll need a big garment bag, sheet, something."

"Shower curtain," said Angelina. "Little blue fish on it. I took care of it."

Angelina drove. They took the Buffalo Skyway south along the lake. It was snowing very hard now, visibility was limited to the two cones of headlights filled with flurries, and the elevated highway was treacherous with black ice. Only the Lincoln Town Car's massive weight kept them moving as the rear-wheel drive slipped and then gripped for pavement. Kurtz had the clear image of them getting stuck and a friendly patrolman stopping to help them out, a need to look in the trunk for the chains or somesuch. . . .

"We going far?" he asked.

"Not far. Near Hamburg."

"What's near Hamburg?"

"My father and older brother used to keep an ice-fishing shack just offshore in February. Sometimes they'd drag Little Stevie along, whining and pouting. I went a few times. If there's anything more stupid than sitting in a freezing shack staring at a hole in the ice, I don't what it might be. But some of the old *capos* still set up the shack even though there are no Farinos around to use it."

"I didn't know that people ice-fished on Lake Erie. Is the ice thick enough to walk on?"

"We're going to drive this car out onto it."

"But aren't there big ships still moving out there?"

"Yeah."

That was all Kurtz wanted to know about that subject. He concentrated on staying awake while the big car crept along through blowing snow. Once off the Skyway and moving along Highway 5 through little shoreline communities like Locksley Park and Mount Vernon, the black ice was less frequent but the snow was worse.

"Are you still with me on this, Kurtz?"

The woman's voice made him blink awake. "With you on what?"

"You know. Gonzaga."

"I don't know."

Angelina drove in silence for a few minutes.

"Why don't you tell me what your real plan is," Kurtz said. "What your objectives are, long term goals. So far you've just tried to use me like some damned Hamas suicide bomber."

"And you used me," she said. "You were ready to get me killed today just so you could get to Emilio."

Kurtz shrugged at that. He waited.

"If Little Skag gets out of Attica this spring, it's too

late," Angelina said at last. "I'm screwed. The Farino Family is finished. Stevie thinks he can ride this tiger, but Emilio will gobble him up in six weeks. Less."

"So? You can always go back to Italy or something. Can't you?"

"No," said Angelina, throwing the word like a javelin. "Fuck that. The Gonzagas have been planning this . . . this extermination . . . of the Farinos for a long, long time. It was Emilio's father who had my father ambushed and crippled sixteen years ago. Emilio raped me seven years ago as much out of Gonzaga contempt as anything else. There's no way on earth that I'm going to let them destroy the family without a fight." She slowed, hunted for a street sign in the blizzard, and turned right toward the lake.

"So say I'd killed Gonzaga for you," said Kurtz. "Either you or one of the New York families would have had me killed, but then where are you? Little Skag is still running things from Attica."

"But he can't get out without the judges and parole-board people on the Gonzaga payroll," said Angelina. "It buys me time to try to consolidate things. If the rebuilt Farino Family is earning money for them, the New York bosses won't care who's actually running the action here in Buffalo."

"But Little Skag still has the leverage and control of the money," said Kurtz. "In a vacuum, he'll just find a way to buy the Gonzaga judges and parole-board people."

"Yes." The asphalt road ended at a snowy boat ramp dropping down onto the lake. Two rows of red flares were dimly visible stretching across the snowy ice, marking a makeshift road onto Lake Erie. A few truck and snowmobile tracks were gradually being erased by the wind. "The goddamned Gonzagas," muttered Angelina as she slowly descended the boat ramp. She was talking without thinking about it, just to relieve the tension of the driving. "While Papa and my family were consolidating gambling and prostitution and paying off just a few tame judges, the Gonzagas spent their money to buy top officials. Hell, most of the top cops in the Buffalo P.D. are on their pad."

"Stop!" said Kurtz.

The big Lincoln slewed to a stop with only its front wheels on the ice. "What?" snapped Angelina. "Goddammit, Kurtz. I told you, the ice is thick enough now to hold ten Town Cars. Quit being so fucking nervous."

"No," said Kurtz. The windshield wipers pounded wildly, trying to knock away the blowing snow. "Say that again . . . about the cops."

"Say what? The Gonzagas have been paying the top cops for years. It's how Emilio's family gets away with moving the huge volume of drugs it does."

"Do you have a list of those cops?"

"Sure. So what?"

Kurtz was too busy thinking to answer.

The Farino ice-fishing shack was only a few hundred yards out on the ice, but in the dark and the snow and the howling wind, it seemed like miles from shore. A few other shacks were visible in the headlights, but there were no vehicles. Even idiots who thought ice fishing was a sport weren't out tonight.

Kurtz and Angelina Farino Ferrara wrestled the stiffened bundle out of the trunk and carried it into the shack. There was a large hole centered where men could sit on plywood seats on either side and watch their lines—the whole building reminded Kurtz of an oversized outhouse—but a film of new ice had grown over the hole.

Angelina took a long-handled shovel from the corner and bashed away the scrim of ice. The wind literally howled, and icy pellets pounded the north wall of the shack.

Angelina had added some chains to the package so there was no need to hunt for additional weights. They lowered Leo through the hole, his shoulders barely squeezing through and bunching up the plastic shower curtain, and watched the last bubbles rise in the middle of the black circle.

"Let's get out of here," said Kurtz.

Back on Highway 5, Angelina said, "It's a good thing you chose Leo."

"Why?"

"Marco wouldn't have fit through that hole. We would've had to chop a new one."

Kurtz let that go.

Angelina glanced at him in the light of the instrument console. There was almost no traffic going through Lackawanna and back into town. "Did it occur to you that Leo might have had a family, Kurtz? A loving wife? Couple of kids?"

"No. Did he?"

"Of course not. As far as I could find out, he left New Jersey because he'd beaten his stripper girlfriend to death. He'd killed his brother the year before over some gambling debt. But my point was, he *might've* had a family. You didn't know."

Kurtz wasn't listening. He was trying to fight away fatigue long enough to work through this thing.

"Okay," Angelina said. "Tell me. What was this about the cops?"

"I don't know."

She waited. As they drove into the Marina Towers basement garage, Kurtz said, "I may have a way. For us to get to Gonzaga and survive. Maybe even put you in the position you want to be in and take Little Skag out of the equation."

"Kill Stevie?" She did not sound shocked at the idea.

"Not necessarily. Just get rid of his leverage."

"Tell me."

Kurtz shook his head. He looked around the garage and realized that his Volvo was still parked at the Buffalo Athletic Club. That cute little Boxster would never get through this snow. *And where am I going?* Hansen probably had his room at the Royal Delaware Arms and the office staked out. Kurtz thought of how crowded Gail's tiny apartment was tonight—violinist on the sofa, wino on the floor, whatever—and it made him more tired than ever.

"You have to drive me back to the Athletic Club," he said dully. Maybe he could sleep in the car there.

"Fuck that," Angelina said in conversational tones. "You're staying in the penthouse tonight."

Kurtz looked at her.

"Relax. I'm not after your body, Kurtz. And you look too wasted to make a pass. I just need to hear about this plan. You're not leaving until you tell me."

"I need a B-and-E expert tomorrow," said Kurtz. "Your family has to know someone really good at defeating security systems. Maybe cracking safes as well."

Angelina laughed.

"What's so funny?" said Kurtz.

"I'll tell you upstairs. You can sleep on the sectional in the living room. We'll build a fire, you can pour us a couple of brandies, and I'll tell you what's so funny. It'll be your bedtime story."

CHAPTER
TWENTY-FIVE

James B. Hansen awoke on Wednesday morning refreshed, renewed, and determined to go on the offensive. He made love to his very surprised wife—only Hansen knew that it would almost certainly be for the last time, since he planned to move on before the approaching weekend was past—and even while he made her moan, he was thinking that he had been passive in this Frears/Kurtz thing far too long, that it was time for him to reassert his dominance. James B. Hansen was a Master chess player, but he much preferred offense to defense. He had been reacting to events rather than being proactive. It was time for him to take charge. People were going to die today.

His wife moaned her weak little orgasm, Hansen dutifully had his—offering a prayer to his Lord and Savior as he did so—and then it was time to shower, strap on his Glock-9, and get to work.

Hansen went to the office long enough to have "Captain Millworth" clear his schedule except for a mandatory meeting with Boy Scout Troop 23 at 11:30 and a lunch with the Chief and the Mayor an hour after that. He called the two detectives: Myers was on the stakeout at Kurtz's secretary's house in Cheektowaga after a few hours' sleep; Brubaker had checked the Royal Delaware Arms and Kurtz's office downtown—no joy there. Hansen told Brubaker to join Myers in Cheektowaga, he would meet them there.

He went down to the precinct basement to requisition tactical gear.

"Wow, Captain," said the sergeant behind the cage wire, "you starting a war?"

"Just running a tactical exercise for a few of my boys," said Hansen. "Can't let the detectives get fat and lazy while ESU and SWAT are having all the fun, can we?"

"No, sir," said the sergeant.

"I'm going to back my Cadillac sport ute around," said Hansen. "Would you pack all this stuff in two ballistic-cloth bags and get it up to the rear door?"

"Yes, sir," said the sergeant in an unhappy tone. It wasn't his job to hump gear bags up the back stairs. But Captain Robert Gaines Millworth had a reputation as a humorless, unforgiving officer.

Hansen drove out through heavy snow to Cheektowaga, thinking about how easy this apprehension would be if he could just call a dozen of his detectives into the ready room and send them searching for Frears and Kurtz: checking every hotel and motel in the Buffalo area, running credit-card searches, going door to door. He had to smile at this. After years of being the ultimate loner, James B. Hansen was being contaminated by the group-effort persona of Captain Millworth. *Well. I'll just have to get by with Brubaker and Myers.* It was too bad that he had to rely on a venial, corrupt cop and a fat slacker, but he'd use them and then discard them within the next couple of days.

The venial, corrupt cop and the fat slacker were eating doughnuts in Myers's Pontiac, across the street from Arlene DeMarco's house.

"Nothing, Captain," reported Brubaker. "She hasn't even come out for her paper."

"Her car's still in the garage," said Myers, belaboring the obvious. The driveway showed six inches of fresh snow and no tire tracks.

Hansen glanced at his watch; it was not quite 8:30 A.M. "Why don't we go in and say hello?"

The two detectives stared at him over their gnawed doughnuts and steaming coffee. "We got a warrant, Captain?" asked Myers.

"I've got something better," said Hansen. The three men got out in the falling snow. Hansen opened his trunk and handed the pneumatic battering ram to Myers. "Brubaker, you ready your weapon," said Hansen. He took his own Glock-9 out, chambered a round, and crossed the street to the DeMarco house.

He knocked three times, waited a second, stood to one side, and nodded to Myers. The fat man looked at Brubaker as if questioning the order, but then swung the ram. The door burst inward, ripping its bolt chain off as it fell.

Hansen and Brubaker went in with pistols held high in both hands, swinging their weapons as they moved their heads. Living room—clear. Dining room—clear. Kitchen—clear. Bedrooms and bathrooms—clear. Basement and utility room—clear. They returned to the kitchen and holstered their weapons.

"That bugger packs a wallop," said Myers, setting the battering ram on the table and shaking his fingers.

Hansen ignored him. "You're sure someone was home when you started the stakeout?"

"Yeah," said Myers. "I could see a woman moving around in the living room yesterday afternoon before she pulled the drapes. Then the lights went off about eleven."

"The lights could have been on a timer," said Hansen. "When was the last time you saw someone move?"

Myers shrugged. "I dunno. It wasn't dark yet. Maybe, I dunno, four. Four-thirty."

Hansen opened the back door. Even with the new snow, faint tracks were visible crossing the backyard. "Stay a few paces back," he said. Not bothering to pull his Glock from its holster, he followed the faint depressions in the snow across the backyard, through a gate, across the alley, and through another backyard.

"We got another warrant for this house?" asked Brubaker from the yard as Hansen went to the back door.

"Shut up." Hansen knocked.

A woman in her seventies peered fearfully through the kitchen curtains. Hansen held his gold badge to the window. "Police. Please open the door." The three detectives waited while a seemingly endless number of bolts and locks and chains were released.

Hansen led the other two into the woman's kitchen. He nodded at Brubaker, who beckoned to Myers, and the two began searching the other rooms of the house while the old lady wrung her hands.

"Ma'am, I'm Captain Millworth of the Buffalo Police Department. Sorry to bother you this morning, but we're looking for one of your neighbors."

"Arlene?" said the woman.

"Mrs. DeMarco, yes. Have you seen her? It's very important."

"Is she in some kind of trouble, Officer? I mean, she asked me not to mention to anyone . . ."

"Yes, ma'am. I mean no, Mrs. DeMarco's not in any trouble with us, but we have reason to believe that she may be in danger. We're trying to find her. What is your name, ma'am?"

"Mrs. Dzwrjsky."

"When did you see her last night, Mrs. Dzwrjsky?"

"Yesterday afternoon. Right after *Wheel of Fortune*."

"About four-thirty?"

"Yes."

"And was she alone?"

"No. She had a Negro man with her. I thought that was very strange. Was she his hostage, Officer? I mean, I thought it very strange. Arlene didn't act frightened, but the man . . . I mean, he seemed very nice . . . but I thought it was very strange. Was he kidnapping her?"

"That's what we're trying to find out, Mrs. Dzwrjsky. Is this the man?" Hansen showed her the photo of John Wellington Frears.

"Oh, my, yes. Is he dangerous?"

"Do you know where they went?"

"No. Not really. I loaned Arlene Mr. Dzwrjsky's car. I mean, I almost never drive it anymore. Little Charles from down the street drives me when I have to—"

"What kind of car is it, Mrs. Dzwrjsky?"

"Oh . . . a station wagon. A Ford. Curtis always bought Fords at the dealership out on Union, even when—"

"Do you remember the make and year of the station wagon, ma'am?"

"Make? You mean the name? Other than Ford, you mean? My heavens, no. It's big, old, you know, and has that fake wood trim on the side."

"A Country Squire?" said Hansen. Brubaker and Myers came back into the kitchen, their weapons out of sight. Brubaker shook his head. No one else in the house.

"Yes, perhaps. That sounds right."

"Old?" said Hansen. "From the seventies perhaps?"

"Oh, no, Officer. Not that old. Curtis bought it the year Janice's first daughter was born. Nineteen eighty-three."

"And do you know the license number on the Ford Country Squire, ma'am?"

"No, no . . . but it would be in that drawer there, with the registration forms and the car-insurance stuff. I always . . ." She paused and watched as Brubaker rifled through the drawer, coming up with a current license-registration form. He said the tag number aloud and put the form in his coat pocket.

"You're being very helpful, Mrs. Dzwrjsky. Very helpful." Hansen patted the old woman's mottled hands. "Now, can you tell us where Arlene and this man were going?"

Mona Dzwrjsky shook her head. "She did not say. I'm sure she did not say. Arlene just said that something very important had come up and asked if she could borrow the station wagon. They seemed in a hurry."

"Do you have any idea where they might have been going, Mrs. Dzwrjsky? Anyone that Arlene might try to contact if there were trouble?"

The old woman pursed her lips as she thought. "Well, her late husband's sister, of course. But I imagine you've spoken with Gail already."

"Gail," repeated Hansen. "What's her last name, ma'am?"

"The same as Alan's and Arlene's. I mean, Gail was married, twice, but never had children, and she took back her maiden name after the second divorce. I used to tell

Arlene, you can never trust an Irish boy, but Gail was always . . ."

"Gail DeMarco," said Hansen.

"Yes."

"Do you know where she lives? Where she works?"

Mrs. Dzwrjsky looked as if she might cry. "Gail lives near where Colvin Avenue becomes Colvin Boulevard, I think. Arlene took me to visit her once. Yes, right near Hertel Plaza, north of the park."

"And where does she work?" asked Hansen, his voice more impatient than he meant it to be.

The old woman looked afraid. "Oh, Gail has always worked at the Erie County Medical Center. She's a surgical nurse there."

Hansen patted her hands again. "Thank you, Mrs. Dzwrjsky. You've been a huge help." He nodded for Brubaker and Myers to head back to the DeMarco house.

"I hope that Arlene is all right," said the old woman from the back door. She was weeping now. "I just hope Arlene is all right."

Back in Arlene DeMarco's kitchen, Brubaker used his cell phone to call Dispatch. They got Ms. Gail DeMarco's address on Colvin and the phone number, and Hansen called. There was no answer. He called the Erie County Medical Center, identified himself as a police officer, and was informed that Nurse DeMarco was assisting in surgery right now but would be available in about thirty minutes.

"Okay," said Hansen. "You two get over to the house on Colvin Avenue."

"You want us to go in?" asked Myers, lifting the battering ram off the table.

"No. Just stake it out. Check the driveway and call me if the Ford wagon is there. You can ask neighbors if they've seen the car or Arlene DeMarco or Frears or Kurtz, but don't go in until I get there."

"Where will you be, Captain?" Brubaker seemed half-amused by all this urgency.

"I'm going to stop at the Medical Center on the way. Get going."

Hansen watched from the front window as the two drove off in their unmarked cars. Then he walked back across the yard, through the carport, across the alley, and knocked on Mrs. Dzwrjsky's back door again.

When the old woman opened the door, she was holding the phone but it appeared that she hadn't dialed a number yet. She set the phone back in its cradle as Hansen stepped into the kitchen. "Yes, Officer?"

Hansen pulled the Glock-9 and shot her three times in the upper chest. Any other time, he would take the chance that the woman would call someone rather than take the chance of leaving a body behind, much less leave two detectives as witnesses, but this was an unusual situation. All he needed was a day or two and none of this would matter for Captain Robert Gaines Mill-worth. Probably just one day.

Hansen stepped over the body, making sure not to step in the widening pool of blood, picked up his ejected brass, and took time to reload the three cartridges in the Glock's magazine before walking back through the yards to his waiting Cadillac Escalade.

CHAPTER
TWENTY-SIX

Earlier that morning, Kurtz and Angelina Farino Ferrara sat in the front seat of her Lincoln and watched Captain Robert Millworth drive away from his home. It was 7:15 A.M.

"There was another car in the garage," said Angelina. "A BMW wagon."

Kurtz nodded and they waited. At 7:45, a woman, a teenage boy, and an Irish setter backed out in the station wagon. The woman beeped the garage door shut and drove off. "Wife, kid, and dog," said Angelina. "Any more in there?"

Kurtz shrugged.

"We'll find out," said Angelina. She drove the Town Car right up the long Millworth driveway and they both got out, Angelina carrying a heavy nylon bag. Kurtz stood back while she knocked several times. No answer.

"Around back," she said. He followed her through the side yard and across a snowy patio. The nearest neighbor was about a hundred yards away behind a privacy fence.

They paused by the sliding doors to the patio as Angelina crouched and studied something through the glass. "It's a SecureMax system," she said. "Expensive but not the best. Would you give me that glass cutter and the suction cup? Thanks."

Yesterday evening, in front of the fire over brandies, with Kurtz almost too tired to concentrate, she had told him her story . . . or at least the part of it that had made her laugh when he'd told her that he would need a B&E man.

Angelina Farino had always wanted to be a thief. Her father, Don Byron Farino, had worked to keep her sheltered from the facts of his life and would never have considered allowing her to take part in the family business. But Angelina did not want to be involved in every aspect of the business—not then. She just wanted to be the best thief in New York State.

Her brother David introduced her to some of the legendary old second-story men and in high school Angelina would visit them, bringing wine, just to hear their stories. David also introduced her to some of the rising young thugs in their father's organization, but she didn't care much for them; they bragged about using guns, violence, and frontal assaults. Angelina wanted to know about the smart men, the subtle men, the quiet men, the patient men. Angelina did not want to be another mobster; she wanted to be a cat burglar; she wanted to be The Cat; she wanted to be Cary Grant in *To Catch a Thief.*

She had put herself in harm's way with Emilio Gonzaga when she was in her early twenties because she thought that Gonzaga was going to introduce her to a safecracker she'd always wanted to meet. Instead, as she put it, Emilio introduced her to his dick.

Exiled to Sicily to have the baby, she had married a local mini-don, an idiot exactly her age but with half her

IQ, "to keep up appearances." After appearances were kept up and after the baby died and after the young don had his unfortunate hunting accident—or accident cleaning his pistol, Angelina let them choose the story they wanted—she flew to Rome to meet the famous Count Pietro Adolfo Ferrara. Eighty-two years old and suffering the effects .of two strokes, the count was still the most famous thief in Europe. Trained by his legendary thief of a father between the wars, active in the Italian resistance, and credited with stealing the communiques from Gestapo headquarters that led to the interdiction and assassination of Mussolini and his mistress, it was often said that the handsome, daring Count Ferrara had been the *model* for that Cary Grant character in *To Catch a Thief.*

Angelina had married the bedridden old man four days after they met. The next four years were, in her words, a training camp for becoming a world-class thief.

"What are you doing?" said Kurtz. He was moving from foot to foot on Hansen's patio. It was damned cold and his hair was wet with snow.

Angelina had cut a circular hole from the lower part of the patio door, had removed the glass carefully, and was reaching inside with a long instrument. She ignored Kurtz.

"Isn't that security system set for motion or messing with the glass?" asked Kurtz. "Haven't you tripped it already?"

"Would you shut up, please?" She reached in to clip on red and black wires and connected them to a module that connected with a Visor digital organizer. She studied the readout for a second, shut off the Visor, and unclipped the wires. "Okay," she said, standing and throwing her heavy black bag over her shoulder.

"Okay what?"

"Okay we open the door the usual way and have eight seconds to tap in the six-digit code on the keypad."

"And you know the code now?"

"Let's see." She studied the back door a minute, removed a short crowbar from her bag, broke the glass, and reached in to slip the chain lock and undo the main lock. It seemed to Kurtz that she had used the full eight seconds just to do that.

Angelina walked into the rear hallway, found the keypad on the wall, and tapped in the six-character alphanumeric code. An indicator on the security keypad went from red to green to amber. "Clear," she said.

Kurtz let out his breath. He pulled his pistol out from under his coat.

"You expecting someone else to be home?" said Angelina.

Kurtz shrugged.

"You going to tell me now whose house this is and how it relates to Gonzaga?"

"Not yet," said Kurtz. They went from room to room together, first the large downstairs, then all the bedrooms and guest rooms upstairs.

"Jesus," said Angelina as they came back downstairs. "This place is the definition of retro anal retentive. It's like we broke into Mike and Carol Brady's house."

"Who the hell are Mike and Carol Brady?"

Angelina paused at the top of the basement stairs. "You don't know the Brady Bunch?"

Kurtz gave her a blank look.

"Christ, Kurtz, you've been locked away longer than twelve years."

The basement had a laundry room, a bare rec room with a dusty Ping-Pong table, and a room locked away behind a steel door with a complicated security keypad.

"Wowzuh," said Angelina and whistled.

"Same code as upstairs?"

"No way. This is a serious piece of circuitry." She started pulling instruments and wires from her bag.

Kurtz glanced at his watch. "We don't have all day."

"Why not?" said Angelina. "You have things to see and people to do today?"

"Yeah."

"Well, don't get your jockey briefs in a bunch. In two minutes, we'll either be in or we'll have armed private-security people all over our ass here."

"Private security," said Kurtz. "This guy's alarms don't go to the cop house?"

"Get serious." She focused her attention on removing the keypad from the wall and connecting her wires to its wires without setting off the silent alarm.

Kurtz wandered back upstairs and looked out the front window. Their black Town Car was parked in plain sight, although the increasing snowfall made visibility more problematic. Kurtz was thankful that Hansen had bought a relatively isolated house with such a long driveway.

"Holy shit!" Angelina's voice sounded far away.

Kurtz trotted down the stairs and went through the open door. It was quite a private office—mahogany-paneled walls, a lighted gun case running from floor to ceiling, a heavy, expensive-looking wooden desk. On the wall above and behind that desk were photographs of James B. Hansen posing with various Buffalo worthies, plus a scad of certificates—Florida Police Academy diplomas, shooting awards, and commendations for Lieutenant and Captain Robert G. Millworth, Homicide Detective.

Angelina's eyes were narrow when she wheeled on

Kurtz. "You had me break into a fucking *cop's* home?"

"No." He walked over to the large wall safe. "Can you get into this?"

She quit staring daggers at Kurtz and looked at the safe. "Maybe."

He looked at his watch again.

"If this were a small, round safe, we'd have to pry the fucker out of the wall and take it with us," said Angelina. "You just can't get any blast leverage on a round safe. But our boy went in for the heavier, more expensive type."

"So?"

"So anything with corners, I can get into." She set her bag down near the safe door and began removing timers, primers, thermite sticks, and wads of plastique.

"You're going to blow it?" Kurtz was wishing that he'd gone to check on Arlene, Frears, and Pruno before doing this errand.

"I'm going to burn our way into the lock mechanism and get at the tumblers that way," said Angelina. "Why don't you make yourself useful and go make us some coffee?" She worked for a few seconds and then looked up at Kurtz standing there. "I'm *serious*. I didn't get my full three cups this morning."

Kurtz went up to the kitchen, found the coffeemaker, and made the coffee. He found some cannoli in the refrigerator. By the time he started down the stairs with two mugs and a dish with the cannoli, there came a loud hiss, a muffled *whump,* and an acrid odor filled the air. The safe looked intact to Kurtz's eye, but then he saw a fissure around the combination lock. Angelina Farino Ferrara had attached a slim fiberoptic cable to the Visor organizer and was watching a monochrome display as she clicked the combination.

The heavy safe door swung open. She accepted the

cup of coffee and drank deeply. "Blue Mountain roast. Good stuff. Cannoli's just okay."

Kurtz began removing things from the safe. A heavy nylon bag contained more than a dozen carefully wrapped cubes of what looked to be gray clay nestled in with foam-wrapped detonators, delicate-looking timers, and coils of primer cord.

"Military C-Four," said Angelina. "What the hell does your homicide captain want with C-Four in his home?"

"He likes to burn down and blow up his homes," said Kurtz. Shelves in the safe held more than $200,000 in cash and bearer's bonds, a bunch of certificates and policies, and a titanium case. Kurtz ignored the money and carried the case to the desk.

"Excuse me," Angelina said. "You forgetting something?"

"I'm not a thief."

"I am," she said and began transferring the money and bonds to her bag.

"Shit," said Kurtz. The locks on the case were also titanium and did not give when he went at them with the small crowbar.

"That little case may take longer to crack than the safe," said Angelina.

"Uh-uh," said Kurtz. He took out his .40-caliber Smith & Wesson and blew the locks off. The gap allowed the crowbar to get a grip and he popped the briefcase open.

Angelina finished loading the contents of the safe, lifted her heavy bag, and came over to the desk where Kurtz had laid out some of the photographs. "So what exactly are you . . . Holy Mother of God!"

Kurtz nodded.

"Who *is* this motherfucking pervert?" whispered Angelina.

Kurtz shrugged. "We'll never know his real name. But I was sure that he'd keep trophies. And he did."

It was Angelina's turn to look at her watch. "This is taking too long."

Kurtz nodded and hefted the bag of C-4 over his shoulder.

Angelina was sipping her coffee and heading for the door. She gestured. "Bring the other bag with the money and my burglar's stuff. Leave the cannoli."

CHAPTER
TWENTY-SEVEN

Hansen showed his badge to three nurses and two interns before being told where Nurse Gail DeMarco was.

"She's out of the O.R. and is . . . ah . . . right now, she's in the Intensive Care Unit on nine." The fat, black nurse was checking her computer monitor. Evidently all the hospital personnel were tracked by electronic sensors.

Hansen went up to the ICU and found the nurse speaking on a cell phone while looking down at a sleeping or comatose teenage girl. The girl had bruises and bandages and at least three tubes running in and out of her.

"Mrs. DeMarco?" Hansen showed his badge.

"I have to go," the nurse said into the phone and punched the disconnect button, but kept the phone in her hand. "What is it, Captain?"

Hansen showed his most engaging smile. "You know that I'm a captain of detectives?"

"It said so right on the ID you just showed me, Captain. Let's step out of this room."

"No, we're all right here," said Hansen. "I'll just be a minute." He liked the glass doors and walls separating them from the nurses' station. He went closer to the bed and leaned over the sleeping girl. "Car accident?"

"Yes."

"What's the kid's name?"

"Rachel."

"How old?"

"Fourteen."

Hansen gave his winning smile again. "I have a fourteen-year-old son. Jason. He wants to be a professional hockey player."

The nurse did not respond. She checked one of the monitors and adjusted the IV drip. She was still carrying the stupid cell phone in her left hand.

"She going to make it?" asked Hansen, not giving the slightest damn if the kid survived or went into cardiac arrest right then and there, but still wanting to get on Gail DeMarco's good side. Most women were blown away by his smile and affable persona.

"We hope so," said the nurse. "Can I help you, Captain?"

"Have you heard from your sister-in-law Arlene, Mrs. DeMarco?"

"Not for the last week or so. Is she in some sort of trouble?"

"We don't know." He showed the Frears photo. "Have you ever seen this man?"

"No."

No hesitation. No questions. No sign of alarm. Gail DeMarco wasn't responding according to the script. "We think perhaps this man abducted your sister-in-law."

The nurse didn't even blink. "Why would he do that?"

Hansen rubbed his chin. In other circumstances, he would take great pleasure in using a knife on this uncooperative woman. To calm himself, he looked down at the sleeping girl. She was just at the high end of the age group he liked. He raised her wrist and looked at the sea-green hospital bracelet there.

"Please don't touch her, Captain. We're worried about infection. Thank you. We shouldn't be in here."

"Just one more minute, Mrs. DeMarco. Your sister-in-law works for a man named Joe Kurtz. What can you tell me about Mr. Kurtz?"

The nurse had moved between Hansen and the sleeping girl. "Joe Kurtz? Nothing, really. I've never met him."

"So you haven't heard from Arlene in the last few days?"

"No."

Hansen graced the woman with a last glimpse of his most charming smile. "You've been very helpful, Mrs. DeMarco. We *are* concerned about your sister-in-law's whereabouts and well-being. If she gets in touch, please call me immediately. Here's my card."

Gail DeMarco took the card but immediately slipped it into her smock pocket as if it was contaminated.

Hansen took the elevator down to the reception level, spoke briefly with the nurse there, and took the elevator the rest of the way to the parking garage. He had learned several things. First, Kurtz's secretary had been in touch with her sister-in-law, but Arlene probably had not told her any details concerning Frears or what was going on. The nurse had known just enough not to be concerned about her sister's safety. Second, Gail almost certainly knew where Arlene was hiding. And probably Kurtz as well. Third, odds were good that Arlene and her boss, probably with Frears, were hiding at Nurse DeMarco's home on Colvin Avenue. Finally, and perhaps most important, Hansen had recognized the girl's name on the ID bracelet—Rachel Rafferty. Most people would not have made the connection, but James B. Hansen's memory was near photographically perfect. He recalled the notes in Joe Kurtz's file: former partner in their private investigation firm, Samantha Fielding, one daughter—Rachel—two years old when Ms. Fielding had been murdered; Rachel later adopted by Fielding's ex-husband, Donald Rafferty. And the nurse at reception, after being prodded by his badge, gave the details of the Raffertys' auto accident—black ice on the Kensington Expressway, Donald Rafferty recovering well but under suspicion of sexually abusing his daughter, the investigation currently on hold until the girl either recovered consciousness or died.

Hansen smiled. He loved subtle connections. Even more, he loved leverage over other people, and this injured child might make wonderful leverage.

Kurtz and Angelina had just driven away from the Hansen house in Tonawanda when Kurtz's cell phone rang. It was Arlene. "Gail just called from the hospital."

"You told her that you were all staying at her place?" said Kurtz.

"I called her earlier this morning," Arlene said. "She called a minute ago because she was in Rachel's ICU room and her friend at reception called up from downstairs to tell her that a plainclothes detective was there at the hospital looking for her. Gail was on the phone with me when the cop came in and she left the line open while they talked . . . it was Millworth. *Hansen.* He even *sounded* crazy, Joe. And scary."

"What did Gail tell him?"

"Nothing. Not a thing."

Kurtz doubted that. Even with the titanium briefcase full of incriminating evidence in the car with him, it was no time to start underestimating the creature Kurtz thought of as James B. Hansen.

"You and Pruno and Frears have to get out of there," he said.

"We'll go now," said Arlene. "I'll take the station wagon."

"No," said Kurtz. He checked where they were. Angelina had chosen the Youngman Highway to get them back to the city, and the Lincoln was approaching the Colvin Boulevard exit. "Get off here," he snapped at Angelina.

She gave him an angry look but glanced at the titanium case and roared down the off-ramp onto Colvin Boulevard South.

"We'll be there in ten minutes," Kurtz said to Arlene. "Less."

Hansen had just left the Medical Center when his private cell phone rang.

"We just got to the DeMarco place on Colvin," came Brubaker's voice. "A black Lincoln Town Car just pulled into the driveway—either the DeMarco drive or the one belonging to the duplex next door, we can't tell from down the block. Wait a minute, it's pulling out again . . . the Lincoln's coming by us . . . I see a woman driving, not Kurtz's secretary. There was someone in the passenger seat, but Myers and me couldn't see because of the reflection and I can't see in the back because of the goddamned tinted windows . . . sorry for the language, Captain. You want us to stake out the duplex or follow the Lincoln?"

"Did you see anyone get into the car from the DeMarco house?"

"No, sir. But we can't see that side door from where

we're parked. Someone might have had time to jump in. But the Lincoln wasn't in the driveway for more than ten seconds. It was more like a car turning around than anything else."

"Is the Country Squire station wagon in the driveway?"

"Yeah. I can see it."

"Did you get the tag numbers on the Lincoln?"

There was a short silence that sounded to Hansen like Brubaker sulking at being asked if they'd carried out such an elementary bit of detective work. Hansen wouldn't have been surprised if they'd neglected to get the tag numbers.

"Yeah," Brubaker said at last. He read the numbers. "There's no parking on the street here, Captain. We pulled into a driveway a couple of houses down. You want us to go after the Lincoln? We can catch up to it if we hurry."

"Brubaker," said Hansen, "tell Myers to follow the Lincoln. Tell him to run a DMV check while he's tailing it. You stay there and keep watch on the house. Try to be inconspicuous."

"How do I look inconspicuous while I'm standing out on the sidewalk in the snow?" said Brubaker.

"Shut up and tell Myers to catch that Lincoln," said Hansen. "I'll be at the duplex in five minutes." He broke the connection.

"Where's Pruno?" said Kurtz, turned in the passenger seat to look at the two in the rear. When they had swept into the driveway, only Arlene and John Wellington Frears had run to the Lincoln and jumped in.

"He left early this morning," said Arlene. "About dawn. All dressed up in his pinstripe suit. He said something about hiding in plain sight. I think he's going to check into a hotel or something until all this blows over."

"Pruno in a hotel?" said Kurtz. It was hard to picture. "Did he have any money?"

"Yes," said Frears.

"There's a Pontiac following us," said Angelina.

Kurtz swiveled back and looked in the rearview mirror. "Where'd it come from?"

"It was parked a couple of houses down from the place we picked these two up. It's been moving fast in traffic to catch up."

"It could be coincidence," said the violinist in back, looking out the rear window of the Lincoln.

Kurtz and Angelina exchanged glances. Obviously neither of them believed in coincidences.

"The car across the street from my house yesterday was a Pontiac," Arlene said.

Kurtz nodded and looked at Angelina. "Can we lose them?"

"Tell me who we're losing. I'm beginning to feel like the hired help today."

Kurtz thought of her black bag with the $200,000 next to Hansen's bag of C-4 in the trunk. "You have to admit, the pay's pretty good," he said.

Angelina shrugged. "Who's behind us? Mr.—?" She tapped the titanium briefcase Kurtz was holding on his lap.

"One or more of the detectives who are working for him," said Kurtz.

"You mean working for him or working for *him*?"

"For him personally," said Kurtz. "Can we lose them? I don't think you want this guy visiting you." He tapped the case.

Angelina Farino Ferrara checked the mirror again.

"He's only one car behind. They probably made the license plate."

"Still . . ." said Kurtz.

"Everyone buckle up," said Angelina.

CHAPTER
TWENTY-EIGHT

The light was red by Nichols School at the intersection of Colvin and Amherst where the street ended at the park. The Lincoln was second in line. Kurtz glanced back and could see the silhouette of only one head in the Pontiac two cars back.

Without warning, Angelina swung the Lincoln around the old car ahead of them, almost hit a Honda turning left from Amherst, and accelerated through the red light—cutting off two other cars that had to brake wildly. She headed east on Amherst for a hundred yards and then swung south again on Nottingham Terrace along the edge of the park.

"The car's following," called Arlene from the back seat.

Angelina nodded. They were doing seventy miles per hour on the residential street. She braked hard and swung the big vehicle up a ramp onto the Scajaquada Expressway. A hundred yards back, almost lost in the snowfall, the Pontiac bounced and roared its way up the same ramp.

Cutting more cars off as she made the exchange from the Scajaquada to 190, she accelerated to one hundred

miles per hour as they roared south over snow and black
ice along the elevated sections paralleling the river.

For a minute, the Pontiac was lost in traffic, and Angelina braked hard enough to send the Lincoln into a
slide. Going lock to lock with the steering wheel, tapping
the brake and hitting the gas again to bring the rear end
around, Angelina cut off a rusty Jetta and zoomed down
another ramp, drove through a red light in front of an
eighteen-wheeler to drive east on Porter and then swung
around behind the old pumping-station building in La
Salle Park.

The street here—old AmVets Drive—had not been
plowed for hours, and Angelina slowed as the black Lincoln kicked up rooster tails of snow. To their right, the
Niagara River widened toward Lake Erie, but it was all
ice, all snow, as featureless gray-white as the frozen
fields in the empty park to their left. The back street
connected to the maze of local loops and streets around
the Erie Basin Marina and the Marina Towers. The Pontiac did not reappear.

Hansen did not use the battering ram. He and Brubaker
kicked in the side door of Gail DeMarco's duplex and
went up the stairs with their guns drawn.

The tiny little apartment up there was empty. Photographs on the bedroom dresser showed the nurse Hansen
had interviewed, Gail DeMarco, Kurtz's secretary Arlene, and a man who was probably Arlene DeMarco's
dead husband. Hansen and Brubaker searched the rooms,
but there was no sign that the secretary or Frears or
Kurtz had been there.

"Shit," said Brubaker, holstering his weapon and ignoring the frown at the use of such language. Brubaker

gave Hansen a shrewd, ferret look. "Captain, what the hell is going on?"

Hansen stared at the detective.

"You know what I mean, Captain. You couldn't care less about this Kurtz, and now you've got Myers and me running all over town and back trying to find him and his secretary and this violinist. We've violated about three dozen department procedures. What's going on?"

"What do you mean, Fred?"

"Don't Fred me, Millworth." Brubaker was showing his smoker's teeth in a leer. "You say you're going to cover my back in an Internal-Affairs investigation, but why? You're the original straight-arrow, aren't you? What the fuck is going on here?"

Hansen lifted the Glock-9 and laid the muzzle against Detective Brubaker's temple. Thumbing the hammer back for effect, Hansen said, "Are you listening?"

Brubaker nodded very slightly.

"How much did Little Skag Farino pay you to get Kurtz, *Detective* Brubaker?"

"Five thousand in advance to arrest him and get him into the system. Another five when someone whacked him at County."

"And?" said Hansen.

"Fifteen K promised if I killed him myself."

"How long have you been on the Farino payroll, *Detective* Brubaker?"

"December. Just after Jimmy died."

Hansen leaned closer. "You sold your gold badge for five thousand dollars, *Detective*. This situation—with Frears, with Kurtz—is worth a hundred times that. To you, Myers, me."

Brubaker rolled his eyes toward Hansen. "Half a million dollars? Total?"

"Apiece," said Hansen.

Brubaker licked his lips. "Drugs then? The Gonzagas?"

Hansen denied nothing. "Are you going to help me, *Detective*? Or are you going to continue asking insulting questions?"

"I'm going to help you, Captain."

Hansen lowered the Glock-9. "What about Tommy Myers?"

"What about him . . . sir?"

"Can he be trusted to do as he's told?"

Brubaker looked calculating. "Tommy's not on anybody's payroll except the department's, Captain. But he does what I tell him to. He'll keep his mouth shut."

Hansen saw the shrewd glint in Brubaker's eyes and realized that the detective was already planning on how to eliminate Tommy Myers from the payoff once the work was done. Half of a million and a half dollars was seven hundred and fifty thousand for Detective Frederick Brubaker. Hansen didn't care—there was no drug money, no money of any sort involved—as long as Brubaker did what he was told.

Hansen's phone rang.

"I lost them on the downtown section of the Thruway," said Myers. He sounded a little breathless. "But I got a make on the license plates. Byron Farino of Orchard Park."

Hansen had to smile. The old don was dead and the Orchard Park estate closed up, but evidently someone in the family business was still using the vehicle. A woman had been driving, Myers had said. The daughter back from Italy? Angelina?

"Good," said Hansen. "Where are you?"

"Downtown, near the HSBC arena."

"Go over to the Marina Tower building and find a place to watch the garage exit."

"The Farino bitch's penthouse?" said Myers. "Sorry, Captain. You think this Frears and the others are there?"

"I think so. Just keep a good watch, Detective. I'll be down to talk to you in a bit." He disconnected and told the other detective what Myers had said.

Brubaker was standing at the front window of the duplex, watching the snow pile up on the small rooftop terrace there. He seemed to have no hard feelings after having a 9mm pistol pressed against his head. "What next, Captain?"

"I'm going to drop you at the main precinct garage to get another car. Take the battering ram with you. I want you to knock in the door at Joe Kurtz's office. Make sure that no one's there and then join Myers at the stakeout at Marina Towers."

"Where will you be, sir?"

Hansen holstered his Glock and adjusted his suit jacket. "I've got a meeting with the Boy Scouts."

CHAPTER
TWENTY-NINE

"According to the radio," said Angelina, "the real storm's going to hit this evening."

"Lake Effect," said Arlene.

John Wellington Frears looked up from the book he was perusing. "Lake Effect? What is that?"

Like true Buffalonians, both Arlene and Angelina were eager to explain the meteorological wonder that was a cold arctic air mass sweeping across Lake Erie, depositing incredible amounts of snow on the Buffalo area, especially in the "snow belt" south of the city along the lake.

Frears looked out the twelfth-story window at the blowing snow and blue-black clouds moving toward them across the frozen river and lake. "*This* isn't the snow belt?"

The penthouse was a pleasant enough place of refuge during the long winter day. Kurtz knew that it was literally the lull before the storm.

A little before noon, Angelina brought the bodyguard Marco into the corner kitchen, where Kurtz stood with binoculars, looking down at the Pontiac and the old Chevy parked back-to-back along Marina Drive. Seeing

Marco, Kurtz touched the pistol on his belt.

"It's all right," said Angelina. "Marco and I have had several long talks and he's in this with us."

Kurtz studied the big man. Marco had a good poker face, but there was no denying the intelligence behind those gray eyes. Obviously Angelina had appealed to the bodyguard's loyalty and good nature—and then promised him shitloads of money when this dustup with the Gonzagas was over. With the $200,000 she'd taken from James B. Hansen's safe that morning, she could afford a few payoffs.

Kurtz nodded and went back to watching the watchers.

James B. Hansen's audience with the Boy Scouts and their troop leaders went well. Captain Millworth gave a short speech in the briefing room and then the scouts and their leaders came up to have their photographs taken with the homicide detective. There was a photographer there from the *Buffalo News*, but no reporter.

Later, Hansen walked across the street to the courthouse for a private lunch with the Mayor and the Chief. The topic was the bad press the city and Department were getting because of the increased drug trade flowing through Buffalo to and from Canada and the resulting increase in murders, especially in the African-American community. The Mayor also had concerns about Buffalo being the first stop for Islamic terrorists carrying explosives in from Canada, although one glance exchanged between the Chief and Hansen communicated their skepticism about someone wanting to bomb Buffalo.

All during these activities, Hansen was considering the complicated mess that had blotched out like an ink stain on felt over the past few days. If possible, he would like to continue in his Captain Millworth persona for another year or so, although the events of the past twenty-four hours made that very problematic. A lot of people would have to be buried, and soon, in order for him to maintain this identity.

Well, thought Hansen, *I've already buried a lot of people. A few more won't matter.*

Hansen had always been excellent at multitasking, so he easily made comments and handled the occasional question from the Chief or Mayor while pondering strategies for the resolution of this Kurtz-Frears problem. It bothered him that he still could not get in touch with Dr. Howard Conway in Cleveland. Perhaps the old fairy had taken his muscled pretty-boy and gone on vacation.

When Hansen's cell phone first rang, he ignored it. But it rang again. And then again.

"Excuse me, Chief, Mr. Mayor," he said, "I have to take this." He stepped into the small sitting room next to the courthouse dining room and answered the phone.

"Honey, Robert, you've got to come home. Someone's broken in and—"

"Whoa, whoa, slow down, sugar. Where are you?" Donna should have been at the library until three.

"They closed the library because of the storm, Robert. The schools are shutting down early as well. I picked Jason up during his usual lunch hour and we came home and . . . someone's broken in, Robert! Shall I call the police? I mean, I did, you are, but you know what I mean—"

"Calm down," said Millworth. "What did they steal?"

"Nothing, I think. I mean, Jason and I can't find anything missing from the house. But they left the door to your basement office open, Robert. I peeked in . . . I'm sorry, but I thought they might still be in there . . . but the door was open and the door to a big safe is open in there, Robert. I didn't go in, but they obviously did, the thieves, I mean. I didn't know you had a safe down there, Robert. Robert? Robert?"

Hansen had gone cold all over. Spots danced in front of his eyes for a minute. He sat down on the small couch in the sitting room. "Donna? Don't call the police. I'm coming home. Stay upstairs. Don't go in the office. You and Jason stay where you are."

"Robert, why do you think—"

Hansen broke the connection and went in to tell the Chief and the Mayor that something important had come up.

Marco showed them the marina pay phone where Little Skag would be calling for his weekly information update. Marco said that Leo usually did the talking. Kurtz, Angelina, and the bodyguard had left the apartment tower by its south door, out of sight of Brubaker and Myers, parked on the street to the north. Angelina told Marco to return to the penthouse, and Kurtz rigged the small cassette recorder and microphone wire the don's daughter had supplied.

The call came precisely at noon. Angelina answered it. With the additional earphone, Kurtz could eavesdrop on the conversation.

"Angie . . . what the fuck are you doing there?"

Angelina winced. She had always hated the nickname.

"Stevie, I wanted to talk to you . . . privately."

"Where the fuck are Leo and Marco?"

"Busy."

"Miserable incompetent motherfuckers. I'm going to fire their asses."

"Stevie, we need to talk about something."

"What?" To Kurtz's ear, his former fellow convict sounded not only irritated but alarmed.

"You've been hiring cops to whack people. Detective Brubaker, for instance. I know you've put him on the payroll that used to go to Hathaway."

Silence. Little Skag obviously didn't know what his sister was up to, but he wasn't about to encourage his own entrapment. Finally, "What the fuck are you talking about, Angie?"

"I don't care about Brubaker," said Angelina, her breath fogging in the cold air, "but I've gone over the family notes and I see that Gonzaga's got a captain of detectives on the arm. A guy named Millworth."

Silence.

"Millworth's not really Millworth," said Angelina. "He's a serial killer named James B. Hansen . . . and a bunch of other aliases. He's a child-killer, Stevie. A rapist and a killer."

Kurtz heard Little Skag let out a breath. If this dealt with Gonzaga, it was not his sister trying to entrap him. "So?" said Little Skag.

"So do you really want me doing this deal with Emilio when he has a child-killer on his payroll?"

Little Skag laughed. It was an unpleasant laugh and every time Kurtz had heard it in Attica, it had been at someone else's expense.

"Do I give a flying fuck who Emilio hires?" said Little Skag. "If this cop is a killer like you say, it just means that the Gonzagas own him. They got him by the balls. Now put Leo on."

"I wouldn't expect *you* to do anything about someone who rapes kids," said Angelina.

"What the fuck is that supposed to mean?"

"You know what it means, Stevie. You and that high-school Connors girl who disappeared twelve years ago.

Emilio kidnapped her, but you were in on it—you raped her, didn't you?"

"What the fuck are you talking about? Have you gone out of your mind? Who gives a shit about something that happened twelve years ago?"

"I do, Stevie. I don't want to do business with a man who pays a serial child-killer."

"*Fuck* what you want!" screamed Little Skag. "Who the fuck asked you what *you* want, you stupid cunt? Your job is to finish those dealings with Gonzaga so his people can get me the fuck out of here. Do you understand? If I want to fuck kindergarten kids up the ass, you're going to shut the fuck up about it. You're my sister, Angie, but that won't stop me from—"

The line hissed and crackled.

"Stop you from what, Stevie?" Angelina said after a minute. "From having me whacked the way you did Maria?"

The cold wind blew in off the lake during the next silence. Then Little Skag said, "You're my sister, Angelina, but you're a stupid bitch. You meddle in my business again . . . in Family business . . . and I'll do worse than have you whacked. Understand me? I'm gonna get my lawyer to set up another call at noon tomorrow and you'd goddamn better have Leo and Marco there."

The line went dead.

Kurtz disconnected the small microphone, rewound, and hit "Play" on the micro-cassette recorder long enough to hear the voices loud and clear. He clicked off the machine.

"How the hell is that going to help with anything?" said Angelina.

"We'll see."

"Are you going to tell me your plan about how to get

to Gonzaga now, Kurtz? It's time, unless you want me to toss you and your friends out in the snow."

"All right," said Kurtz. He told her the plan as they walked back to Marina Towers.

"Jesus fuck," whispered Angelina when he was finished. They were silent riding up in the elevator.

Arlene was standing in the foyer. "Gail just called me," she said to Kurtz. "They're going to discharge Donald Rafferty from the hospital in about thirty minutes."

CHAPTER
THIRTY

Donna and Jason were waiting when James B. Hansen arrived home. He calmed them, spoke soothingly, told them to put the dog outside and that nothing important could have been stolen from his basement gun room, inspected the point of breaking and entering, and went downstairs to look in his room.

They had stolen everything important. Hansen saw black dots dancing in his vision and had to sit down at his desk or faint. His photographs. The $200,000 in cash. They had even stolen his C-4 explosive. Why would thieves take that?

He had more money hidden away, of course—$150,000 tucked away with the cadavers in the rental freezer unit. Another $300,000 in various banks under different names in various cities. But this was not a small setback. Hansen would love to believe that this robbery was just a coincidence, but there was no chance of that. He would have to find out if Joe Kurtz was a skilled thief—whoever had bypassed those two expensive alarm systems and blown the safe knew his business—but it had to be someone working for or with John Wellington Frears. All of the recent events suggested a conspiracy afoot to destroy James B. Hansen. The theft of the souvenir photos left Hansen no choice as to his next actions. And Hansen despised being left without choices.

He looked up to find Donna and Jason peering into his basement sanctum sanctorum.

"Wow, I didn't know you had so many guns," said Jason, staring at the display case. "Why didn't they steal your guns?"

"Let's go upstairs," said Hansen.

He led them up to the second floor.

"Nothing was stolen or disturbed very much up here as far as I can tell," said Donna. "I'm glad Dickson was at the vet's. . . ."

Hansen nodded and led them into the guest bedroom with its two twin beds. He gestured for his wife and stepson to sit on one of the beds. Hansen was still wearing his topcoat and now he reached into the pocket. "I'm sorry this happened," he said, his voice smooth, reassuring, controlled. "But it's nothing to be alarmed about. I know who did it."

"You do?" said Jason, who never seemed to quite trust his stepfather's pronouncements. "Who? Why?"

"A felon named Joe Kurtz," said Hansen with a smile. "We're arresting him today. In fact, we've already found the weapon he's used in similar robberies." Hansen brought out the .38 that he had reloaded.

"How did you get his gun?" asked Jason. The boy did not sound convinced.

"Robert," said Donna in her bovine way, "is there anything wrong?"

"Not a thing, dear," said Hansen and fired from the hip, hitting Donna between the eyes. She flopped backward on the bed and lay still. Hansen swiveled the muzzle toward Jason.

The boy did not wait to be shot. He was off the bed

in a single leap, reacting faster than Hansen would have ever guessed the boy could move. He hit his stepfather in a full body check—an against-the-boards hockey crash—before Hansen could aim or pull the trigger again. They both went backward off the bed, Jason struggling to get his hands on the weapon, Hansen fighting to keep it away from the tall boy. Jason's reach was actually longer than Hansen's, but he was sixty pounds lighter. Hansen used his body mass to shove the boy off him and against the dresser. Then both of them were on their feet, still struggling for the weapon, Jason sobbing and cursing at the same time, Hansen fighting hard but smiling now, smiling without knowing it, amused by this sudden and unexpected opposition. Who would have expected this surly teenage slacker to put up such a fight?

Jason still had Hansen's right wrist in a death grip, but the boy freed his right arm, made a fist, and tried to slug his stepfather in the best Hollywood tradition. A mistake. Hansen kneed the teenager in the balls and backhanded him in the face with his left hand.

Jason cried out and folded over but kept his grip on Hansen's wrist, trying to foil his stepfather's aim.

Hansen kicked the boy's feet out from under him and Jason flew backward onto the empty bed, pulling Hansen with him. But Hansen was succeeding in swiveling the muzzle lower, even as Jason clung to his right arm with both hands, panting and swearing. Now the boy was sobbing entreaties. "Please, no, no. Mom, help. No, no, no. God *damn* you—"

Hansen got the angle and shot the kid in the chest.

Jason gasped, his mouth flopping open like a landed fish's, but still clung to Hansen's wrist, trying to deflect a second shot. Hansen put his knee on the boy's bloody chest, forcing the last of the air out of his lungs, and wrenched his right arm free of the boy's weakening grip.

"Dad . . ." gasped the wounded teenager.

Hansen shook his head . . . no . . . set the muzzle against the boy's forehead, and pulled the trigger.

Gasping, out of breath and almost shaking from the exertion, Hansen went into the guest bathroom. Somehow he had avoided getting blood or brain matter on his topcoat and trousers. His black shoes were spattered, however. He used one of the pink guest towels to clean his shoes and then he splashed water on his face and hands, drying them with the other towel.

The guest room was a mess—dresser knocked askew, mirror broken, the green coverlet on one of the beds crumpled under Jason's sprawled body. The boy's mouth was still open wide as if in a silent scream. Hansen went to the window and looked out for a minute, but he had no real concern that the neighbors had heard the shots. The houses were too far away and sealed for winter.

The snow was falling more heavily and the sky was very dark to the west. Dickson, their Irish setter, ran back and forth in the dog run.

Hansen felt light, his mind clear, energy flowing much as it did after a good workout at the gym. The worst had happened—someone taking his souvenir briefcase—but he still had options. James B. Hansen was too intelligent not to have backup plans beneath his backup plans. This was a setback, one of the most bizarre he'd ever encountered, but he had long anticipated someone discovering not only the falsehood of one of his identities, but the full chain of his lives and crimes. There was a plastic surgeon waiting in Toronto, a new life in Vancouver.

But first, details. It was too bad that the thief—Kurtz or whoever it was—had taken his C-4 explosive. That would have reduced this part of the house to such sham-

bles that it would take an explosives forensic team weeks
or months to figure out what had happened here. But
even a basic fire would give him time. Especially if there
was the usual third body in the house.

Sighing, aggrieved that he had to spend the time,
Hansen went out, locked the door behind him, and drove
the big Cadillac SUV to the rental freezer. There he retrieved all of the cash from the body bags, chose Cadaver Number 4 from the shelves, tossed the frozen
corpse into the back of the Escalade, and drove home,
taking care not to speed in the heavy snow. He passed
several snowplows working but almost no traffic. Donna
must have been correct about schools closing early.

The house was just as he'd left it. Hansen put the
Cadillac Escalade in the garage, brought his dog, Dickson, inside, and closed the garage door before hauling
the cadaver up the stairs, removing it from its plastic
wrapping and laying it on the bed next to Donna. The
corpse was in street clothes from two years ago when
he had killed the man, but Hansen went into his own
closet and pulled out a tweed jacket he had never liked
very much. The body's arms were frozen at its sides, but
Hansen draped the jacket over its shoulders. He also removed his Rolex from his wrist and set it on the cadaver's wrist. Thinking he would need a watch of his
own, he undid Jason's and slid it in his trouser pocket.

He carried in the five jerricans of gasoline stored in
the garage. Burn the place now and leave forever? Cau-
tion said that he should, but there were still elements left
to be resolved. Hansen might need something from the
house—some of the guns, perhaps—and he had no time
to pack now.

Leaving the cans of gas with Dickson in the living
room. Hansen carefully locked the house, pulled the
Cadillac SUV out of the garage, beeped the garage door

shut, and drove back downtown to plant the .38 in
Kurtz's room.

Donald Rafferty was glad to get out of the hospital.

He had a broken wrist, bruises on his ribs and ab-
domen, and bandages on his head. The mild concussion
still hurt like a sonofabitch, but Rafferty knew that he'd
hurt a lot worse than that if he didn't get the hell out of
the hospital and the hell out of town.

He'd been lucky with the child-abuse/molestation rap.
Rafferty had indignantly denied everything to the cops
when they interviewed him, pointed out that his adopted
daughter Rachel was a typical teenager—hard to handle,
given to lying and blaming others for her problems—
and that he'd done nothing but go down to the bus station late that night to retrieve her after she'd run away.
He was afraid, he told the cops, that she was doing
drugs. They'd had a fight—Rachel hated the idea of Rafferty remarrying, even though her real mother had been
dead for more than twelve years—and she was still angry at him in the car when he'd hit the black ice and
the car had spun off the Kensington.

Yes, Rafferty admitted to the cops, since they had the
blood-alcohol test results anyway, he'd been drinking
that evening at home—hell, he was worried sick about
Rachel, why wouldn't he have a few drinks at home—
but what was he supposed to do when she called from
the bus station at 2:30 A.M., leave her there? No, the
drinking didn't cause the accident—the goddamned
snowstorm and black ice had.

Luckily, when Rachel regained consciousness in the
ICU, the cops had interviewed her and she'd retracted
the story about Rafferty trying to rape her. She seemed
confused to the police, probably because of the anesthe-

sia and pain from the surgery. But she'd taken back the accusations she'd made to the paramedics as the firemen were cutting her out of the wreckage of the Honda.

Rafferty felt vindicated. Shit, he'd not come anywhere close to raping her. It was just that the girl was wearing pajamas two sizes too small when she came down to the kitchen to get some cake, Rafferty had been drinking all evening and was frustrated that DeeDee couldn't see him for the next couple of weekends, and he'd made the slight mistake of coming up behind Rachel as she stood at the counter and running his hands over her budding breasts, down her stomach and thighs.

Waiting in the hospital lounge for his taxi to arrive, Rafferty felt himself stir at that memory, even through the pain and the painkillers. He was sorry the brat had screamed and rushed to her room, locking the door and then going out the window and down the garage trellis while he stood like a dork in the hallway, threatening to kick the door down if she didn't come to her senses. She'd taken the last bus from Lockport into the city station, but then realized she didn't have the money to get out of Buffalo. Sobbing, cold—she'd only had time to grab a sweatshirt—she'd finally called Rafferty. This also made him smile. The girl had no one else to go to, which was probably why she'd recanted on her accusations. If she was going to go home at all, she'd have to go home to Donald Rafferty.

Normally, Rafferty would face the driving-under-the-influence charges and take his lumps, but when one of the nurses—not that bitch Gail Whatever, who kept looking in on Rachel and staring at Rafferty like he was some sort of amphibian, but that pretty nurse—had said that Rafferty's *brother* had stopped in to see him the morning after the accident, his blood had literally run cold. Donald Rafferty's brother was serving time in an

Indiana prison. From the nurse's description, this man sounded like Joe Kurtz.

It was time to leave town for a while.

He'd called DeeDee in Hamilton, Ontario, telling her to get her cellulite ass down here to pick him up, but she couldn't get off work until after five and she griped about the storm coming in off the lake, so there was no way that Rafferty was going to wait for her. He'd had the nurse call him a cab and he was going to get to Lockport, pack the things he needed—including the .357 Magnum he'd bought after that asshole Kurtz threatened him—and then he was going to take a little vacation. Rafferty was sorry that Rachel had gotten hurt—he didn't mean the kid harm—but if she did have a setback and failed to pull through, well, hell, that was one way to be sure that she wouldn't change her mind and rat him out to the authorities again. All he'd wanted was a little feel, a touch, maybe a blow job from the kid; it wasn't like he was going to take her virginity from her or anything. She had to grow up sooner or later. Or maybe not.

An orderly came into the lounge and said, "Your cab is here, Mr. Rafferty."

He tried to stand but the nurse he didn't like shook her head and he settled back into the wheelchair. "Hospital policy," she said, wheeling him out under the overhang. Big deal, hospital policy, thought Rafferty. They make sure you stay in the wheelchair until you're out of the building and then you're on your own. You can go home and die that day as far as they're concerned. Tough titty.

The cabdriver didn't even get out to open the door or to help Rafferty into the back seat. Typical. The ugly nurse steadied him with one hand while Rafferty struggled out of the wheelchair, his injured wrist hurting like hell and his head spinning. The concussion was worse than he'd thought. He collapsed into the seat and took some deep breaths. When he turned around to tell the nurse that he was okay, she'd already turned away and pushed the chair back into the hospital. *Bitch.*

For a second, Rafferty considered telling the driver to drop him off at one of his favorite bars, maybe the one on Broadway. A few drinks would probably help more than these wimpy Tylenol Threes they'd grudgingly given him. But then Rafferty thought better of it. First, it was snowing like a bastard, and if he waited too long, the goddamn roads would be closed. Second, he wanted to get his stuff and be ready when DeeDee got there. No time to waste.

"Lockport," he told the driver. "Locust Street. I'll tell you which house to stop at."

The driver nodded, hit the meter, and pulled away into the falling snow.

Rafferty rubbed his temples and closed his eyes for a minute. When he opened them, the taxi had pulled onto the Kensington but was going in the wrong damned direction, toward the downtown instead of east and then north. *Fucking idiot,* Rafferty thought through his headache. He rapped on the bulletproof glass and slid the open partition wider.

The driver turned. "Hello, Donnie," said Kurtz.

CHAPTER
THIRTY-ONE

Hansen was driving to the Royal Delaware Arms to plant the .38 in Kurtz's room when his cell phone rang. He considered not answering it—the life of Captain Robert Millworth was effectively at an end—but decided that he'd better respond; he didn't want people at the precinct to notice his absence for at least twenty-four hours.

"Hansen?" said a man's voice. "James B. Hansen?"

Hansen was silent but he had to pull the Escalade to the side of the road. It was Joe Kurtz's voice. It had to be.

"Millworth then?" said the voice. The man went on to name a half dozen of Hansen's other former personae.

"Kurtz?" Hansen said at last. "What do you want?"

"It's not what I want, it's what you might want."

The shakedown, thought Hansen. *All this has been leading up to the shakedown.* "I'm listening."

"I thought you might. I have your briefcase. Interesting stuff. I thought you might like it back."

"How much?"

"Half a million dollars," said Kurtz. "Cash, of course."

"Why do you think I have that much cash around?"

"I think the two hundred K I liberated from your safe today was just the tip of the iceberg, Mr. Hansen," said Kurtz. "A lot of the people you've been posing as earned a lot of money—a stockbroker, a Miami realtor, a plastic surgeon, for Christ's sake. You have it."

Hansen had to smile. He'd hated the thought of leaving Kurtz and Frears behind him, alive. "Let's meet. I have a hundred thousand in cash with me right now."

"So long, Mr. Hansen."

"Wait!" said Hansen. The silence on the line showed that Kurtz was still there. "I want Frears," said Hansen.

The silence stretched. "That would cost another two hundred thousand," Kurtz said at last.

"All I can get in cash is three hundred thousand."

Kurtz chuckled. It was not a pleasant sound. "What the hell. Why not? All right, Hansen. Meet me at the abandoned Buffalo train station at midnight."

"Midnight's too late—" started Hansen, but Kurtz had disconnected.

Hansen sat for a minute by the curb, watching the Escalade's wipers bat away the falling snow, trying to think of nothing, allowing the neutral Zen state to fill his mind. It was impossible to clear this noise, these events—they kept falling on him like the snow. Hansen had not played tournament chess for years, but that part of his mind was fully engaged. Frears and Kurtz—he had to think of them as a unit, partners, a single opponent with two faces—had made this chess game interesting, and now Hansen had the option of walking away and always remembering the pieces frozen in mid-play, or the option of clearing the chessboard with his forearm, or of beating them at their own game.

So far, the Frears-Kurtz team had been on the attack even when Hansen had thought he was playing offense. Somehow, they had stumbled upon his current identity—

probably John Wellington Frears's contribution to the game—and their moves after that had been predictable enough. The robbery of his home to obtain the evidence had been shocking, though obvious enough in retrospect. But they had not yet gone to the police. This meant one of three endgames had to be in play—A) Frears-Kurtz wanted to kill him; B) Kurtz was actually double-crossing his partner to carry out the blackmail and might actually tell Hansen of Frears's whereabouts if he was paid; or C) Frears-Kurtz wanted him dead *and* wanted the blackmail money.

From what Hansen remembered of John Wellington Frears, the black man was too civilized for his own good. Even twenty years of stewing about his daughter's death probably had not prepared Frears for murder; he would always opt for turning Hansen in to the proper authorities. Hansen also remembered that the violinist had used the phrase "proper authorities" frequently back during their political discussions at the University of Chicago.

So that left Kurtz. The ex-convict must be running the show now, overriding Frears's protests. Perhaps Kurtz had made contact with the Farinos for help. But James B. Hansen knew how limited the Farino Family clout was in this new century—almost nonexistent with the old don dead, the core of the Family scattered, and the drug addict Little Skag locked up in Attica. There were intelligence reports of a few new people being recruited for the Farinos, but they were middle-management people: numbers runners, a few body-guards, accountants—no real muscle to speak of. Which left only the Gonzagas as a power in Buffalo.

Kurtz had demanded half a million dollars, with a bonus for Frears, which was certainly enough to get the Farinos involved on spec, but Hansen suspected that Kurtz was too greedy to spread the money out. Perhaps this Farino daughter, Angelina, was giving Kurtz some logistical support without knowing the whole situation. That seemed probable.

I could leave now, thought Hansen, his thoughts tuned to the metronomic pulse of the windshield wipers. *Plant this .38, make an anonymous 911 call fingering the murderer of the old lady in Cheektowaga, and leave now.* This would be the forearm-clearing-the-chess-pieces answer to the dilemma and it had a certain elegance to it. *But who does this Kurtz think he is?* was the immediate follow-on thought. By attempting blackmail, Kurtz had raised the game to a new and more personal level. If Hansen did not play out the rest of the game, he would be tipping his own king in defeat. That weakling Frears and this sociopath of an ex-convict would have beaten James B. Hansen at his own game.

Not fucking likely, thought Hansen, immediately offering a prayer of apology to his Savior.

Hansen turned the Cadillac SUV west and got on the expressway, heading north along the river.

Kurtz had driven to the empty alley near Allen Street, parked the taxi next to the Lincoln, transferred Rafferty to the trunk of the Town Car and the bound, gagged and blindfolded cabdriver from the Lincoln to the taxi, then called Hansen while driving back to the Farino penthouse. Something about actually hearing James B. Hansen's smooth, oily voice had made Kurtz's head pulse with migraine pain.

Back at Marina Towers, he left Rafferty in the trunk and took the elevator up. Everyone was chowing down on lunch and Kurtz joined them. Angelina Farino Ferrara had told her cook, servants, and the eleventh-floor accountants to take the day off—don't try to get in through the storm, she'd said—so the motley crew in the pent-house had thrown together a big meal of chili, John Frears's recipe, and various types of cheese, good French bread and taco chips and hot coffee. Angelina offered wine, but no one was in the mood for it. Kurtz was in the mood for several glasses of scotch, but he decided to forgo it until the day's errands were all run.

After the lunch, he stepped onto the icy and wind-blown west balcony to clear his head. A few minutes later, Arlene joined him, lighting one of her Marlboros.

"Can you believe it, Joe? She's a Mafia don's daughter but she doesn't allow smoking in her apartment. What's La Cosa Nostra coming to?"

Kurtz didn't answer. The sky to the northwest was as black as a curtain of night sliding toward the city. The lights along the marina and the walkways below had already come on.

"Rafferty?" said Arlene.

Kurtz nodded.

"Can we talk about Rachel for a minute, Joe?"

Kurtz neither answered nor looked at her.

"Gail says that she's showing some improvement to-day. They're keeping her sedated much of the time and watching for infection in her remaining kidney. Even if there is drastic improvement, it will be several weeks—maybe a month and a half—before she can leave the hospital. And she'll need special care at home."

Kurtz looked at her now. "Yeah? And?"

"I know you won't let Rachel become a ward of the state, Joe."

He didn't have to say anything to show his agreement with that.

"And I know how you go straight at things. Like this Hansen situation. You've always gone straight at things.

But maybe in this case you should consider taking the long way."

"How?" Tiny pellets of ice were pelting his face.

"I shouldn't be Rachel's guardian . . . I've had my child, raised him as best I could, mourned his death. But Gail has always wanted a child. It's one of the main reasons she and Charlie broke up . . . that and the fact that Charlie was a total asshole."

"Gail . . . adopt Rachel?" Kurtz's voice was edged.

"It wouldn't have to be a full-scale adoption," said Arlene. "Rachel is fourteen. She'll just need a court-appointed guardian until she turns eighteen. That would be perfect for Gail."

"Gail is single."

"That's not so important for a guardian. Plus, Gail has friends in social services and Niagara Frontier Adoption Option, and she knows several of the child-care legal people. She's been an excellent nurse—remember, her specialty is pediatric surgery—and she has tons of time off coming to her."

Kurtz looked back at the approaching storm.

"You could spend time with her, Joe. With Rachel. Get to know her. Let her get to know you. Someday you could tell her—"

Kurtz looked at her. Arlene stopped, took a drag on her cigarette, and looked up to meet his gaze. "Tell me you'll think about it, Joe."

He went back through the sliding doors into the penthouse.

Hansen crossed the bridge to Grand Island and drove to Emilio Gonzaga's compound. The guards at the gatehouse looked astonished when he showed his badge and said that he was there to see Mr. Gonzaga, but they conferred with the main house via portable radios, searched him carefully to make sure he was not wearing a wire, appropriated his service Glock-9—Hansen had stowed the .38 under the passenger seat—transferred him to a black Chevy Suburban, and drove him up to the main house, where he was searched again and left to wait in a huge library in which the hundreds of leather-bound books looked as if they had never been opened. Two bodyguards, one an Asian man with absolutely no expression on his smooth face, stood against the far wall with their hands at their sides.

When Gonzaga came in, smoking a Cuban cigar, Hansen was struck by how truly ugly the middle-aged don was. The man looked like a toad that had been molded into human form, with an Edward G. Robinson mouth minus the touch of humor.

"Captain Millworth."

"Mr. Gonzaga."

Neither man offered to shake hands. Gonzaga remained standing; Hansen remained sitting. They looked at one another.

"You want something, Detective?"

"I need to talk to you, Don Gonzaga."

The tall, ugly man made a gesture with his cigar.

"You paid my predecessor," said Hansen. "You sent me a check last December. I sent it to charity. I don't need your money."

Gonzaga lifted one heavy black eyebrow. "You come out here in a fucking blizzard to tell me that?"

"I came out here in a blizzard to tell you that I need something more important and that I can give you something very important."

Gonzaga waited. Hansen glanced at the bodyguards. Gonzaga shrugged and did not tell them to leave.

James B. Hansen removed a photograph of Joe Kurtz

that he'd pulled from the felon's file. "I need to have this man killed. Or to be more specific, I need help in killing him."

Gonzaga smiled. "Millworth, if you are wearing a wire which somehow my boys did not discover, I shall kill you myself."

Hansen shrugged. "They searched me twice. I'm not wearing a wire. And if I were, what I said is a felony by itself—suborning you to be an accomplice to murder."

"And entrapment also in addition," said Gonzaga. The way the man spoke made Hansen think that human language was not the don's native tongue.

"Yes," said Hansen.

"And what is it that I would receive in exchange for this hypothetical quid-pro-quo service, Detective Millworth?"

"It's *Captain* Millworth," said Hansen. "Of Homicide. And what you will receive is years of a service that you could not otherwise buy."

"Which would be?" said Gonzaga, implying that he'd already bought every service the Buffalo Police Department had to offer.

"Impunity," said Hansen.

"Im—what?" Emilio Gonzaga removing a long cigar from his mouth made Hansen think of a frog wrestling with a turd.

"Impunity, Don Gonzaga. Freedom not only of prosecution when murders are required of you, but freedom even from serious investigation. A get-out-of-jail card with no jail attached. Not only as far as Homicide is concerned, but Vice, Narcotics . . . all of the departments."

Gonzaga relit the cigar and furrowed his brow. He was an ostentatious thinker, Hansen could see. Finally

Hansen saw the lightbulb over the toad's head as Gonzaga realized what he was being offered.

"One-stop shopping," said the don.

"I will be a veritable Wal-Mart," agreed Hansen.

"So you're so fucking sure that you're going to be chief of police?"

"Indubitably," said Hansen and then, as the toadman's brow furrowed again, "Without doubt, sir. In the meantime, I can make sure that no homicide investigation even turns in your direction."

"In exchange for whacking one guy?"

"In exchange for simply *helping* me whack one guy."

"When?"

"I'm supposed to meet him at the old train station at midnight. That means he'll probably be there by ten o'clock."

"This guy," said Gonzaga, looking at the photograph again. "He looks fucking familiar but I can't place him. Mickey."

The Asian glided over from the wall.

"You know this guy, Mickey?"

"That's Howard Conway." The man's voice was smooth as his gait, very quiet, but the words made Hansen's head spin, and for the second time that day he saw black spots dancing in his vision.

Kurtz has been playing with me. If he knows Howard's name, then Howard is dead. But why tell Gonzaga? Have they foreseen this move as well?

"Yeah," said Gonzaga, "Angie Farino's new fucking bodyguard." He flapped the photo at Hansen. "What's going on here? Why are you after this Raiford jailbird?"

"He's not a Raiford ex-con," Hansen said smoothly, blinking away the dancing spots while trying not to look distressed. "He's an Attica ex-con named Kurtz."

The don looked at the Asian. "Kurtz. Kurtz. Where've we heard that name, Mickey?"

"Before Leo, our guy in their camp, disappeared, he said that Little Skag was putting out some nickels and dimes to whack an ex-P.I. named Kurtz," said Mickey Kee, showing no special deference to Gonzaga.

Gonzaga's brow furrowed more deeply. "Why would Angie hire some guy that her brother's trying to whack?"

"She has her own agenda," said Hansen. "And my bet is that it doesn't include you in the picture, Mr. Gonzaga."

"How many men you want?" grunted Gonzaga.

"I don't care how many," said Hansen. "The fewer the better. I just want them to be the best. I need a guarantee that Kurtz—and anyone he brings with him—won't leave that train station alive. Are any of your men so good that you can give me that guarantee?"

Emilio Gonzaga smiled broadly, showing great horses' teeth like yellowed ivory. "Mickey?" he said.

Mickey Kee did not smile. But he nodded.

"Kurtz said midnight but he'll get there early," Hansen said to Mickey Kee. "I'm going to be there at eight with two men. It'll be dark in that old station. Make sure you don't mistake us for Kurtz. Can you get there through this storm?"

Emilio Gonzaga removed his cigar and gave a phlegmy laugh. "Mickey owns a fucking Hummer."

CHAPTER
THIRTY-TWO

The afternoon and early evening in Marina Towers had a strangely sweet, almost elegiac calm to it.

Pruno had taught Joe Kurtz the word "elegiac" during their long correspondence while Kurtz was in Attica. Before Kurtz had gone behind bars, Pruno had given him a list of two hundred books he should read to begin his education. Kurtz had read them all, beginning with *The Iliad* and ending with *Das Kapital*. He had to admit that he'd enjoyed Shakespeare the most, spending weeks on each play. Kurtz had a hunch that before the night was over, the Buffalo train station might look like the last act of *Titus Andronicus*.

After the chili lunch, Frears had gone to one end of the big penthouse living room to tune his violin and it was Arlene who asked him to play. Frears had only smiled and shaken his head, but Angelina had joined in the request. Then—surprisingly—so had Marco, and even Kurtz had looked up from his brooding by the window.

While everyone sat around on sectionals and bar stools, John Wellington Frears had walked to the center of the room, removed a linen handkerchief from his suit pocket and draped it on the chin rest of the impossibly expensive violin, stood almost on his tiptoes with bow poised, and had begun playing.

To Kurtz's surprise, it was not classical. Frears played the main theme from *Schindler's List*, the long, plaintive passages holding notes that seemed to die with a sigh, the dying-away parts echoing against the cold glass windows like the half heard cries of children in the trains being pulled to Auschwitz. When he was done, no one applauded, no one moved. The only sound was the snow pelting against the glass and Arlene's soft snuffling.

Frears took Hansen's titanium briefcase with its photographs and went into the library. Angelina poured herself a tall scotch. Kurtz went back to the window to watch the storm and the growing darkness.

He met with Angelina in her private office at the northwest corner of the penthouse.

"What's happening tonight, Kurtz?"

He held up one hand. "I've given Hansen blackmail demands. We're supposed to meet at midnight. I suspect he'll be there early."

"You going to take the money if he brings it?"

"He won't bring it."

"So you're going to kill him."

"I don't know yet."

Angelina raised a dark eyebrow at that. Kurtz came over and sat on the edge of her modern rosewood desk. "I'll ask you again, what are your goals? What have you been trying to get out of all this bullshit?"

She studied him for a minute. "You know what I wanted."

"Gonzaga dead," said Kurtz. "Your brother . . . neutralized. But what else?"

"I'd like to rebuild the family someday, but along different lines. In the meantime, I'd like to be the best thief in the state of New York."

"And you have to be left alone to do both those things."

"Yes."

"And if I help you get those things, are you going to leave *me* the fuck alone?"

Angelina Farino Ferrara hesitated only a second. "Yes."

"Did you print out that list I asked for?" said Kurtz.

Angelina opened a drawer and produced three sheets of paper stapled together. Each page held columns of names and dollar amounts. "We can't use this for anything," she said. "If I were to release it, the Five Families would have me killed within the week. If you release it, you'll be dead within a day."

"You're not going to release it and neither am I," said Kurtz. He told her the last version of his plans.

"Jesus," whispered Angelina. "What do you need tonight?"

"Transportation. And do you have two walkie-talkie-type radios? The kind with earphones? They're not necessary, but could be useful."

"Sure," said Angelina. "But they're only good within a range of a mile or so."

"That'll work."

"Anything else?"

"That pair of handcuffs you used on Marco."

"Anything else?"

"Marco. I have some heavy lifting to do."

"Are you going to arm him?"

Kurtz shook his head. "He can bring a knife if he wants to. I'm not asking him to get mixed up in a gunfight, so he doesn't need to come heavy. There'll probably be enough guns there in the dark anyway."

"What else?"

"Long underwear," said Kurtz. "Thermal long johns if you've got them."

"You're kidding."

Kurtz shook his head. "It may be a long wait and it's going to be cold as a witch's teat in there."

He went into the library, where John Wellington Frears was sitting in an Eames chair, the briefcase open on the ottoman, photographs of dead children reflecting light from the soft halogen spotlight above. Kurtz assumed that Frears's daughter Crystal was one of the corpses on display, but he did not look and he did not ask.

"Can I talk to you a minute?" said Kurtz.

Frears nodded. Kurtz took a seat in a second leather Eames chair across from the violinist.

"I need to talk to you about what's going to happen next with Hansen," said Kurtz, "but first I have a personal question."

"Go ahead, Mr. Kurtz."

"I've seen your files. All of your files. Arlene pulled information off the Net that's usually kept confidential."

"Ah," said Frears, "the cancer. You want to know about the cancer."

"No. I'm curious about the two tours in Vietnam back in nineteen sixty-eight."

Frears blinked at this and then smiled. "Why on earth are you curious about that, Mr. Kurtz? There was a war on. I was a young man. Hundreds of thousands of young men served."

"Hundreds of thousands of guys were drafted. You volunteered for the army, were trained as an engineer, specialized in disarming booby traps over there. Why for Christ's sake?"

Frears was still smiling slightly. "Why did I specialize in that area?"

"No. Why volunteer at all? You'd already gone to Princeton for a couple of years, graduated from Juilliard. You had a high draft number, I checked. You didn't have to go at all. And you volunteered. You risked your life."

"And my hands," said Frears, holding those hands in the beam of light from the halogen spot. "Which were much more important to me than my life in those days."

"Why did you go?"

Frears scratched his short, curly beard. "If I try to explain, Mr. Kurtz, I do so at the real risk of boring you."

"I've got some time."

"All right. I entered Princeton with the idea of studying philosophy and ethics. One of my teachers there was Dr. Frederick."

"Pruno."

Frears made a pained face. "Yes. During my junior year at Princeton, Dr. Frederick shared some early research he was doing with a Harvard professor named Lawrence Kohlberg. Have you heard of him?"

"No."

"Most people haven't. Professors Kohlberg and Frederick were just beginning their research to test Kohlberg's theory that human beings pass through stages of moral development just as they have to pass through the Piagetian stages of development. Have you heard of Jean Piaget?"

"No."

"It doesn't matter. Piaget had proved that all children pass through various stages of development—being able

to cooperate with others, say, which happens for most
children around the age of kindergarten—and Lawrence
Kohlberg reasoned that people—not just children, but all
people—pass through discrete stages of moral development as well. Since Professor Frederick taught both philosophy and ethics, he was very interested in Kohlberg's
early research, and that was what our class was about."

"All right."

Frears took a breath, glanced at the obscene photographs lying on the ottoman, scooped them into the
briefcase, and closed the briefcase. "Kohlberg had classified six stages of moral development. Level One was
simple avoidance of punishment. Moral boundaries are
set only to avoid pain. Essentially the moral development of an earthworm. We've all known adults who stop
at Level One."

"Yes," said Kurtz.

"Level Two was a crude form of moral judgment motivated by the need to satisfy one's own desires," said
Frears. "Level Three was sometimes called the 'Good
Boy/Good Girl' orientation—a need to avoid rejection
or the disapproval of others."

Kurtz nodded and shifted his weight slightly. The .40
Smith & Wesson was cutting into his hip.

"Stage Four was the Law and Order level," said
Frears. "People had evolved to the moral degree that
they had an absolute imperative not to be criticized by
a duly recognized authority figure. Sometimes entire na-
tional populations appear to be made up of Stage Four
and lower citizens."

"Nazi Germany," said Kurtz.

"Exactly. Stage Five individuals seem motivated by
an overwhelming need to respect the social order and to
uphold legally determined laws. The law becomes a
touchstone, a moral imperative unto itself."

"ACLU types who allow the Nazis to march in Skokie," said Kurtz.

John Wellington Frears rubbed his chin through his beard and looked at Kurtz for a long minute, as if reappraising him. "Yes."

"Is Stage Five the top floor?" asked Kurtz.

Frears shook his head. "Not according to the research that Professors Kohlberg and Frederick were carrying out. A Level Six individual makes his moral decisions based on his own conscience in attempts to resonate with certain universal ethical considerations . . . even when those decisions fly in the face of existing laws. Say, Henry David Thoreau's opposition to the war with Mexico, or the civil-rights marchers in the South in the nineteen sixties."

Kurtz nodded.

"Professor Frederick used to say that the United States was founded by Level Six minds," said Frears, "protected and preserved by Level Fives, and populated by Level Fours and below. Does this make any sense, Mr. Kurtz?"

"Sure. But it hasn't done a damned thing toward telling me why you left Juilliard and went to the Vietnam War."

Frears smiled. "At the time, this idea of moral development was very important to me, Mr. Kurtz. Lawrence Kohlberg's dream was to find a Level Seven personality."

"Who would that be?" said Kurtz. "Jesus Christ?"

"Precisely," Frears said with no hint of irony. "Or Gandhi. Or Socrates. Or Buddha. Someone who can *only* respond to universal ethical imperatives. They have no choice in the matter. Usually the rest of us respond by putting them to death."

"Hemlock," said Kurtz. Pruno had made Plato's dialogues required reading for him in Attica.

"Yes." Frears set his long, elegant fingers on the metal briefcase. "Lawrence Kohlberg never found a Stage Seven personality."

Surprise, thought Kurtz.

"But he did find something else, Mr. Kurtz. His testing showed that there were many people walking the street who can only be classified as Level Zeroes. Their moral development has not even evolved to the point where they will avoid pain and punishment if their whim dictates otherwise. Other human beings' suffering means absolutely nothing to them. The clinical term is 'sociopath,' but the real word is 'monster.' "

Kurtz looked at Frears's fingers tensed against the lid of the briefcase as if trying to keep it closed. "This Kohlberg and Pruno had to do university research to find this out? I could have told them that when I was five years old."

Frears nodded. "Kohlberg committed suicide in nineteen eighty-seven—walked into a marsh and drowned. Some of his disciples say that he couldn't reconcile himself to the knowledge that such creatures walk among us."

"So you went to Vietnam to find out what rung of Kohlberg's ladder you were on," said Kurtz.

John Wellington Frears looked him in the eye. "Yes."

"And what did you find out?"

Frears smiled. "I discovered that a young violinist's fingers were very good at disarming bombs and booby traps." He leaned forward. "What else did you want to talk to me about, Mr. Kurtz?"

"Hansen."

"Yes?" The violinist was completely attentive.

"I don't think Hansen has cut and run yet, but he's close to doing that. Very close. Right now I think he's waiting a few hours just because I've been a factor he doesn't understand. The miserable son of a bitch is so smart that he's stupid . . . he thinks he understands everything. As long as we appear to be one step ahead of him, he hangs around to see what the fuck is going to happen—but not much longer. A few hours maybe."

"Yes."

"So, Mr. Frears, the way I see it, we can play this endgame one of three ways. I think you should decide."

Frears nodded silently at this.

"First," said Kurtz, "we hand over this briefcase to the authorities and let them chase down Mr. James B. Hansen. His modus operandi is shot to hell, so he won't be repeating his imposter kill-the-kids routine in the same way. He'll be on the run, pure and simple."

"Yes," said Frears.

"But he might stay on the run and ahead of the cops for months, even years," said Kurtz. "And after he's arrested, the trial will take months, or years. And after the trial, the appeals can take more years. And you don't have those months and years. It doesn't sound like the cancer's going to give you very many weeks."

"No," agreed Frears. "What is your second suggestion, Mr. Kurtz?"

"I kill Hansen. Tonight."

Frears nodded. "And your third suggestion, Mr. Kurtz?"

Kurtz told him. When Kurtz finished talking, John Wellington Frears sat back in the Eames chair and closed his eyes as if he was very, very tired.

Frears opened his eyes. Kurtz knew immediately what the man's decision was going to be.

• • •

Kurtz wanted to leave by six-thirty so he could get to the train station no later than seven. The storm had come in with nightfall, and there was a foot of new snow on the balcony when he stepped out for a final look at the night.

Arlene was smoking a cigarette there.

"Today was Wednesday, Joe."

"So?"

"You forgot your weekly visit to your parole officer."

"Yeah."

"I called her," said Arlene. "Told her you were sick." She flicked ashes. "Joe, if you manage to kill this Hansen and they still think he's a detective, every cop in the United States is going to be after you. You're going to have to hide so far up in Canada that your neighbors'll be polar bears. And you hate the out-of-doors."

Kurtz had nothing to say to that.

"We get kicked out of our basement in a week," said Arlene. "And we never got around to looking for new office space."

CHAPTER
THIRTY-THREE

The meeting with Kurtz was set for midnight. Hansen arrived at ten minutes after eight. Both Brubaker's and Myers's cars had trouble getting through the snow near the courthouse, so they'd had dinner downtown and waited for their captain to pick them up in his expensive sport utility vehicle. Brubaker was half-drunk and decided to confront Millworth on the ride to wherever the hell they were going.

"Whatever's going on," Brubaker said from the front passenger seat, "it sure and hell isn't department procedure. You said there was going to be something in this for us, Captain. It's time we saw what it was."

"You're right," said Hansen. He was driving carefully—he always drove carefully—following a snow-plow east on Broadway. The plow's flashing orange lights reflected off the silent buildings and low clouds.

Hansen took two thick envelopes out of the Cadillac Escalade's center console and tossed one to Brubaker and the other back to Myers.

"Holy shit," said Detective Myers. Each envelope contained $20,000.

"That's just a down payment," said Hansen.

"For what?" asked Brubaker.

Hansen ignored him and concentrated on driving the last two miles along Broadway and side streets. Except for snowplows and the occasional emergency vehicle, there was almost no traffic. Broadway had six inches of new snow but was being plowed regularly; the side streets were wastelands of drifting snow and snow-covered vehicles. The Escalade powered its way along on permanent all-wheel drive, but Hansen had to switch into four-wheel drive and then into four-wheel-low to make the final mile to the abandoned train station.

The driveway rising up the hill to the station was empty. There was no sign that another vehicle had been there. It was the first time Hansen had seen the station in real life, but he had studied floor plans of the complex all afternoon. He knew it by heart now. He parked by the boulders that sealed off the huge parking lot and nodded to the detectives. "I have tactical gear in the back."

He issued each man a bulletproof vest—not the thin Kevlar type that cops could wear under a shirt, but bulky SWAT flak vests with porcelain panels. Hansen pulled out three AR-15 assault rifles, rigged for rapid-fire, and handed one to Brubaker and one to Myers. Each man got five magazines, the extra going into the Velcroed pockets on the flak vests.

"We going into combat, Captain?" asked Myers. "I'm not trained for this shit."

"My guess is that there'll be one man in there," said Hansen.

Brubaker locked and loaded his AR-15. "That man named Kurtz?"

"Yes."

Myers was having trouble Velcroing shut the flak vest. He was too fat. He tugged at a nylon cord, found the fit, and patted the vest into place. "We supposed to arrest him?"

"No," said Hansen. "You're supposed to kill him." He handed each man a black SWAT helmet with bulky goggles on a swing-down visor.

"Night-vision goggles?" said Brubaker, swinging his down and peering around like a bug-eyed alien. "Wild. Everything's greenish and as bright as day."

"That's the idea, Detective." Hansen pulled on his helmet and powered up the goggles. "It's going to be dark as a coal mine in there for a civilian, but there's enough ambient light for us to see fine."

"What about civilians?" asked Myers. He was swinging his assault rifle around while peering through his goggles.

"No civilians in there. If it moves, shoot it," said Hansen. *If this Mickey Kee gets in the way, too bad.*

"No tactical radios?" said Brubaker.

"We won't need them," said Hansen. He pulled a pair of long-handled wire cutters from his bag. "We're going to stay together. Brubaker, when we're inside, you and I will be at SWAT-ready, covering forward fields of fire, you on the left, me on the right. Myers, when we're moving together inside, you face rear, keeping your back against Brubaker's back. Questions?"

There weren't any.

Hansen used his key remote to lock the Cadillac, and the three men crossed the parking lot toward the looming station. The blowing snow covered their tracks in minutes.

Kurtz had arrived only half an hour earlier.

He'd planned to get to the station by seven, but the blizzard slowed them down. The drive that normally would have taken ten minutes, even in traffic, took almost an hour; they almost got stuck once and Marco had to get out and push to get them moving again. It was seven-thirty before the Lincoln came to a stop at the base of the drive leading up to the station. Kurtz and Marco got out. Kurtz leaned into the open passenger door.

"You know where to park this down the side street so you can see this whole driveway area?"

John Wellington Frears nodded from his place behind the wheel.

"I know it's cold, but don't leave the engine on. Someone could see the exhaust from the street here. Just hunker down and wait."

Frears nodded again and touched a button to pop the trunk.

Kurtz went around back, tossed a heavy black bag to Marco, who set it on the passenger seat and closed the door. Kurtz lifted the other bundle from the trunk. It was wiggling slightly, but the duct tape held.

"I thought you wanted me to do the heavy lifting," said Marco.

"It's a hundred yards to the train station," said Kurtz. "By the time we get there, you can have it."

They walked up the hill and kept near the high cement railing as they approached the tower. Kurtz heard the Lincoln shoosh away but he did not look back. Marco used the wire cutters on the fence and they slipped through, keeping close to the station as they went around to the north side, where Kurtz knew how to get in through a boarded-up window. It was dark up here near the hilltop complex of the abandoned station, and the tower loomed over them like a skyscraper from hell, but the light from the sodium-vapor streetlights in the ghetto nearby reflected off the low clouds and lit everything in a sick, yellow glow.

The blowing snow stung Kurtz's eyes and soaked his hair. Before going through the window, he shifted the taped and gagged man from his shoulder to Marco's and took a flashlight out of his peacoat pocket.

Holding the flashlight in his left hand and the S&W semiautomatic in his right, Kurtz led the way into the echoing space.

It was too cold for pigeons to be stirring. Marco came in, and their two flashlight beams stabbed back and forth across the huge waiting room.

If Hansen got here first, we're dead, thought Kurtz. *We're perfect targets.*

Their shoes crunched on the cold stone floor. Wind howled beyond the tall, boarded-up windows. At the far end of the waiting room, Kurtz pocketed his pistol and pointed upward with the flashlight.

"That balcony should be a good vantage point for you," whispered Kurtz. "The stairway's mostly closed off and you could hear anyone climbing up it toward you. There's no reason for them to go up there—it's a dead end. If they come in the tower way, I'll see them. If they come in the way we did, they'll have to pass you here."

Kurtz fumbled in his left coat pocket, felt the Compact Witness .45 that Angelina had insisted he take—"It's served me well," she'd said as they stood in the penthouse foyer—and then found the extra two-way radio. They'd tested it in the penthouse but he wanted to make sure it worked here.

Marco dumped the groaning man and set his own earphones and radio in place.

"You don't have to actually speak into it," whispered Kurtz. "Just leave it on and thumb the transmit button if anyone passes you here. I'll hear it when you break squelch. Once if he's alone, twice if there are two guys, and so on. Give it a try."

Marco thumbed the button twice. Kurtz clearly heard the two interruptions of static. "Good."

"What if nobody shows?" whispered Marco. They'd shut off the flashlights while they huddled under the balcony, and Kurtz could barely see the big man three feet away.

"We wait until one and go home," whispered Kurtz. The cold in the waiting room was worse than outside. It made Kurtz's forehead ache.

"If I see anybody, I'm going to beep you and that's it. Soon as they're past me, I'm out of here. No one's paying me enough for this shit."

Kurtz nodded. Switching on his flashlight, he bent down, inspected the duct tape and cords, and lifted the heavy bundle. Marco climbed the littered and barricaded staircase carefully, but still made noise. Kurtz waited until the bodyguard was in place, out of sight but able to peer through the railings, and then he continued the next hundred feet or so up the main walkway into the tower rotunda.

CHAPTER
THIRTY-FOUR

"Jesus God, it's cold," whispered Myers.

"Shut up," hissed Brubaker.

James B. Hansen said nothing, but he made a fist and pounded both men on the chest plates of their flak vests, demanding silence.

They'd come in from the south side, through the acres of empty service buildings, across the rusted and snow-buried tracks, across the windswept boarding platforms, through the fenced-over south portal, up the boarding ramps, and now were crossing the vast main waiting room. The view was uncanny through the night-vision goggles: brilliant, glowing green-white outside, a dimmer, static-speckled greenish gloom here in the deeper darkness. But enough reflected light filtered through the boarded-up skylights and windows to allow them to see a hundred feet across the waiting room. Abandoned benches glowed like tombstones; smashed kiosks were a tumble of shadows; stopped clocks looked like skulls on the wall.

Hansen felt a strange exhilaration. Whatever happened, he knew there would have to be a sea change in his behavior. The shifting personae and the self-indulgent Special Visits would have to stop—at least for a few years. If a dullard like this ex-con Kurtz could find the pattern there, then it was no longer safe. Hansen would have to settle into the deep-cover identity he'd prepared in Vancouver and practice self-restraint for years as far as the teenage girls were concerned. In the meantime, this unaccustomed public action was exciting.

The three detectives crossed the wide space in respectable SWAT search-and-clear form: Brubaker and Hansen holding their weapons cocked and ready, swinging the muzzles as they turned their heads; Tommy Myers, his shoulder touching Brubaker, walking backward with his weapon and goggles in constant motion, covering their backs.

The loading platforms had been clear. The ramps had been clear. This waiting room and the rooms on either side—clear. That left the main rotunda and the tower.

If Kurtz had not arrived four hours early—and Hansen would be amazed if the man showed that much discipline and foresight—then the plan was for the three detectives to take up a shooting position in a front room of the tower, preferably on one of the mezzanine levels surrounding the entry rotunda. If Kurtz approached across the parking lot on the north side, or from the driveway to the west, they could ambush him from the front windows. If he came in from the east or south, they would hear him approaching up the staircase now in front of them and have a free field of fire down into the rotunda.

That was the plan.

Right now, Hansen was busy using his goggles to sweep the small balcony on the south wall to the left of the main staircase. There was enough ambient light to show no one standing there, but the darkness between the rungs of the old railings was a jumble of green static.

He checked the narrow staircase to the balcony—barricaded and littered. Still, it was probably worth clearing before going on to the rotunda, so—

"Listen!" whispered Brubaker.

A sound from the rotunda beyond the main staircase. A rattling. The scrape of shoes on marble or wood.

Hansen held the AR-15 steady with his left hand and used his right hand to shake the collar of each man's flak vest, enforcing silence and continued discipline. But he was thinking—*Got you, Kurtz! Got you!*

Marco stayed flat against the floor of the small balcony, raising his head just high enough to peer through the thick marble slats of the railing. He couldn't *see* who was down there—it was too fucking dark—but he could hear footsteps and once he heard urgent whispers. Whoever it was, they were moving through the blackness without flashlights. Maybe they were using those night-vision lenses or something, like the ones he'd seen in the movies.

As the soft shuffling came closer and paused ten yards below his balcony, Marco pressed his face against the floor. No use exposing himself when he couldn't see the fuckers anyway.

Marco clearly heard a man hiss "Listen!" and then the shuffling became footsteps hurrying up the main staircase toward the rotunda and tower where Kurtz had gone. Marco was alone in the huge waiting room. He took a breath and got to his feet, straining to see in the blackness. Even after twenty minutes here, his eyes had not completely adapted to such darkness.

He lifted the two-way radio, but paused before thumbing the transmit button. How many men had there been? Marco didn't know. But just beeping Kurtz twice wouldn't warn him that the opposition was moving around easily in the dark, using some high-tech shit or something. He could whisper into the radio, warn Kurtz.

Fuck him. Marco had decided that his best bet after the scary cocksucker had wasted Leo was to stick with Ms. Farino, at least until the shit quit flying, but he didn't owe anything to Kurtz. Still, if Kurtz got out of this alive, Marco didn't want him pissed at him. But that didn't warrant Marco risking even a whisper with hostiles in the building.

Marco silently thumbed the transmit button twice, heard the clicks on his earphone and then turned off the radio, pulled the earphone free, and crammed it all into his pocket. *Time to get the fuck out of here.*

When the long blade swept across Marco's throat from behind, slicing his jugular and windpipe and almost severing his spinal cord, he didn't even know what it was, it happened so fast and cut so deep. Then there was the sound sort of like a fountain, but Marco's brain did not associate it with the geyser of his own blood flowing out onto the cold marble floor.

Then his knees buckled and the big man fell, hitting his face on the stone railing but feeling nothing, seeing nothing. The midnight blackness of the train station filled his brain like black fog and that was that.

Mickey Kee wiped his eight-inch blade on the dead man's shirt, folded it back with his gloved hand, and glided back down the dark staircase as silently as he had ascended.

CHAPTER THIRTY-FIVE

The dim green glow of the corridor above the main staircase brightened considerably as Hansen, Brubaker, and Myers stepped out under the rotunda ceiling. Ambient light from the windowed tower rooms above filled the junk-cluttered space with green-white static and ghostly, glowing shapes.

Suddenly Joe Kurtz's voice—completely identifiable as Kurtz's voice—called from across the rotunda. "Hansen. Is that you? I can't see you."

"There!" Brubaker said aloud.

Directly across the rotunda floor, perhaps sixty-five feet away, against the west wall—a human form, standing, moving behind a bench, turning as if searching out the source of the shout. Hansen could see the bright glow of a titanium briefcase in the man's left hand.

"Don't fire!" Hansen called, but too late. Brubaker had opened up on full auto with his assault rifle. Myers swiveled and fired a second later.

God's will be done, thought Hansen. He thumbed the AR-15 to full auto and squeezed the trigger. The muzzle flare blinded him through the night-vision goggles. Hansen closed his eyes to shake away the retinal afterimages and listened while the rotunda echoed from the rifle blasts and the last ricochets whined away.

"We got him," yelled Brubaker. The detective ran across the open rotunda floor toward the man slumped over the bench. Myers followed.

Hansen went to one knee, waiting for the inevitable gunfire from one or more of the mezzanines above. Kurtz was too smart to be cut down like this. Wasn't he? This had to be an ambush.

No gunfire.

Hansen used his goggles to check out the darkest shadows under the mezzanine overhang as he moved carefully around the rotunda, staying back against the wall, keeping his rifle trained on any bench or tumbled kiosk that might give a man cover for an ambush.

Nothing.

"He's dead!" called Myers, the fat man's voice echoing.

"Yeah, but who the fuck is it?" said Brubaker. "I can't see his face through these fucking things."

Hansen was fifteen feet from the two detectives and the corpse when Brubaker's flashlight beam bloomed like a phosphorous bomb in his goggles.

Hansen sought cover behind a fallen bench and waited for the gunfire from above.

Nothing.

He flipped up his own goggles and looked over to where Brubaker's flashlight was swinging back and forth.

The man in the dark jacket was dead—at least three shots to the chest and one in the throat. It wasn't Kurtz. The man had been handcuffed to a wall pipe and still half hung from it, his upper torso draped across a bench. Hansen could see the face; the corpse's eyes were wide and staring in terror. Tape covered the mouth and ran all the way around the head. James B. Hansen's titanium briefcase had been taped to the man's left hand with twist after twist of the same silver duct tape.

Myers was tugging a billfold out of the corpse's pocket. Hansen ducked low, expecting an explosion.

"Donald Lee Rafferty," read Myers. "Ten-sixteen Locus Lane, Lockport. He's an organ donor."

Brubaker laughed.

"Who the fuck is Donald Lee Rafferty?" whispered Myers. The two detectives were beginning to realize how exposed they were.

Brubaker shut off the flashlight. Hansen could hear their goggles being swung down on the helmets' visor hinges.

In the green glow, Hansen duck-walked over to the trio, pulled the dead man's left hand back over the bench, and pried the taped briefcase open. It was empty.

What kind of stupid joke is this? Hansen remembered exactly who Donald Rafferty was, remembered the man's adopted daughter lying in the hospital, remembered the connection to Joe Kurtz and Kurtz's dead partner from twelve years ago. But none of this added up. If Kurtz really wanted the blackmail money, why this idiocy? If Kurtz's goal was to kill him, again why this complication? Even if Kurtz had his own night-vision goggles, there could have been no way he could distinguish one of the detectives from the other here in the rotunda. Kurtz should have fired when he had a clear field of fire.

If he was still here.

Hansen suddenly felt the deep cold of the place creep into him. It took him a few seconds to recognize the phenomenon—fear.

Fear of the inexplicable. Fear of the absolutely unreasonable action. Fear that came from not understanding what in hell your opponent was up to or what he might do next.

Quit trying to turn him into Moriarty, thought Hansen. *He's just an ex-con screw-up. He probably doesn't know why he's doing what he's doing. Maybe it just amused him to have us kill Rafferty for him. He'll probably call me tomorrow with another time and place for the handover of the money and photographs.*

Well, thought Hansen, *fornicate that*. No more games. Let Frears and Kurtz have the photographs. Let them do their worst. Time to leave. Time to leave the train station. Time to leave Buffalo. Time to leave all of this behind.

Myers and Brubaker were crouched behind the bench with him.

"Time to leave," Hansen whispered to them.

"We get to keep the money?" Myers whispered back, his breath hot and fetid on Hansen's face. "Even though it wasn't Kurtz?"

"Yes, yes," whispered Hansen. "Brubaker. Five yards to your left is the stairway to the front door. Wide stairs. Just twelve of them. The doors and windows down there are boarded over. Clear the staircase while we give you cover. Kick the boards off the door or window. Shoot an opening if you have to. We're getting out of here."

Brubaker hesitated a second but then nodded and scuffed to his right and down the staircase.

Hansen and Myers stayed behind the bench, muzzles swinging to cover the mezzanine levels across the rotunda, then the opposite main-staircase doorway. Nothing moved. No shots from the front staircase. Hansen heard Brubaker kicking the hell out of the boarded door and then the shout, "Clear!"

Hansen had Myers cover him while he shuffled to the

staircase and then covered the fat man while he wheezed and panted past him and down the stairs.

Outside, the night-vision goggles were almost too bright. It was still snowing hard, but the drifted expanse of the parking lot glowed like a green desert in bright sunlight. The three detectives abandoned all pretext of proper SWAT procedure and just loped away from the station, running flat-out across the parking lot. Each man ran hunched, obviously half-expecting a bullet between the shoulder blades. But as they reached a hundred feet from the tower, then two hundred, then a hundred yards and better, they began to relax slightly under their heavy flak vests. It would take a master marksman with a high-velocity rifle, night-scope, and much luck to get off a good shot at this distance, in this snow.

No shot came.

Panting and wheezing loudly now, they passed the low boulders blocking access to the lot and came down the slippery driveway. The goggles gave them a view of everything for sixty yards in each direction. Nothing moved. No other cars were visible. The only tire tracks in the driveway, mostly drifted over now, were those of the Cadillac Escalade, which had accumulated two inches of new snow in the forty-five minutes or so they had been in the station.

"Wait," panted Hansen. He used the remote to beep the Cadillac unlocked and they checked the lighted interior before approaching. Empty.

"Myers," said Hansen between gasps. "Keep your goggles and vest on and keep watch while Brubaker and I get out of this gear."

Myers grumbled but did as he was told as the other two detectives tossed their heavy vests, rifles, and helmets into the back of the SUV.

"All right," said Hansen, pulling the .38 from his coat

pocket and standing guard while Myers divested himself of his tactical gear. There was enough light out here to allow Hansen to see the fat man's grin when he was free of the heavy equipment. Despite the cold and snow, Myers wiped sweat from his face.

"That was fucking weird," said the heavyset detective.

"How many times have I asked you not to use profanity?" Hansen said, and shot Myers in the forehead.

Brubaker began groping in his jacket for his gun, but Hansen had plenty of time to fire twice—hitting the man first in the throat and then in the bridge of the nose.

He dragged the bodies out of the way so he could back the Escalade down to the street and then went through their jackets, pulling out the two envelopes of cash.

Breathing more easily now, Hansen looked back at the distant tower and train station. Nothing moved across the wide expanse of snow. If Mickey Kee had ever shown up, he was on his own in there now. Settling into the big SUV, Hansen felt a twinge of regret—he'd probably never know what game Joe Kurtz and John Wellington Frears had been playing. But he no longer cared. It was time to leave it all behind.

CHAPTER
THIRTY-SIX

Suddenly Kurtz knew that he was not alone on the mezzanine.

It had been a long, cold wait for Hansen and his pals, first waiting at the broken window of the front mezzanine office. The parking lot had been dark, but Kurtz was sure he could see any moving figure against the snow, even though his view from the third-floor window was partially obscured by the large steel-and-plaster ornamental awning directly beneath his perch.

When Marco had broken squelch twice on the radio, Kurtz had slipped the earpiece into his pocket and moved as quietly as he could—the floor was littered with broken plaster and glass—to the rotunda mezzanine outside the office. From there he didn't have long to wait until Hansen and the other two detectives showed up and blasted Rafferty to bits.

Kurtz never had a clear shot with his pistol. The rotunda got more light than most of the rest of the train station's interior, but it was still too dark for Kurtz to see anything clearly, even with his eyes adapted to the dark. One of the men had turned a flashlight on briefly when they were inspecting their kill, but Kurtz had only a brief glimpse of SWAT-garbed men more than eighty feet across the circle of the rotunda. Too far for a shot from the .40-caliber SW99 semiauto in his hand or the .45 Compact Witness in his coat pocket. Besides, even that brief glimpse of the men—he couldn't tell them apart in their black helmets and SWAT vests—showed that their body armor would stop a pistol shot.

Then the three had gone down the front stairway and battered their way out the front door and Kurtz had scuttled back to his place by the shattered window.

The entrance canopy below blocked his view until the three running men were again out of range, then lost to the darkness and falling snow of the parking lot.

Kurtz didn't even try following their retreat. He sat with his back against the wall and slowed his breathing.

There was the slightest hint of noise from either the mezzanine outside the office or the rotunda below. The whispering-gallery effect worked both ways.

Marco? He didn't think the unarmed bodyguard would be stupid enough to come *toward* the sound of automatic weapons fire. *Could Rafferty still be alive and stirring?* No. Kurtz had seen the wounds in the few seconds of the flashlight's inspection.

Getting silently to his feet, Kurtz raised the pistol and crossed the littered floor as quietly as he could. Glass still crunched underfoot.

Pausing at the doorway, he stepped out onto the mezzanine, pistol ready.

A shadow against the wall to his right moved with impossible speed. The .40 S&W went flying out across the railing and Kurtz felt his right wrist and hand go numb from the kick.

He leaped back, pawing with his left hand for the .45 in his peacoat pocket, but the shadow leaped and a two-footed kick caught him in the chest, breaking ribs and throwing Kurtz backward into the office.

Rolling, Kurtz got to his feet and lifted both arms in defense even as the shadow hurtled at him and three more fast kicks numbed his right forearm, smashed another rib, and kicked Kurtz's feet out from under him. He landed hard and felt broken glass rip at his back even as the wind rushed out of him.

Hansen? No. Who?

Kurtz staggered to his knees and grabbed for the extra gun again but his peacoat had been torn open and twisted around by the fall and he couldn't find the pocket. Maybe the gun had been knocked free but Kurtz couldn't see it in the dim light through the broken window.

His assailant came up behind him silently, grabbed Kurtz by the hair and pulled him to his feet.

Instinctively, Kurtz threw his left hand up tight to his chin—the right hand was useless—and felt a long blade cutting his forearm to the bone rather than severing his neck. Kurtz gasped and kicked backward as hard as he could.

The man danced away.

Kurtz was reeling, barely able to stand, feeling the shattered rib where it had cut into his right lung. He was bleeding badly, right hand dangling useless, legs shaky. He had only a few seconds he could stay standing, maybe thirty seconds before he lost consciousness.

His attacker moved to his left, a shadow in shadows.

Kurtz backed toward the window. A tall shard of sharp glass stuck upward from the windowsill. If he could maneuver the man toward the . . .

The man-shaped darkness leaped from the shadows. Kurtz abandoned the window-glass strategy, tugged his coat around with his bloody left hand, and reached for his pocket just as there came a blinding flash of light.

The figure, who had kicked him in the chest again, was not distracted by the light. The man body-blocked Kurtz with a sharp shoulder, lifted him, and threw him backward through the window even as Kurtz's left hand became entangled in his own coat pocket.

Kurtz was dimly aware that he was somersaulting through the cold air, looking up at the dark rectangle of window fifteen feet above, his assailant's face white against the blackness there. Then Kurtz hit the solid canopy with his back, smashed through the rotten plaster and lathing and rebar, and fell another fifteen feet to the snowy pavement below.

A hundred yards away through blowing snow, snug in the driver's seat of the Cadillac SUV, Hansen heard none of this. He turned the ignition, heard the V-8 roar to life, set the heater to maximum, and flipped on the halogen headlights.

He had just raised his hand to the gearshift when there came a soft *tik-tik* and thirty-two pounds of C-4 explosive rigged under the floorboards, in the engine compartment, behind the dash, and especially carefully around the 40-gallon fuel tank, exploded in tight sequence.

The first wad of explosive blew off Hansen's feet just above the ankles. The second batch of C-4 blew the hood a hundred feet into the air and sent the windshield flying. The main packet ignited the fuel tank and lifted the two-and-a-half-ton vehicle five feet into the air before the SUV dropped back onto burning tires. The interior of the Cadillac immediately filled with a fuel-air mixture of burning gasoline.

Hansen was alive. Even as he breathed flames, he thought, *I'm alive!*

He tried the door but it was buckled and jammed. The passenger seat was twisted forward and on fire. Hansen himself was on fire. The wood-and-polymer steering wheel was melting in his hands.

Not knowing yet that his feet were gone, Hansen lurched forward and clawed at the dashboard, pulling himself through the jagged hole where the windshield had been.

The hood was gone; the engine compartment was a well of flames.

Hansen did not stop. Reaching up and over with hands of molten flesh, he grabbed the optional roof rack of the Cadillac and pulled his charred and burning legs out of the wreck, twisting free of the interior, dropping himself away from the flaming mass of metal.

His hair was on fire. His face was on fire. Hansen rolled in the deep snow, smothering the flames, screaming in agony.

He crawled on his smoking elbows farther from the wreck, rolling on his back, trying to breathe through the pain in his lungs. He could see everything clearly, not knowing that his eyelids had fused with his brow and could not be closed. Hansen held his hands in front of his face. They hurt. He saw in a surge of disbelief bordering on a weird joy that his fingers had bloated like hot dogs left too long on the charcoal grill and then burst and melted. He saw white bone against the black sky. The flames illuminated everything in a sixty-yard radius.

Hansen tried to scream for help but his lungs were two sacks of carbon.

A silhouette walked between him and the burning vehicle. A man. The dark shape knelt, leaned closer, showed a face to the flames.

"Hansen," said John Wellington Frears. "Do you hear me? Do you know who I am?"

I am not *James B. Hansen,* Hansen thought and tried to say, but neither his jaws nor tongue would work.

Frears looked down at the burned man. Hansen's clothes had peeled off and his skin hung in greasy folds, smoking like charred rags. The man's face showed exposed and burned muscles like cords of slick red-and-yellow rope. Hansen's scorched lips had peeled back from his teeth, so he seemed to be caught in the middle of a wild grin. The staring gray eyes could not blink. Only the thin column of Hansen's breath rising into the frigid air from the open mouth showed that he still lived.

"Can you hear me, Hansen?" said Frears. "Can you see who I am? I did this. You killed my daughter, Hansen. And I did this. Stay alive and suffer, you son of a bitch."

Frears knelt next to the charred man for several minutes. Long enough to see the pupils in the monster's eyes widen in recognition and then become fixed and dilated. Long enough to see that the only vapor rising into the cold air from Hansen now was no longer breath, but steam and smoke from the cooked flesh.

Distant sirens rose from the direction of the lighted city—the habitat, John Wellington Frears thought, of the other men, the civilized men. He rose and was ready to walk back to the Lincoln parked a block away when he saw something that looked like an animal crawling toward him through the snow of the parking lot.

CHAPTER
THIRTY-SEVEN

Mickey Kee stood at the open window for a minute, staring down at Kurtz's body through the hole in the metal canopy and then glancing up at the vehicle burning in the distance. He was curious about the explosion, but he hadn't let it deter him from his work.

His charge from Mr. Gonzaga had been—kill Kurtz, then kill Millworth. In Mr. Gonzaga's words, "Any fucking cop crazy enough to hire me to kill somebody is too fucking crazy to be left alive." Mickey Kee had not disagreed. Mr. Gonzaga had added that he wanted Kurtz's head—literally—and Kee had brought a gunny sack on his belt to transport the trophy. Mr. G planned to give Ms. Angelina Farino a surprise present.

Kee had been mildly disappointed twenty minutes earlier when Millworth and his two sidekicks had come into the station like the Keystone Kops shuffling along in body armor. He'd followed them to Kurtz, knowing that the time was not right to take care of Millworth, that it was too risky with all of that firepower in the hands of clowns. Now this explosion. With any luck, Millworth was no longer a factor. If it hadn't been the homicide detective's pyre, then Mickey Kee would drive to Millworth's house and take care of things there. The evening was young.

Moving silently even over broken glass, Kee circled the mezzanine and went down the stairs, across the rotunda, and out the front door. Kurtz's body had not moved.

Kee slipped his Beretta out of its holster and approached carefully. Kurtz had made a mess coming through the overhang. Rebar hung down like spaghetti. Plaster and rotted wood were scattered around the body. Kurtz's right arm was visibly broken, the bone visible, and his left leg looked all twisted out of position. His left arm was pinned under his body just as he had fallen on it. There was blood soaking the snow around Kurtz's head and his eyes were wide and staring fixedly at the sky through the hole he'd made in the overhang. Snowflakes settled on the open eyes.

Mickey Kee straddled the body and counted to twenty. No breath rising in the cold air. Kee spat down onto Kurtz's open mouth. No movement. The eyes stared past Kee into intergalactic space.

Kee grunted, slipped away the Beretta, pulled the gunny sack from his belt, and clicked open the eight-inch blade on his combat knife.

Kurtz blinked and brought his left hand up and around, squeezing the trigger of the Compact Witness .45 he'd pulled out during his fall. The bullet hit Mickey Kee under the chin, passed through his soft palate and brain, and blew the top of his skull off.

The .45 suddenly grew too heavy to hold so Kurtz dropped it. He would have liked to have closed his eyes to go away from the pain, but Kee's body was too heavy on his damaged chest to let him breathe, so he pulled the body off him with his left hand, rolled over painfully, and began crawling on his belly toward the distant flames.

CHAPTER
THIRTY-EIGHT

John Wellington Frears drove Kurtz to the Erie County Medical Center that night. It wasn't the hospital closest to the train station, but it was the only one he knew about since he'd driven past it several times on the way to and from the Airport Sheraton. Despite the storm, or perhaps because of it, the emergency room was almost empty, so Kurtz had no fewer than eight people working on him when he was brought in. The two real doctors in the group didn't understand the injuries—severe cuts, lacerations, concussion, broken ribs, broken wrist, damage to both legs—but the well-dressed African-American gentleman who'd brought the patient in said that it had been an accident at a construction site, that his friend had fallen three stories through a skylight, and the shards of glass in Kurtz seemed to bear that story out.

Frears waited around long enough to hear that Kurtz would live, and then he and the black Lincoln disappeared back into the storm.

Arlene made it through the weather to the hospital that night, stayed until the next afternoon, and came back every day. When Kurtz regained consciousness late the next morning, she was reading the *Buffalo News*, and she insisted on reading parts of it aloud to him every day after that.

On that first day after the murders, Thursday, the carnage at the train station almost crowded out the news about the blizzard. "The Train Station Massacre," the papers and TV news immediately christened it. Three homicide detectives were dead, a civilian named Donald Rafforty, a petty criminal from Newark named Marco Dirazzio, and an Asian-American not yet identified. It was obvious to the press that some sort of straight-from-the-movies shoot-out between the crooks and the cops had taken place that night, probably while Captain Robert Gaines Millworth and his men were working undercover.

By that afternoon, the chief of police and the mayor of Buffalo had both vowed that this cold-blooded murder of Buffalo's finest would not go unavenged—that every resource, including the FBI, would be used to track down the killers and bring them to justice. It would, they said, be the largest manhunt in the history of Western New York. The vows were made in time to be picked up by the prime-time local and network news. Tom Brokaw said during the lead-in to the report, "A real—and deadly—game of cops-and-robbers took place in Buffalo, New York, last night, and the body count may not be finished yet." That odd prediction came true when the authorities announced late Thursday that the dead bodies of Captain Millworth's wife and son, as well as another unidentified body, had been discovered that morning at the captain's home in Tonawanda. One city alderman was quoted during the late news saying that it was inappropriate for a captain of Homicide on the Buffalo Police Department to *live* in Tonawanda, that city law and department policy required residence within the city limits of Buffalo for all city employees. The alderman was largely ignored.

On Friday, the second day after the murders, the dead Asian-American was identified as Mickey Kee, one of alleged Mafia Don Emilio Gonzaga's enforcers, and rumors were circulating that Detective Brubaker, one of the fallen hero cops, had been on the payroll of the Farino crime family. Chief Podeski's sound bite that night was: "Whatever the complicated circumstances of this heinous crime, we must not let it blind us to the incredible bravery of one man—Captain Robert Gaines Millworth—who gave his life and the lives of his beloved family for the people of Erie County and the Niagara Frontier." A hero's funeral was being planned for Captain Millworth. It was rumored that the President of the United States might attend.

Kurtz had surgery for his left leg, right lung, and both arms that day. He slept all that evening.

On Saturday, the third day, Arlene attended the funeral of her neighbor, Mrs. Dzwrjsky, and brought a tuna casserole to the family afterward. That same day, the *Buffalo News* ran a copyrighted story that canceled the President's visit: a world-famous violinist named John Wellington Frears had come forward with documents, photographs, and audio tapes showing that Captain Robert Gaines Millworth was an imposter, that the city had hired a serial child-killer with no history of law enforcement in his background, and that this imposter had once been James B. Hansen, the man who had murdered Frears's daughter twenty years earlier. Furthermore, Frears had evidence to show that Millworth/Hansen had been in the pay of crime boss Emilio Gonzaga and that the Train Station Massacre had not been a cops-versus-robbers fight at all, but a complicated gangland killing gone terribly wrong.

The Mayor and the chief of police announced on Saturday afternoon that there would be an immediate grand jury investigation into both the Gonzaga and Farino alleged crime families.

On that third evening, the CBS, NBC, ABC, Fox, and CNN news all led with the story.

On the fourth morning, Sunday, it was revealed by the *Buffalo News* and two local TV stations that Mr. John Wellington Frears had produced an audio tape of a telephone conversation between Angelina Farino Ferrara—a young woman recently returned from Europe, a widow, and someone never connected to the Farino family's business of crime—and Stephen "Little Skag" Farino, calling from Attica over his lawyer's secure phone. The transcript ran in that morning's edition of the *Buffalo News*, but copies of the tape were played on radio and TV stations everywhere.

Ms. Farino: **You've been hiring cops to whack people. Detective Brubaker, for instance. I know you've put him on the payroll that used to go to Hathaway.**

Stephen Farino: **What the [expletive deleted] are you talking about, Angie?**

Ms. Farino: I don't care about Brubaker, but I've gone over the family notes and I see that Gonzaga's got a captain of detectives on the arm. A guy named Millworth.

Stephen Farino: [no response]

Ms. Farino: Millworth's not really Millworth. He's a serial killer named James B. Hansen . . . and a bunch of other aliases. He's a childkiller, Stevie. A rapist and a killer.

Stephen Farino: So?

And so on. Along with the transcript, the *Buffalo News* released a list of forty-five names that included cops, judges, politicians, parole-board members, and other Buffalo-area officials shown to be on the Gonzaga family payroll, along with the amount they were paid each year by Gonzaga. There was a shorter list—eight names—of lesser cops and minor politicians who were in the pay of the Farino Family. Detective Fred Brubaker's name was on the second list.

On the fifth day, Monday, three of the most expensive lawyers in the United States, including one famous law-

yer who had been successful in the O.J. Simpson defense
years ago, all now in the hire of Emilio Gonzaga, held
a press conference to announce that John Wellington
Frears was a liar and a scoundrel, as well as someone
intent upon slandering Italian-Americans everywhere,
and they were prepared to prove it in a court of law.
Their client, Emilio Gonzaga, was suing John Wellington Frears for slander to the tune of one hundred million
dollars.

That evening, Frears appeared on *Larry King Live*
The violinist was sad, dignified, but unwavering. He
showed photographs of his murdered daughter. He produced documents showing that Gonzaga had hired Mill-
worth/Hansen. He showed carefully edited photographs
of Millworth/Hansen posing with other murdered children—and with Frears's own daughter. When Larry
King pressed Frears to tell how he had come by all this
material, Frears said only, "I hired a skilled private investigator." When confronted with the news of the
hundred-million-dollar lawsuit, Frears talked about his
battle with colon cancer and said simply that he would
not live long enough to defend his name in such a lawsuit. Emilio Gonzaga and Stephen Farino, said Frears,
were murderers and child molesters. They would have
to live with that knowledge, Frears said. He would not.

"Shut that damned thing off," Kurtz said from his
hospital bed. He hated Larry King.

Arlene shut it off but lit a cigarette in defiance of all
hospital rules.

On the sixth day after the massacre, Arlene came into
the hospital to find Kurtz out of his bed and room. When
he returned, pale, shaking, trailing his IV stand, he
would not say where he had been, but Arlene knew that

he had gone one floor up to look in on Rachel, who was in a private room now. The doctors had saved the girl's remaining kidney and she was on the road to recovery. Gail had put in the necessary papers to become Rachel's legal guardian, and the two spent hours together in Rachel's room each evening when Gail got off work.

On the seventh day, Wednesday, Arlene came in with a copy of *USA Today*: Emilio Gonzaga had been found in New York City that morning, stuffed in the trunk of a Chevrolet Monte Carlo parked near the fish market, two .22 bullets in the back of his head. "A double tap, obviously a professional hit," said the experts in such things. The same experts speculated that the Five Families had acted to end the bad publicity. "They're sentimentalists when it comes to kids," said one source.

But Kurtz was gone on that seventh morning. He'd checked himself out during the night. The previous evening, an inquiring mind from one of the newspapers had come by the hospital to ask Kurtz if he was the "skilled private investigator" mentioned by John Wellington Frears.

Arlene checked the office and the Royal Delaware Arms, but Kurtz had taken some essentials from both places and disappeared.

CHAPTER
THIRTY-NINE

The week Joe disappeared, she'd had to move everything out of their basement office so the city could tear down the building. Gail and some friends helped her with the move. Arlene stored the computers and files and miscellaneous stuff in her garage out in Cheektowaga.

The week after that, Angelina Farino Ferrara phoned her. "Did you hear the news?" asked Ms. Ferrara.

"I'm sort of avoiding the news," admitted Arlene.

"They got Little Skag. Shanked him eleven times in the Attica exercise yard last night. I guess it's true that cons don't like Short Eyes any more than the Five Family bosses do."

"Is he dead?" asked Arlene.

"Not quite. He's in some sort of high-security secret infirmary somewhere. They won't even let me—his only surviving family member—visit him. If he lives, they'll move him out of Attica to some undisclosed location."

"Why are you telling me?"

"I just thought Joe would like to know if you happen to talk to him. Do you talk to him?"

"No. I have no idea where he is."

"Well, if he gets in touch, tell him that I'd like to talk

to him sometime. We don't exactly have any unfinished business between us, but I might have some business opportunities for him."

"I'll tell Mr. Kurtz that you called."

That same afternoon, Arlene received a check for $35,000 from John Wellington Frears. The note on the check said only: "Wedding Bells.com." Arlene vaguely remembered discussing her idea with him the day they were together at her house. The news that evening reported that the violinist had checked himself into a hospital—not Erie County, but an expensive private hospital in the suburbs. A few days later, the newspaper said that Frears was on a respirator and in a coma.

Three and a half weeks after the Train Station Massacre, there was hardly anything about it in the papers except for the continuing string of city resignations and ongoing investigations and commissions. On that Wednesday in early March, Rachel came home to Gail's duplex on Colvin Avenue. Arlene visited them the next day and brought some homemade cake.

The next morning, early, Arlene's doorbell rang. She'd been sitting at the kitchen table, smoking her first cigarette of the day and sipping coffee, staring at the unopened paper, and the sound of the doorbell made her jump. She left her coffee but took her cigarette and the .357 Magnum she kept in the cupboard and peered out the side window before opening the door.

It was Kurtz. He looked like shit. His hair was rumpled, he hadn't shaved for days, his left arm was still in a sling, his right wrist was in a bulky cast, and he stood stiffly as if his taped ribs were still hurting him.

Arlene set the big pistol on her curio cabinet and opened the door. "How're they hanging, Joe?"

"Still low, wrinkled, and to the left."

She batted ashes out onto the stoop. "You came all the way over from whatever Dumpster you've been sleeping in to tell me that?"

"No." Kurtz peered up at the strange, glowing orb that had appeared in the sky over Buffalo that morning. "What the hell is that?"

"The sun," said Arlene.

"I just wondered," said Kurtz, "if you'd like to go out today to look for some office space."

On the day he was shot in the head, things were going strangely well for Joe Kurtz. In fact, things had been going strangely well for weeks. Later, he told himself that he should have known that the universe was getting ready to readjust its balance of pain at his expense.

And at the much greater expense to the woman who was standing next to him when the shots were fired.

He had a two P.M. appointment with his parole officer and he was there at the Civic Center on time. Because curb parking around the courthouse was almost impossible at that time of day, Kurtz used the parking garage under the combined civic, justice, and family court complex. The best thing about his parole officer was that she validated.

Actually, Kurtz realized, that wasn't the best thing about her at all. Probation Officer Margaret "Peg" O'Toole, formerly of the Buffalo P.D. narcotics and vice squad, had treated him decently, knew and liked his secretary—Arlene DeMarco—and had once helped Kurtz out of a deep hole when an overzealous detective had tried to send him back to County lock-up on a trumped-up weapons charge. Joe Kurtz had made more than a few enemies during his eleven and a half years serving time for manslaughter in Attica, and odds were poor that he'd last long in general population, even in County. In addition to validating his parking tickets, Peg O'Toole had probably saved his life.

She was waiting for him when he knocked on the door and entered her second-floor office. Come to think of it, O'Toole had never kept him waiting. While many parole officers worked out of cubicles, O'Toole had earned herself a real office with windows overlooking out the Erie County Holding Center on Church Street. Kurtz figured that on a clear day she could watch the winos being dragged into the drunk tank.

"Mr. Kurtz." She gestured him to his usual chair.

"Agent O'Toole." He took his usual chair.

"We have an important date coming up, Mr. Kurtz," said O'Toole, looking at him and then down at his folder.

Kurtz nodded. In a few weeks it would be one year since he left Attica and reported to his parole officer. Since there had been no real problems—or at least none she or the cops had heard about—he should be visiting her once a month soon rather than weekly. Now she asked her usual questions and Kurtz gave his usual answers.

Peg O'Toole was an attractive woman in her late thirties—overweight by current standards of perfection but all the more attractive in Kurtz's eyes for that, with long, auburn hair, green eyes, a taste for expensive but conservative clothing, and a Sig Pro nine-millimeter semiautomatic pistol in her purse. Kurtz knew the make because he'd seen the weapon.

He liked O'Toole—and not just for helping him out of the frame-up a year ago this coming November—but also because she was as no-nonsense and non-condescending as a parole officer can be with a "client." He'd never had an erotic thought about her, but that wasn't her fault. There was just something about the act of imagining an ex-police officer with her clothes off that worked on Kurtz like a 1,000-cc dose of Anti-Viagra.

"Are you still working with Mrs. DeMarco on the Sweetheart Search dot com business?" asked O'Toole. As a felon, Kurtz couldn't be licensed by the state of New York for his former job—PI—but he could operate this business of finding old high school flames, first via the Internet—that was his secretary Arlene's part of it—then by a bit of elementary skip-tracing. That was Kurtz's part of it.

"I tracked down a former high-school football captain this morning in North Tonawanda," said Kurtz, "to hand him a handwritten letter from his former cheerleader girlfriend."

O'Toole looked up from her notes and removed her tortoise-shell glasses. "Did the football hero still look like a football hero?" she asked, showing only the faintest trace of a smile.

"They were both from Kenmore West's Class of '61," said Kurtz. "The guy was fat, bald, and lived in a trailer that's seen better days. It had a Confederate flag hung on the side of it and a clapped-out '72 Camaro parked outside."

O'Toole winced. "How about the cheerleader?"

Kurtz shrugged. "If there was a photo, it was in the sealed letter. But I can guess."

"Let's not," said O'Toole. She put her glasses back on and glanced back at her form. "How is the Wedding Bells dot com business going?"

"Slowly," said Kurtz. "Arlene has the whole Internet

thing set up—all the contacts and contracts with dress-makers, cardmakers, cakemakers, musicians, churches and reception halls set in place—and money's coming in, but I'm not sure how much. I really don't have much to do with that side of the business."

"But you're an investor and co-owner?" said the parole officer. There was no hint of sarcasm in her voice.

"Sort of," said Kurtz. He knew that O'Toole had seen the articles of incorporation during a visit the parole officer had made to their new office in June. "I roll over some of my income from Sweetheart Search back into Wedding Bells and get a cut in return." Kurtz paused. He wondered how the felons and shankmeisters and Aryan Brotherhood boys in the exercise yard at Attica would react if they heard him say that. The D-Block Mosque guys would probably drop the price on his head from $15,000 to $10,000 out of sheer contempt.

O'Toole took off her glasses again. "I've been thinking of using Mrs. DeMarco's services."

Kurtz had to blink at that. "For Wedding Bells? To set up all the details of a wedding on-line?"

"Yes."

"Ten percent discount to personal acquaintances," said Kurtz. "I mean, you've met Arlene."

"I know what you meant, Mr. Kurtz." O'Toole put her glasses back on. "You still have a room at . . . what is the hotel's name? Harbor Inn?"

"Yes." Kurtz's old flophouse hotel, the Royal Delaware Arms near downtown, had been shut down in July by the city inspectors. Only the bar of the huge old building remained open and the word was that the only customers there were the rats. Kurtz needed an address for the parole board and the Harbor Inn served as one. He hadn't gotten around to telling O'Toole that the little hotel in the south side was actually boarded up and abandoned or that he'd leased the entire building for less than the price of his room at the old Delaware Arms.

"It's at the intersection of Ohio and Chicago Streets?"

"Right."

"I'd like to drop by and just look at it next week if you don't mind," said the parole officer. "Just to verify your address."

Shit, he thought. "Sure," he said.

O'Toole sat back and Kurtz thought that the short interview was over. The meetings had been getting more and more pro forma in recent months. He wondered if Officer O'Toole was becoming more laid back after the hot summer just past and with the pleasant autumn just winding down—the leaves on the only tree visible outside her window were a brilliant orange but ready to blow off.

"You seem to have recovered completely from your automobile accident last winter," said the parole officer. "I haven't seen even a hint of a limp the last few visits."

"Yeah, pretty much full recovery," said Kurtz. His "automobile accident" the previous February had included being knifed, thrown out of a third story window, and crashing through a plaster portico at the old Buffalo train station, but he hadn't seen any pressing need for the probation office to know the details. The cover story had been a pain for Kurtz, since he'd had to sell his perfectly good twelve-year-old Volvo—he could hardly be seen driving around in the car he was supposed to have wracked up on a lonely stretch of winter highway—and now he was driving a much older red Pinto. He missed the Volvo.

"You grew up around Buffalo, didn't you, Mr. Kurtz?"

He didn't react, but he felt the skin tighten on his face. O'Toole knew his personal history from the dossier on her desktop, and she'd never ventured into his pre-Attica history before. *What'd I do?*

He nodded.

"I'm not asking professionally," said Peg O'Toole. "I just have a minor mystery—very minor—that I need solved, and I think I need someone who grew up here."

"You didn't grow up here?" asked Kurtz. Most people who still lived in Buffalo had.

"I was born here, but we moved away when I was three," she said, opening the bottom right drawer of her desk and moving some things aside. "I moved back eleven years ago when I joined the Buffalo P.D." She brought out a white envelope. "Now I need the advice of a native and a private investigator."

Kurtz stared flatly at her. "I'm not a private investigator," he said, his voice flatter than his gaze.

"Not licensed," agreed O'Toole, evidently not intimidated by his cold stare or tone. "Not after serving time for manslaughter. But everything I've read or been told suggests you were an excellent PI."

Kurtz almost reacted to this. *What the hell is she after?*

She removed three photographs from the envelope and slid them across the desk. "I wondered if you might know where this is—or was?"

Kurtz looked at the photos. They were color, standard snapshot size, no borders, no date on the back, so they'd been taken sometime in the last couple of decades. The first photograph showed a broken and battered Ferris wheel, some cars missing, rising above bare trees on a wooded hilltop. Beyond the abandoned Ferris wheel was a distant valley and the hint of what might be a river. The sky was low and gray. The second photo showed an dilapidated bumper-car pavilion in an overgrown meadow. The pavilion's roof had partially collapsed and there were overturned and rusted bumper cars on the pavilion floor and scattered outside among the brittle winter or late-autumn weeds. One of the cars—Number 9 emblazened on its side in fading gold script—lay upside down in an icy puddle. The final photograph was a close-up of a merry-go-round or carousel horse's head, paint faded, its muzzle and mouth smashed away and showing rotted wood.

Kurtz looked at each of the photographs again and said, "No idea."

O'Toole nodded as if she expected that answer. "Did you used to go to any amusement parks around here when you were a kid?"

Kurtz had to smile at that. His childhood hadn't included any amusement park visits.

O'Toole actually blushed. "I mean, where did people go to amusement parks in Western New York in those days, Mr. Kurtz? I know that Six Flags at Darien Lake wasn't here then."

"How do you know this place is from way back then?" asked Kurtz. "It could have been abandoned a year ago. Vandals work fast."

O'Toole nodded. "But the rust and . . . it just seems old. From the seventies at least. Maybe the sixties."

Kurtz shrugged and handed the photos back. "People used to go up to Crystal Beach, on the Canadian side."

O'Toole nodded again. "But that was right on the lake, right? No hills, no woods?"

"Right," said Kurtz. "And it wasn't abandoned like that. When the time came, they tore it down and sold the rides and concessions."

The parole officer took off her glasses and stood. "Thank you, Mr. Kurtz. I appreciate your help." She held out her hand as she always did. It had startled Kurtz the first time she'd done it. They shook hands as they always did at the end of their weekly interviews. She had a good, strong grip. Then she validated his parking ticket. That was the other half of the weekly ritual.

He was opening the door to leave when she said, "And I may really give Mrs. DeMarco a call about the other thing."

Kurtz assumed that "the other thing" was the parole officer's wedding. "Yeah," he said. "You've got our office number and website address."

Later, he would think that if he hadn't stopped to take a leak in the first-floor restroom, everything would have been different. But what the hell—he had to take a leak, so he did. It didn't take reading Marcus Aurelius to know that *everything* you did made everything different, and if you dwelled on it, you'd go nuts.

He came down the stairway into the parking garage corridor and there was Peg O'Toole, green dress, high heels, purse and all, just out of the elevator and opening the heavy door to the garage. She paused when she saw Kurtz. He paused. There was no way that a probation officer wanted to walk into a underground parking garage with one of her clients, and Kurtz wasn't keen on the idea either. But there was also no way out of it unless he went back up the stairs or—even more absurdly—step into the elevator. *Damn.*

O'Toole broke the frozen minute by smiling and holding the door open for him.

Kurtz nodded and walked past her into the cool semi-darkness. She could let him get a dozen paces in front of her if she wanted. He wouldn't look back. Hell, he'd been in for manslaughter, not rape.

She didn't wait long. He heard the clack of her heels a few paces behind him, heading to his right.

"Wait!" cried Kurtz, turning toward her and raising his right hand.

O'Toole froze, looked startled, and lifted her purse where, he knew, she usually carried the Sig Pro.

The goddamned lights had been broken. When he'd come in less than half an hour earlier, there had been fluorescent lights every twenty-five feet or so, but half of those were out. The pools of darkness between the remaining lights were wide and black.

"Back!" shouted Kurtz, pointing toward the door from which they'd just emerged.

Looking at him as if he were crazy, but not visibly afraid, Peg O'Toole put her hand in her purse and started to pull the Sig Pro.

The shooting started.

When Kurtz awoke in the hospital, he knew at once that he'd been shot, but he couldn't remember when or where it happened, or who did it. He had the feeling that someone had been with him but he couldn't bring back any details and any attempt to do so hammered barbed spikes through his brain.

Kurtz knew the varieties and vintages of pain the way some men knew wines, but this pain in his head was already beyond the judging stage and well into the realm where screaming was the only sane response. But he didn't scream. It would hurt too much.

The hospital room was mostly dark but even the dim light from the bedside table hurt his eyes. Everything had a nimbus around it and when he attempted to focus his eyes, nausea rose up through the pain like a shark fin cutting through oily water. He solved that by closing his eyes. Now there were only the inevitable, ambient hospital sounds from beyond the closed door—intercom announcements, the squeak of rubber soles on tile, inaudible conversations in that muffled tone heard only in hospitals and betting parlors—but each and every one of these sounds, including the rasp of his own breathing, was too loud for Joe Kurtz.

He started to raise his hand to rub the right side of his head—the epicenter of this universe of pain—but his hand jarred to a halt next to the metal bedrail.

It took Kurtz two more tries and several groggy seconds of mental effort and the pain of opening his eyes again before he realized why his right arm wouldn't work; he was handcuffed to the metal frame of the hospital bed.

It took him another minute or two before he realized that his left hand and arm were free. Slowly, laboriously, Kurtz reached that hand across his face—eyes squinted to keep the nausea at bay—and touched the right side of his head, just above his ear, where the pain was broadcasting like the concentric radio-wave ripples in the beginning of one of those old RKO films.

He could feel that the right side of his head was a mass of bandages and tape. But when he saw that there were only two IV's visibly punched into his body and only one monitoring machine beeping a few feet away, and no doctors or nurses huddled around with their rescuscitation crash cart, he figured he wasn't on the verge of checking out yet. Either that, or they'd already given up on him, issued a "Do Not Resuscitate" order, and gone off for coffee to leave him to die here in the dark.

"Fuck it," said Kurtz and winced as the pain went from 7.8 to 8.6 on his own private Agony Richter Scale. He was used to pain, but this was . . . silly.

He dropped his hand on his chest, closed his eyes, and allowed himself to float out of the line of fire.

"Mr. Kurtz? Mr. Kurtz?"

Kurtz awoke with the same blurred vision, same nausea, but different pain. It was worse. Some fool was pulling his eyelids back and shining a light in his eyes.

"Mr. Kurtz?" The face making the sound was brown, male, middle-aged and mild-looking behind black rimmed glasses. He was wearing a white coat. "I'm Dr. Singh, Mr. Kurtz. I dealt with your injuries in the ER and just came from surgery on your friend."

Kurtz got the face into focus. He wanted to say "What friend?", but it wasn't worth trying to speak yet. Not yet.

"You were struck in the right side of your head by a bullet, Mr. Kurtz, but it did not penetrate your skull," said Singh in his mild, sing-song voice that sounded like three chainsaws roaring to Kurtz.

Superman, thought Kurtz. *Fucking bullets bounce right off*.

"Why?" he said.

"What, Mr. Kurtz?"

Kurtz had to close his eyes at the thought speaking again. Forcing himself to articulate, he said, "Why . . . didn't . . . bullet . . . penetrate?"

Singh nodded his understanding. "It was a small caliber bullet, Mr. Kurtz. A twenty-two. Before it struck you, it had passed through the upper arm of . . . of the person with you . . . and ricocheted off the concrete pillar behind you. It was considerably flattened and much of its kinetic energy had been expended. Still, if you had been turning your head to the right rather than to the left when it struck you, we would be extracting it from your brain as we speak—probably during an autopsy."

All in all, thought Kurtz, more information than he had needed at the moment.

"As it is," continued Singh, the soft sing-song voice sawing away through Kurtz's skull, "you have a moderate-to-severe concussion and a subcranial hematoma that does not require tripanning at this time, your left eye will not dilate, blood has drained down beneath your eyes and the whites of your eyes are very bloodshot—but that is not important. We'll assess motor skills and secondary effects in the morning.

"Who . . ." began Kurtz. He wasn't even sure what he was going to ask. *Who shot me? Who was with me? Who's going to pay for this?*

"The police are here, Mr. Kurtz," interrupted Dr. Singh. "It's the reason we haven't administered any painkiller since you regained consciousness. They need to talk to you."

Kurtz didn't turn his head to look, but when the doctor moved aside he could see the two detectives, plainclothes, one male, one female, one black, one white. Kurtz didn't know the black male. He had once been in love with the white female.

The black detective, dressed nattily in tweed, vest, and school tie, stepped closer. "Joseph Kurtz, I'm Detective Paul Kemper. My partner and I are investigating the shooting of you and Parole Officer Margaret O'Toole . . ." began the man in a Morgan Freeman–resonant voice.

Oh, shit, thought Kurtz. He closed his eyes and remembered O'Toole opening a door for him.

". . . can be used against you in a court of law," the man was saying. "If you cannot afford an attorney, one will be appointed for you. Do you understand your rights as I've just explained them to you?"

Kurtz said something through the pain.

"What?" said Detective Kemper. Kurtz changed his

mind. The man's voice wasn't nearly as friendly as Morgan Freeman's.

"Didn't shoot her," repeated Kurtz.

"Did you understand your rights as I explained them to you?"

"Yeah."

"And do you wish an attorney at this time?"

I wish some darvocet or morphine at this time, thought Kurtz. "Yeah . . . I mean, no. No attorney."

"You'll talk to us now?"

How many fucking times are you going to ask me? thought Kurtz. He realized that he'd spoken this aloud only when the male detective got a stern don't-fuck-with-me cop look on his face and the female detective still standing against the far wall chuckled. Kurtz knew that chuckle.

"Why were you in the garage with Officer O'Toole?" asked Kemper. The detective's voice sounded more like Darth Vader's to Kurtz now.

"Coincidence." Kurtz had never noticed how many syllables were in that word before today. All four of them hit him like hot spikes behind the eyes. He needed shorter words.

"Did you fire her weapon?"

"I don't remember," said Kurtz, sounding like every perp he'd ever questioned.

Kemper sighed and shot a glance at his partner. Kurtz also looked at her and watched her look back at him. She obviously recognized him. She must have recognized his name before they started this interview. Is that why she wasn't speaking? She was, Kurtz was startled to realize through the pain in his head, as beautiful as ever. More beautiful.

"Did you see the assailant or assailants?" asked Kemper.

"I don't remember."

"Did you enter the garage as part of a conspiracy to shoot and kill Officer O'Toole?"

Kurtz just looked at him. He knew that he was stupid with pain and concussion at the moment, but not that stupid.

Dr. Singh filled the silence. "Detectives, a concussion of this severity is often accompanied by memory loss of the accident that created it."

"Uh-huh," said Kemper, closing his notebook. "This was no accident, Doctor. And this guy remembers everything he wants to remember."

"Paul," said the female detective, "leave him alone. We have the tapes. Let Kurtz get some painkiller and sleep and we'll talk to him in the morning."

"He'll be all lawyered up in the morning," said Kemper.

The woman shook her head. "No he won't."

It'd been twenty years since Kurtz had last seen Rigby King—what was her married name? Something Arabic, he thought—but she still looked like the Rigby he'd known at Father Baker's and again in Thailand. Brown eyes, full figure, short dark hair, and a smile as quick and radiant as Goldie Hawn's or that gymnast from years ago, the one who later played Peter Pan.

Kemper left the room and Rigby came to the side of the bed and raised a hand as if she was going to squeeze Kurtz's shoulder. Instead she gripped the metal railing of the hospital bed and shook it slightly, making Kurtz's handcuffed wrist and arm sway.

"Get some sleep, Joe."

"Yeah."

When they were both gone, Singh called in a nurse and they injected something into the IV port.

"Something for the pain and a mild sedative," said the

doctor. "We've kept you semi-conscious and under observation long enough to let you sleep now without worrying unduly about the concussion's effects."

"Yeah," said Kurtz.

As soon as the two left, Kurtz reached down, ripped away gauze and tape, and pulled the IV out of his left arm.

Joe Kurtz had seen what could happen to a man doped up and helpless in a hospital bed. Besides, he had a lot of thinking to do through the pain before morning came.